CONFLICTS

Conflict: a state of disharmony between incompatible persons, ideas, or interests; a battle or war.

CONFLICTS

Edited by Ian Whates

NEWCON
PRESS

NewCon Press
England

First edition, published in the UK April 2010
by NewCon Press
2nd edition 2012

NCP 024 (hardback)
NCP 025 (softback)

10 9 8 7 6 5 4 3 2 1

ISBN: 978-1-907069-10-9 (hardback)
978-0-907069-86-4 (softback)

Cover art and design by Andy Bigwood

Invaluable editorial assistance from Ian Watson
Text layout by Storm Constantine

Printed in the UK by MPG Biddles of Kings Lynne

CONTENTS

Conflicts:
An Introduction

Ian Whates

This book breaks new ground for NewCon Press, in that it is comprised purely and unashamedly of Science Fiction stories. Previous anthologies have deliberately crossed genre boundaries, with SF featuring alongside fantasy, dark fantasy, horror and slipstream, but not this one.

In part this might be a reaction to the fact that, while compiling and editing this volume, I was also working on *The Bitten Word* – a collection of all new vampire stories (though, in truth, SF even creeps into a couple of those as well) – but essentially this book's here because I *wanted* to produce a Science Fiction anthology. Simple as that.

I also wanted to produce one that was brazenly, almost *defiantly* Science Fiction, not subtly, whimsically, or deceptively so; the sort of book where you can smell the sweat and the engine oil, as muscle-bound marines heft huge death-dealing guns in the face of impossible odds, where space ships cruise between the stars.

The big guns are here – and how! – with Neal Asher's protagonists fighting through a city infested with prehistoric monsters, Andy Remic's Combat-K embarking on a rescue mission which proves to be far more than it seems, and Jim Mortimore's minor disagreement between two super soldiers which escalates rapidly out of control... Yet there *is* subtlety too. No NewCon Press collection has ever been one-dimensional, and I wasn't about to start now. So we have Una McCormack's tale of a wronged man seeking answers, returning to the scene of a bitter war to discover that historical record and even memory can often hide deeper, darker truths, Rosanne Rabinowitz's poignant story of ephemeral love and loss, Martin McGrath's harrowing account of human's turned fugitive on our own world by alien aggression, and Martin Sketchley's chilling vision of the quietest alien invasion imaginable.

And did I mention space ships? Oh yes, there are space ships. In Michael Cobley's manic planet-hopping yarn of deceit, pursuit and ingenuity, in Keith Brooke's clever story of love, lust criminality and choices, in David L. Clements' saga of humanity's last hope fleeing to the stars, pursued by a relentless enemy, and Eric Brown's tale of a man coming to the aid of a damsel in distress only to suspect that he's doing something else entirely; spaceships aplenty.

Some of the stories, such as Chris Beckett's reimagining of the Middle East Conflict translated to Britain, with the Celts reclaiming their homeland and dispossessing the English, and Gareth L. Powell's vision of future Bristol as a radioactive no-go area, are set on Earth, while others are many, many light years away. All are about humans, facing up to challenges.

Yes, I could have asked for tales of mighty warriors and heroic quests, of goblin armies and dark sorceries, of immortal dragons and demon queens, of cunning thieves and fearless barbarians, and still called the book *Conflicts*. But I didn't. Not this time. Maybe someday I will do, and so compile a *Conflicts II*, but for now I'm more than happy with this, the original. It's Science Fiction. With a space ship on the front. I hope that you enjoy it too.

Ian Whates, February 2010

PSI.COPATH

-a Combat K Adventure-

Andy Remic

"Guys, get your shit together, we're going in." Pippa gave a nasty sideways grin, brown, shoulder-length hair bobbing, grey eyes shifting across the scrawled detritus of scattered kit in the Hornet's narrow, cluttered hold.

"About fucking time," snarled Keenan, slamming a mag into his MPK. "I was starting to get bored." His eyes fixed on Pippa like iron shackles. "Are you sure you're – *ready*, for this? After..."

"I'm ready," she said, words harsh, tone as abrupt as a slap in the face. She flashed an apologetic glance, bared her teeth, then finished stuffing her pack with emergency provisions. "Sorry, Kee. Still delicate. Woman's prerogative, yeah?"

"I'm not surprised, babe."

"Guys! I'm here!" boomed Franco Haggis – adventurer, demolitions expert, sexual athlete – as he burst into the hold like a ginger tsunami. He slammed a fully loaded mag into his Kekra quad-barrel machine pistol, waved the weapon negligently, then grinned at his Combat K squad companions who were all ducking, and wincing. "You weren't going to leave without me? Surely?"

"We'd never do that," said Keenan, moving to the Hornet's controls and punching up a navigational HUD. "After all, who'd pack the sausages?"

"Or the horseradish," said Pippa, tone mordant.

Franco frowned. "Hey," he said, "don't be like that."

"Like what?" snapped Pippa. "Last time you packed emergency rations you packed twenty crates of pre-cube tinned cheese, and fifteen *fucking* crates of horseradish. We crashed. I had to exist – *subsist* – on horseradish for a whole damn month. A girl doesn't forget a mistake like that, you bearded foetus."

Franco frowned. "Hey. Well. They don't call me Franco 'Chef Ramsey' Haggis for nothing, you know. I'm the best damn cook in Quad-Galaxy!" Franco was oblivious to sarcasm, ignorant of irony, mindless of mockery. He extracted the corn and munched from scorn, leaving a pointless and pitiful little *s*.

"Right. Stop dicking about. We're five hundred klicks and closing fast. Lock your harnesses. Vor's high altitude systems are a violent bastard's bastard; I can severely do without petty distractions."

Keenan and Pippa locked in, harnesses clicking.

Franco stared at them; hard. Like a man on a mission. "Suppose I'd better put some pants on, then," he said, glancing down at his big, white, ASDA y-fronts.

Pippa winked, little more than a sardonic twitch. "Good idea, sweetie. You might need them when the shit hits the fan."

"Hey." Franco grinned again. "There's nothing like pants in a firefight."

Vor was an out-range rag-end arsetag planet on the SPAW-riddled circumference of an ii-5 Cluster in the Quad-Galaxy Unification Syndicate Outer Shell. Vor, a planet of natural violence, of raging volcanoes and continent-shattering earthquakes, of monumental tidal waves and jagged, ragged, three-klick leering mountains, and jungles spread and smeared like steroidal gonorrhoea so vast they were practically AI. The mission had come in fastlane through PADs and coreAI, routed via General Steinhauer and dropped in Combat K's lap like a tossed and battered pancake.

Shenzar City: formerly a battlezone of brutal savagery, of death and QuickieGenocide – a hundred year battle once raged between combat AIs and a human-like WarSpecies, the GriTags. Now deserted, Shenzar City was a vast ghost town, a monument to war; scarred, crumbling, booby-trapped to its bomb-strapped tits and more dangerous than a nuke-packed SIM. Empty; yes. Dodgy? Hell, more risky than any Japachinese poodle-vindaloo.

During a flight over Vor, a young lady by the name of Kuminyana, W'hore Princess and daughter of Quad-Gal's complex military-political Royal Family, had recently suffered engine problems in her advanced tactical Klasp Fighter, and executed an emergency landing. Upon entering Vor's atmosphere, all contact was lost. Comms died. Kuminyana, pampered to the point of retardation, had nothing but a platoon of eight combat-AI GG machines for company. Which, across a galaxy canvas filled with hardcore soldiers, political assassins, combat gunrunners and plenty of brain-fried tox insane, might well be less than enough.

Combat K howled through Vor's ionosphere, their Hornet fluctuating between howls, groans and growls. Franco, now – thankfully – wearing pants, strapped into his safety harness and chewed down on a big fat German sausage, apparently unperturbed by the impending ramslam down to Vor's surface as he hummed a little tune and glanced up, staring at the back of Keenan and Pippa's heads where they sat up front in the pilot chairs.

"So," he said, through a mouthful of mush-mash, "Kuminyana had eight GG AIs, she was tagged touching down, so we know she didn't crash, and pretty much all hostile forces on the planet wiped out one another decades ago; a kind of neat and neutralising natural selection, yeah?"

"And your point is?" said Pippa, turning to stare in horror at Franco's bratwurst.

"We-*eell*," said Franco, looking suddenly shifty, "if this is such an easy gig, and there's little or no threat, what I was thinking is that you two walk point and sort out this bird, reet, and then I can activate a brave rearward base-operation of integral food and drink caching combined with complex chemical analysis of onboard chemical substances." He beamed, a bit of sausage stuck between incisors.

Pippa considered this. "What you mean is, you'll stay here, watch a movie, stuff your face with sausage and get pissed?"

"Only technically," beamed Franco, oblivious to the sarcastic growl in Pippa's voice.

"No, dickhead. You can't."

"Aww, Pippa, come on, hey Keenan, tell her, mate, tell her I can stay. I don't wanna go rooting around no archaic battle site with only my piles for company. I'm an ill squaddie, I am; I should be on the sick, confined to quarters and all that."

"The only sick part of you is your mind. Now shut up. We're going in."

As if triggered by her words, the Hornet suddenly rocked, a vicious kick to the engine ports, and Keenan's knuckles went white on the controls. The Hornet gave another surge, then dropped a thousand feet in a second making Franco give a sausage-streamer wail from the back. The Hornet bucked, a wild manoeuvre for such a fast combat craft, then dropped. Keenan leant forward, slapping buttons and dials...

"What is it?" snapped Pippa.

"Engine fault."

"Coincidence?" said Pippa.

Keenan glanced at her. "Let's just land first, yeah?"

"Whatever you say, boss."

The Hornet slammed down from ionosphere to thermosphere, then lower. Vor spread before them like a chequered gameboard, a pastel painting filled with brightly coloured daubs. Sunlight glittered green on the Hornet's stubby wings and the nose dipped again to a background wail of engines and shaved, splintered pistons, Keenan fighting controls like a lunatic, and they all watched a world of brightly spilled paint spread out, glimmering with bursts of sunshine, from this height of ersatz paradise, a tropical canvas, an invitation to *dive in*… only now *now* they were diving in way too fast, and Keenan was losing control by the nanosecond.

"Initiating emergency engine drags," snarled Keenan, watching the world coming up slamfast to punch him in the jaw.

"Agreed," said Pippa, hitting the button to second the command which would, effectively, boost their power but halve the Hornet's engine life; the scanner read her prints and DNA. Howls rocked the rocking Hornet.

Keenan banked. Jungles scrolled past, hugging the mountains like a lover.

"It's going to be a bumpy one," said Keenan, voice an octave too high, face dripping sweat, and they skimmed the jungle and embraced the landscape in an undulating rhythm as computers fast-locked for a safe LZ.

The Hornet snarled, bucked, whirled around in a huge arc as fatbelly-jets blasted a five-hundred metre radius of trees into instant flaming charcoal, and the Hornet ejected legs and touched down, feet gently crackling scorched wood into hard-earth charcoal compression.

Engines whined, then shut down one by one by one. Keenan mopped his brow, took a deep breath, and closed his eyes.

"Good landing," said Franco, finishing his sausage with a belch. He unclipped, stood up, and patted Keenan on the back.

"Well done mate. I had every fucking faith in you."

Franco hit the DP and steps ejected. A metre-thick door lifted. Sunlight streamed in. He grinned, illuminated by a green-hue of sunshine; he looked demonic.

Pippa stared at him. "Does nothing upset you?" she snarled, heartbeat still a tattoo of raging palpitation.

Franco shrugged. "It's in the lap of the Gods, chicken," he said, and stepped outside. Then popped his head back in. "And they don't call me Franco 'Lucky Arse' Haggis for nothing, you know?" Then he was gone, leaving a sausage-grease smeared metal plate on his seat for somebody else to wash up.

Pippa glanced at Keenan. "What happened?"

He scowled. "Engine problems my arse. Something spiked our Hornet; and it's obviously the same thing that brought down Kuminyana."

"You thinking rogue War Machines?"

"I'm thinking ancient not-quite-decommissioned alien bastard war technology. I think we need to bring the big guns."

Pippa gave a wry smile. "Don't we always?"

They stood under the Hornet, which hissed and crackled. Beneath hefty boots lay scorched earth, and a few hundred metres away a glowing, still-flaming jungle rim. Franco hoisted his pack and primed his guns. He looked up, shading eyes from the sun. Everywhere, a heat haze shimmered. "We good to go?"

Pippa nodded. She pointed. "North. Five klicks. Shenzar City. The PAD's locating Kuminyana's ship now..." she pursed her lips. "Well. It's located a destroyed shell." She glanced up at Keenan, dressed in black and jungle camouflage. He was smoking a cigarette, filled with harsh Widow Maker tobacco, and squinting.

"Not good," he muttered.

"Maybe she's still alive?" said Pippa.

"We'll see," growled Keenan. "Come on."

They tabbed hard, fast, down little used trails – but trails nonetheless. Created by predators, they all knew; harsh Grey Serles, a five-legged jungle cat; and the even more deadly chameleonic Liz-Liz lizards which could bite a man's head clean off with a single snap of telescopic jaws from a fifty metre hidden vantage point. Pippa kept a nervous eye on her PAD, which scanned using k-waves. Nothing like losing one's head to really *screw* a mission. However, other than indigenous predators, there was no sentient life on Vor. Or so the DropBot reports ran.

Ahead, Keenan stopped, fist up, clenched. He dropped to one knee, and Pippa and Franco emulated. At the back, always at the back, Franco mumbled to himself about always being at the back. Before they left the ship, he'd moaned the continual mantra, "Why am I always at the back?" And Keenan had grinned like a yardie on crack. "It's where you belong, good buddy." Now, Franco was scowling, face flushed red, sweat dripping in his eyes, hands slapping at the investigative procedures of ants on his pants. "Damn and bloody bollocks," he moaned, and shuffled forward to Pippa. "What is it?"

"Keenan's spotted something."

"Oh yeah?"

"Probably a tree. He's always doing that. Spotting trees, and thinking they're something else." Franco sighed. "What I wouldn't give to be in a downtown dregside Slap & Tickle whorehouse right now, with a buxom lass sat on my face."

"Wouldn't you suffocate?"

Franco stared at Pippa as if she were insane; an interesting and ironic reversal. "That's the whole point," he snapped, and moved ahead to Keenan.

"Is there a problem?" whispered Keenan, sliding back from the jungle fringe.

"Yes," moaned Franco. "I'm not in a compromising position with a fat bird. What about you?"

"I've found Kuminyana's Klasp Fighter."

Franco stared past Keenan, eyes narrowed. "I don't see it."

"That's because it's in fifty or so chunks littering the jungle floor."

"Ahh. That'd be the reason, then."

Keenan gestured to Pippa. "Do another scan on the PAD. The Klasp's up ahead, but something cut it up pretty bad. It wasn't an explosion; I see laser scarring on the cubes.'

"So, not a missile." Pippa activated the PAD scan. "That sounds more like an IMS." An IMS, or Industrial Molecule Stripper, was a savage construction *deconstruction* device used in the terraforming of planets – or more precisely, the *un*terraforming of planets. On the right setting, an IMS could cut a mountain in half. Military-grade hull armour stood no chance. That's why they were illegal. And decommissioned on sight.

"That's what I thought. Franco, any signs of detonation?"

Franco lifted his nose to the wind. He sniffed. "Trace elements of G7 HUP explosive. But it's old. Real old." He closed his eyes, brow furrowing in concentration. Despite appearances of acute insanity and trembling sexual deviancy, Franco was an expert in the field of explosives, detonations and basically anything that went *bang*. Including, occasionally, himself. "Nothing else, bomb-wise… but I can smell a faint sulphuric inhibitor."

"Meaning?" said Pippa.

"IMS. As you surmised." The ginger-bearded man opened his eyes and grinned. "Some lunatic carved this ship like a primetime yuletide turkey; and only a lunatic runs wild with an IMS. Maybe some of the GriTags are left over from the war? Or the combat AIs? Maybe even Kuminyana's own platoon went brain-rot craz*ee*; seen it a few times, down on The City's seedier districts, or in Kujoll and Temple Falls, you know, dengfish soldiers stir-crazy and bollock-naked on inhaled vodka-crack and direct plastic brain-stim injections. Affects AIs in strange ways, you know?"

"You've led a colourful life, haven't you, dickhead?" said Pippa.

Franco grinned, rubbing his goatee beard. 'Bet your pretty little pussy on that one, sweetie." He winked.

Grimacing, Pippa crawled up beside Keenan and scanned the jungle. She started to pick out huge chunks of decimated Klasp starship. It made her shiver. This wasn't just somebody making sure Kuminyana couldn't leave the planet; this was a rampage. There was at least one madman still out there. Pippa reached back, and touched her twin yukana swords sheathed beneath her pack; they soothed her soul, calmed her mind, offered solid metal reassurance. Forged from a single molecule, each perfectly balanced blade could cut hull steel.

Once the PAD gave an okay they moved out in a wide line, eyes alert, senses singing. All weapons were primed now and held steady, professional, in gloved hands. Keenan read the – havoc. The jungle itself was torn apart, and he led the way following wide tracks until they came to a clearing and halted. It was filled with machine corpses.

GG AIs, and especially combat models, were lethal to the point of perfection, their development cycle stalled at a peak of hardware climax. They were end of the line; Nano-Tek could make no better. Sentient, very, very tough, streamlined, intelligent, empathic, loyal, a GG in terms of machine evolution was as good as it got. Machine gods. Ultimate guards, hunters or assassins. And here were eight of them, ripped apart, cracked carapaces spewing machine internals, wires and coils and digital valves, bashed limbs, crushed skulls, metal wrenched from metal wrenched from metal in ragged cokehead lines, alloy severed, wire arteries sliced, eyes fused, fingers pulverised.

Combat K eased forward through jungle mist. They stood amidst the carnage.

"This wasn't done with an IMS," said Franco, spinning slowly about.

"So... what kind of creature rips apart eight GGs?" Pippa's face was straight, and a touch pale. Her eyes met Franco's. They hoisted weapons and glanced at Keenan.

"I think she's dead," said Franco. "I think we should get back to the ship."

"Not till we find her," said Keenan, voice a purr.

"It's a suicide mission!" wailed Franco. "Look around you! There's no way she survived."

"Have you no honour?" snapped Keenan. "There's a young, lonely, frightened princess out there. We have been charged with rescuing her. If she lives, we'll find her."

"Yeah," muttered Franco, "and you can carve *that* on my fucking grave."

"Look at this," said Pippa. She held up a torn piece of fabric. It was made from silk, a dashing bright violet, charred at the edges. Pippa poked at something caught there; it was a long length of stripped and burnt flesh, replete with a tangle of gloss black hair.

Keenan and Franco stared at the item.

"Now do you agree she's dead?" muttered Franco with a shudder.

"No." Keenan locked gazes. "She might be injured. We owe her a chance."

"It's got her fucking skin and hair on it! Urgh! It's 'orrible! Face it pal, she's as dead as a dead duck."

"We're going in."

"You're a stubborn mule, Keenan."

"And you're behaving like a coward. Now listen, soldier; get your shit together, and get online, because I need you focused. If there's a chance Kuminyana is still breathing, we're going to find her. So less moaning, more on-task. Capiche?"

"Yeah boss." Franco sighed. "And boss?"

"Yes?" Keenan snapped, and lit a cigarette. He stared at Franco, eyes blazing, weed drooping from his lower lip, smoke stinging his eyes.

"You're a good guy. You know that?"

Keenan laughed. "Well, you can carve *that* on *my* fucking grave."

The jungle smash ended suddenly, and Keenan, Franco and Pippa crouched in knee-high jungle detritus staring out over Shenzar City. It was a sight to behold. For a start, it was vast; perhaps fifty square kilometres of titanic leering skyscrapers, warehouses, depots, towers, tenement blocks, each one interspersed by curving arcs of tiered freeways criss-crossing and entwining so Franco blinked, almost believing he was staring at a plate of splattered concrete spaghetti. But there were two aspects that set this city apart from the usual teeming metropolis they were used to: First, was the obscene, visceral and visual battle decadence, the crumbling concrete, massacred marble, smashed stone, ionised iron, an oil-painted landscape of bomb blasts, crumbled brickwork, bullet holes, a billion *billion* bullet holes so that bullet holes existed *within* bullet holes, of burned out tanks, six-wheeled husks, crashed and blackened fighter jets, the scene as a whole enough to put any chickenhawk off military pornography (or *milporn,* to those canny self-denying milporn academic addicts in the know) in about a nanosecond. Second, came the silence.

Franco thought the jungle was quiet. In retrospect, the jungle had been a blaze of riotous noise, of clicking insects and buzzing hums, of rustles and creaks and cracks and drips. Now, silence drifted up from the vast, barely inhabited space of Shenzar City. Barely inhabited by *ghosts,* at least.

"I'm not going down there," muttered Franco. "It might be dangerous."

Keenan grabbed the collar of Franco's WarSuit. "That's the idea, dickhead." His eyes glowed. "We're Combat K! That's why we're here."

Franco stared again at the vast city, stretching off as far as the eye could see, and riddled with evidence of ancient slaughter. A heat haze hung over the perfect stillness. He could almost feel the tarmac bubbling, the concrete cracking. He shivered.

"Yes. But it gives me the heebie jeebies."

"Found her." Pippa's face glowed triumphant. In her gloved hand, the PAD gave a tiny *blip*. She glanced at Keenan. "Or at least, a trace of life."

"Where is she?" said Keenan.

"Where else? The core of the city."

"How far?"

"Twenty five klicks, or thereabouts."

"Through that?" said Franco, nodding at the buckled towering heat haze.

"Through that," agreed Pippa.

"Let's move out," said Keenan.

"Can't we stop for a brew? And some, y'know," Franco twitched, "some sausage?"

Keenan stared at him. Then stared at him some more.

Franco buckled. "Okay. Okay." He held up his hand. "I'll just have to wait for my injection of über-sausage fat and hypercaffeine. Gods! This is like... like being *in the army*, or something." Keenan led the way down a savage slope of metal scree, boots sliding, gun tracking, eyes narrowed; Pippa and Franco followed, Franco moaning and mumbling – an act which seemed to keep him moderately happy, at least.

They moved slowly down a narrow street, boots crunching glass, metal shards, old bullet casings, stones, crumbled rock, and above them towered buildings, huge blocks of decimated carnage, concrete riddled with a million bullet holes, windowless eyes glaring down with compressed antediluvian malevolence. Thick dark clouds rolled across the sky, like bruises against a virgin's white skin. Darkness started to fall in spirals. A cool air blew down the street, smelling of old metal and stone-dust. The ground seemed to vibrate with a deep and rhythmical bass, a drum rhythm beneath their boots.

"A storm's coming," said Franco.

"It's something else," said Pippa, eyes narrowed. "Quick. Get in the building."

They entered a dark tomb space and crouched behind a wall once eaten by bullets. Along the street, slowly, thumped a six-legged... vehicle. It looked like a normal QGM troop carrier, its hulking shell military green and battered and bashed so many times it looked like a hand-beaten panel of foil. But instead of wheels it had legs. Metal piston legs, which thumped in what would have been a comical fashion if it hadn't been for three automated HMGs on the hull dome, tracking and moving, clicking and clacking.

"I thought this place was long deserted," whispered Franco.

"Automated defences," said Pippa, voice neutral. "That's called a Thumper."

"But the war was over a hundred years ago!" snapped Franco. He frowned. "And why's it called a Thumper? That's a stupid name?"

The machine halted, a sudden movement accompanied by metallic tearing noises. Engines gnashed. Pistons thrummed inside its belly. It turned, as if looking at the hidden forms of Combat K, despite having no eyes. It growled, long and low, and a huge piston slammed from its prow, smashing through the wall in a tumble of bricks and masonry chunks, and nearly taking Franco's face off. The piston withdrew, slowly, trickling dust and bricks, and Franco, still staring straight ahead, his face now a platter of dust, turned and scowled at Pippa.

"That's why," she mouthed. Then... "Shh!"

They eased back from the wall, and a metallic, nasal, anally bureaucratic voice rang through the air. "ORGANIC MACHINES! I CAN SMELL YOU! I CAN HEAR YOUR

LITTLE INSECT VOICES! YOU ARE TO STAND UP! YOU ARE TO WALK OUTSIDE AND NO FUNNY BUSINESS, BUSTER!"

"*Eh?*" snapped Franco.

HMGs whined, charging up, and bullets swept through the air in a sudden roar. Combat K rolled apart as bullets cut through brickwork and stone, screeching, ricochets *pinging,* and their guns turned on the Thumper, roaring, bullets scything across the short space with sudden hot metal impact. Bullets clanged up the Thumper's battered shell, sparks flying, splinters of shaved metal curling off like red-hot glowing embers. Keenan sprinted through several doorways, bullets tracking him through brickwork with little *puffs* of powdered brick, and he dived long and low, rolling, slammed a wall and hurled a Babe Grenade through a gaping-tooth window. A Babe Grenade was so called (in QGM slang) because 'it gave you a good fucking'. It proceeded to do this to the Thumper. Flames roared, and smoke rolled out engulfing the six-legged jittering clattering vehicle. Keenan kept his gun on the Thumper, face blacked, eyes narrowed in a scowl. This was supposed to be a Search and Rescue mission. DropBots said the planet was damn well *clear.* And now they were in the midst of a violent fire fight with an unknown enemy...

"Bastard," he muttered.

The smoke cleared. The Thumper was unharmed.

"YOU ARE NAUGHTY ORGANIC MACHINES!" came the nasal bureaucratic roar. "YOU ARE TO THROW DOWN YOUR WEAPONS IMMEDIATELY! YOU ARE TO SURRENDER IMMEDIATELY! OR I WILL GET *REALLY ANGRY.*" A long thin barrel ejected from the side of the Thumper's battered hull. There came a *hiss* as a pilot-light ignited. It was an IFT. An Industrial Flame Thrower. Or what they called in the business a *Flesh Flame Griller.*

"Stuff this," snapped Franco. "Cover me!" He lobbed out three smoke grenades, and the Thumper stamped its little piston legs and rotated, seeking the source of this *OUTRAGE!* Franco rolled sideways and came up running. Smoke billowed around him, and he heard Keenan and Pippa's MPKs roar, drawing its fire. As he ran, arms pumping, he pulled round his pack and located a G15 funnel charge. "This'll give him a poke up the arse," he mumbled, slamming against a wall which teetered under the force of the blow. Smoke billowed, obscuring his view. He coughed, and ducking low, crept toward the sound of stamping metal feet.

Guns whined. He could feel a chatter of discharge through the ground. Cordite stink rimed his nostrils. Smoke clung to his throat like a rescued fake jumper to a fireman's ladder. He was close now. Close to the bastard. But if it realised, sensed him, it would turn and *crush him.* Gritting teeth, Franco crept closer and primed the charge – originally used for rock blasting in deep dark mines; Franco had found another use for this unusual and *powerful* explosive. The Thumper turned, it had sensed him, and through the smoke he heard guns whining and clacking. He leapt forward, slammed the charge on the Thumper's metal abdomen, and ran for it…

Guns clacked and bullets howled, slamming random shells around Franco in the smoke. He screamed like a girl and hit the ground, rolling, crawling as the Thumper shifted, all six legs striking the battered tarmac and a roar of flames told Franco the IFT had charged… he crept behind a wall, shouted, "Fire up her hole!" and hit the det. There came a deafening metallic *bang,* like a slap in the face, a kick in the balls, and billowing smoke was blasted into nothing as the Thumper was invaded and picked up, spinning into the sky at a diagonal angle where it struck a building, caving in a two-storey wall which followed the bent and twisted and still moaning Thumper all the way back down to the ground. Bricks tumbled and roared, and within a few seconds what remained of the Thumper's twisted chassis was buried.

From the sleeting dust came Keenan and Pippa, and Franco

ran to them, a grin on his face.

"That's some charge," said Keenan, gun tracking, eyes scanning.

"Like a fist up the arse," grinned Franco. "The bugger never saw it coming."

"What was it protecting?" said Pippa, shielding her eyes and gazing up, around.

"There," snapped Keenan.

Amidst the rubble, the crumbled concrete, the detritus, they saw it – a solid, black, alloy missile block. Keenan's eyes narrowed. "If the Thumper discovered we were here, on this deserted world…"

"Then it knows we arrived on a ship," finished Pippa. Even as she spoke, the missile block came to life, grinding on powerful engines as a long, sleek warhead ejected from a barrel and the block moved fast, whirring and shifting, the missile altering trajectory.

Franco frowned. "Don't be silly," he chastised. "What could it possibly want?"

The missile fired in a roar of flames and thick acrid smoke. Combat K choked, stumbling back. The missile flashed into the sky and was gone. Three seconds passed. Distantly, there came a *boom* and a narrow column of smoke rose into the air over the jungle.

Keenan flashed Franco a sour glance. "Our fucking ship," he snarled, and rubbed at his head. "The son of a bitch."

"Confirmed," said Pippa, staring at the PAD. "It took out the Hornet."

"So even if we find Princess Kuminyana, we've no damn exit from the planet," snapped Keenan, slapping his MPK.

Franco gazed around, eyes wide, like a doe watching a sniper. "Bummer," he said.

"It's coming alive," said Pippa, solemnly.

They watched from the trench, three kilometres from where they'd destroyed the Thumper. It had been a gradual thing at first, as they patrolled the streets, hunted down the ghost of the princess; a buzz here, a chirp there, like distant phonecalls, the reawakening of old electricity, but then three BombBlimps spun overhead, thrumming and droning, bomb-chutes open and ready for intruders and Keenan called a time-out.

"It's as if our presence has awoken them," said Franco, in awe.

"Yeah, that or your big mouth," said Pippa.

"Hey, I was only pointing out the obvious!"

"Yeah, that and *bombing* the shit out of the bastard Thumper."

"It needed to be done," said Franco, primly.

"Stop *arguing!*" snapped Keenan. "How far does the PAD read?"

"Five klicks."

"That's a long way with Razor Drones buzzing your arse," said Franco. As if to emphasise his words, a fleet of twenty Razor Drones snapped overhead, razors spinning, scanners on the lookout for enemy. Franco just *knew* he'd fall easily into that category.

"What I don't get," said Pippa, uneasily, "is why they've suddenly come to life."

"Hmm?" Franco raised his eyebrows.

"The automated defences. Shenzar City's unwelcome denizens. The DropBots scanned this place as dead; even for AI. Now, the minute we tramp through, all shit is let loose. It's too much of a coincidence."

"Maybe they sleep," said Franco, eyes wide. "Maybe Kuminyana coming here woke them all up, and now they just want fresh meat!" He cocked his Kekra quad-barrel machine pistol. "Maybe they want a war!" He puffed out his chest. "Hot damn, we can give them one!" He went as if to stand up, and

Keenan grabbed his WarSuit and dragged him back down to the trench.

"Idiot," he hissed. "They've been fighting this thing for centuries. You think three Combat K squaddies with machine guns can make a difference?"

"We can always make a difference," said Franco.

"We're here to find the girl," said Keenan.

"If she's alive," pointed out Franco.

"Yeah. If she's alive."

They spent the next three hours picking their way through ancient trenches. Razor Drones and scanning HovDrones buzzed overhead, banking between the towering walls of skyscrapers and cubeblocks. BombBlimps droned overhead, high and threatening, bomb doors and bomb slides waiting to drop more gratuitous violence on the unsuspecting below. In silence, a silence enforced by Keenan's gun, boot and threat of court marshal and five months in solitary, Combat K crept like criminals through the trenches, streets, dugouts, alleys, backways, tunnels and cesspipes of Shenzar City, with the PAD guiding them towards the only, apparent, organic life in the vicinity.

Eventually, Pippa moved ahead to scout, climbing a high staircase in a half-bombed five-hundred storey residential towerblock to survey the surroundings. When she returned, she seemed excited. "I can see a Klasp Fighter," she said.

"Where?"

"On top of Barb Hill. Up ahead. It has the markings of the Royal Guard. The W'hore Royal Family."

"I thought we saw the ship destroyed?" said Franco, brows furrowed.

"We did. Cut into cubes, in fact."

"But now it's OK? How's that work, then?"

"This gets stranger and stranger," muttered Keenan.

"Not as strange as my pants," said Franco.

Keenan glanced at him. "Meaning?"

"Well, three nights ago I had an amore... an amour... a *romantic* meeting, reet, with this fit bird but she smelt of fish, and I thought to myself about this being a bit of a fishy meeting, reet, but then we went back to..."

Keenan held up a hand. "Enough."

"It's a good story."

"I'm sure it is. Pippa? You get any more signs of life?"

"Only what's on the PAD." She smiled. "Oddly, Franco isn't included."

"Let's move in, then," said Keenan.

With Franco grumbling, they advanced.

Trenches ended, and Combat K edged onto empty ground. There was a steep slope with many points of cover, but also many choke points to halt an advancing enemy. Carrying weapons, ammo and kit, all three were soon sweating heavily under the Vor heat haze, and as they climbed so the city spread around them, a nightmare of jagged buildings, staccato jumps, towering, blackened crumbling teeth. Barb Hill was, it transpired, a solid hill of war-scrap, old steel, rubbish and crap. It grew steeper as they climbed, Shenzar City spreading out like a visual disease, and Combat K kept guns primed and heads low, moving slowly, aware they were sitting ducks and as vulnerable as a stallion's tackle. The Klasp Fighter loomed high above, distant, bullet marked, rocket scarred, but still in good enough order to fly. Keenan halted, panting, and looked off across the shimmering city. Drones buzzed in the distance, and he shielded his eyes.

"Problem?" said Pippa.

Keenan shook his head, and pushed on, until the pile of war-scrap levelled out a full kilometre in the sky, surrounded by staggered jumps of equally vertiginous skyblocks. Keenan tracked his MPK, eyes narrowed, and moved forward with Pippa and a honking, heaving Franco close behind. They formed a tight unit. A triumvirate of heavy firepower. Combat K.

The Klasp was elongated, sleek, black; battered, scarred, and damaged. A door hissed open in the fighter's flank. Kuminyana stood, hands held palms outwards in supplication, her dress spun in rich violet, her dark gloss hair tied back and high in an arty spiral. Her face was beautiful, with a very slight green hue, her cheekbones high and regal, skin flawless.

"Wow," panted Franco, hands on his knees. "Does that mean we can go to the pub?"

Keenan stepped forward. "Your Highness," he said. "We've come to take you home."

Princess Kuminyana surveyed the smoke-stained dirt-smeared group, and she smiled a radiant smile full of warmth, and happiness, and joy. Keenan felt shoulders relax, felt tension leak from his weary shell.

"Wait." Pippa was beside him. She whispered in his ear. "Something's wrong."

"Thank you for travelling... all this way. It was unnecessary." Kuminyana's voice was high-pitched, sing-song, unused to the guttural language of Quad-Gal Central. The W'hores were an ancient race, but tended away from QG politics, sending the minimum number of emissaries and rarely attending political conventions. She frowned a little. "However. The reason my communications died were because... I did not wish to leave. Thank you for your efforts, Combat K. You may now return."

Keenan eyed Kuminyana. Pippa was right. Something about her was deeply disturbing; it was a splinter of *oddness* which ran through the woman; something about her manner, her stance, an indefinable element of character, the tilt of her head, the tone of her voice. Everything seemed, somehow, *fake*.

"We have been assigned to bring you back," said Keenan, voice low, eyes fixed on Kuminyana's relaxed stance. "We cannot leave without you." He clenched his teeth, muscles standing out along his jaw.

"Yes you can," she said, soothingly. And she smiled. It was

the smile that did it. Something here was extraordinarily out of synch. "I insist."

"What happened to your spaceship?" butted in Franco, stepping forward, frowning, big mouth flapping as it always did. "We found it, back there, cut into chunks, it identified as your ship on the PAD, then we found a piece of gruesome scalp and we thought it was yours with skin and hair and everything, ugh, it was quite horrible, so it was." He grinned at her, showing his missing tooth.

"Maybe you should have turned back then," said Kuminyana.

"It was a set-up," said Pippa, intuition sleeting through her. "You wanted us to think you were dead. Head home with that information; false information."

Kuminyana nodded "Yes."

"But why?" blurted out Franco. "Why'd you want to stay here, girl? It's a crazy place! Full of dead technology and war bastards! Why, eh?"

Kuminyana smiled. "Because I'm in love," she said.

They stared at her. Eventually, Pippa snapped, "There are easier ways to sort out your honeymoon than faking your own death, and putting us through the shit."

"No." Kuminyana took a deep breath, and walked down the ramp from the Klasp Fighter. She stood on the mountain of war-scrap, and looked down at the ground for the moment, in consideration. The she looked up, and Keenan caught the dark glint in her semi-alien eyes. "It is illegal in W'hore culture for me to take one of another species. And especially one of such… non organic origins."

"You've fallen in love with an AI?" said Pippa, slowly.

"More than that," said Kuminyana. She spread her arms wide, as if encompassing the world. "He is the Psi.copath. He reads your thoughts, and mine; and this is his place, his world, his army, his war! All the HovDrones and BombBlimps, Thumpers,

Intruders, Razor Skells, leashed SPAWs and second-hand GriTags, all are his, under his command, and he will build his army strong again, he will take the war from Shenza City and I will rule beside him! We will rule Vor together!" Her eyes glinted in madness now, and Combat K saw she carried a small gun. It was black, nestled in her hand, and they froze.

"Are you fucking *insane?*" snarled Pippa. "We're here to rescue you!"

"If you will not leave, then you must die."

Pippa spread her arms wide. "Come with us, girl!"

"As I said." Kuminyana smiled; almost in apology. Almost.

She fired the gun, a hollow bark, but hadn't reckoned on Combat K's well-oiled unit perfection; they rolled apart fast, inhumanly fast, and the bullet clipped Franco's WarSuit which gave a deep *buzz*. Franco scowled. "Hey, bitch, why'd you shoot at *me?*"

Keenan came up, palmed his Techrim 11mm, and slammed a bullet in Kuminyana's shoulder. The bullet exited on a shower of pissing blood and shoulder shards, and Kuminyana staggered back, face pale, gasping, and she began to fire again and Keenan dropped to one knee and levelled his gun. But before he could shoot, there came a *blam* of a D5 shotgun, and Kuminyana accelerated backwards like a ragdoll, limbs flailing, hit the side of the Klasp Fighter, slumped down in a heap, and was still.

"What did you do that for?" raged Keenan, turning on Pippa. "We take her down, then fucking *take her with us!*"

"I rarely shoot to wound," said Pippa, voice cold. "Only to kill."

"You lunatic! You're bringing your personal life into this game, and you're going to get us all dead."

Pippa shrugged, turned, and stared off across Shenzar City. "Big boys games, big boys rules," she said, and sheathed her D5 shotgun, drawing both yukana swords from sheaths on her back. "Anyway. It was a D5 SpreadShot. If I'd wanted her dead," she twirled a sword, "I would have cut her damn head off." She turned back, and seemed to be waiting.

"What are you doing?" said Franco, slowly, glancing about with nerves jangling.

"You don't get it, do you?" said Pippa. She smiled. It was a smile of intrinsic knowledge. "The Psi.copath won't let us leave. We'd ruin its plans. And it knows that; knows we couldn't take Kuminyana with us."

"So you shot her?" said Keenan.

"You're a brutal bitch," said Franco.

"I never claimed to be anything different. Better get your guns ready. It's coming."

"What is?"

"The Psi.copath, idiot."

There came a roar, so low it was below hearing then rose in electronic pitch till it made their eardrums bleed. Wincing in agony, Pippa twirled her swords and scowled and she knew, they were going to fight for their lives and this wasn't a fucking rescue mission, it was a gang rape, a QGM bureaucratic fuck-up of the usual incredible magnitude. The pile of war-scrap beneath their boots began to move, to writhe, and plates of steel and iron rattled across the surface and everything seemed suddenly to be moving, shifting, a quicksand of metal and old bullets, of iron beams and engine parts, and wires snaked and hissed across the surface and Pippa screamed, "We have to get in the Klasp, it's our only chance!" but the fighter was moving also, shifting on the mountain of moving metal rubble and then set off, sliding down the slope, sparks screaming and streaming to turn suddenly, coming to rest at a teetering angle on the brink of a ledge which led to a thousand metre drop. If the Klasp went over the edge… goodbye journey home.

Still, the mountain top rattled and seethed, a bubbling of metal parts, and Combat K watched in confusion at first, then with a gradual understanding as the Psi.copath assembled itself from the garbage of the war-torn world. It rose from the mound like a monster from a tar-pit, and its head was a FukTruk's engine block, its eyes old headlamps, its body the chassis of several conjoined tanks. Its arms were heavy-duty 7.62mm mini-guns, its legs were H-section girders, and even as they watched it became riddled with armoured scales made from tank plates, the tail sections of destroyed R52 MiG fighters and buckled car panels which scampered up its flanks, toppling untidily into place; the engine for its head suddenly roared into life with a belch of exhaust and headlamps illuminated a bright yellow, dazzling beams sweeping the ground searching for Combat K. The Psi.copath rose above a gawping, surprised combat squad and looked down at them with arms spinning, whining, accelerating and the guns came up and the Psi.copath took a heavy clanking step forward and bullets roared as Combat K fled, leaping from the summit of the metal mountain and sliding down the far slope, boots trying to dig in as they were carried in a sudden avalanche of metal debris, old cans and broken guns, buckled panels and crap.

They slid to a halt, panting, perhaps a hundred metres from the summit.

"We have to reach the fighter," said Pippa, a yukana sword in each fist.

Franco, who was glancing nervously up the slope, nodded. "What the hell *is it?*"

"I've seen one before," said Pippa, slowly. "On Hardcore." Hardcore was a prison world, part of Five Grey Moons where once she had served time for eight counts of murder. "It has Psi powers – can read your mind." She grinned. "But it can only read one mind at a time... we need a decoy, something to distract the fucker." Pippa and Keenan both stared at Franco.

"Hey," he said, holding up his hands. "No way, guys."

"I'm the best pilot," said Pippa.

"And I'm the best person to protect the pilot," said Keenan.

"Listen," snarled Franco, "there's no fucking way I'm being a decoy to that, that… that metal dildo! No way. Not on my watch, compadre. A man would have to be…" his eyes glinted. "Insane."

Franco peered over the edge of the slope, mouth pouting, arse clenching. On descent, he'd expected the Psi.copath to come charging after them; now he understood why it had not. The huge metal creature was crouched over the bleeding form of Princess Kuminyana, weeping. However insane Franco might be, he was no fool. He knew tears would come first; and then violence a close second.

OK, he thought. Distractions. Distractions *without* getting killed. He glanced right, where Keenan and Pippa were working their way around the mound of scrap. Keenan gave Franco the thumbs-up. Franco gave Keenan the finger.

Equation:

Franco+Psi.copath=deadFranco.

Franco+Kekra<Psi.copath(withoutweapon). And it had a weapon. *Shit.*

Franco+fastlegs=possiblerunawayscenario?

Franco grinned. Seemed like a winner!

The Psi.copath screamed, an ululation from bass to bleeding ears in a single second, and Franco covered his ears and winced and watched the creature stomp towards him. "Argh," he said, backed away, and slid down the slope. The Psi.copath leapt after him, and Franco found himself back-pedalling through sliding metal plates as the Psi.copath accelerated and armed its mini guns; bullets roared after Franco and, grimacing, the little ginger squaddie returned fire, sliding backwards, on his behind, down a kilometre high pile of metal debris. Bullets whined and howled and slammed and sparked. Franco was a dam good shot, and even as bullets *pinged* and *hissed* around him he kept a cool head and focused and aimed and there came a *crash,* followed by a second. Franco had taken out its headlamp eyes. He slid to a stop, and lay there, panting, leaning back, guns focused, as the Psi.copath stuttered to a halt, feet clanging amidst ancient brass shell casings.

"Ha! Blinded you, fucker!" A hundred bullets nearly took his head off as the machine AI tracked him by sound; Franco rolled violently, and the Psi.copath leapt, scooping him up in mini-gun arms and Franco screamed like a woman, beat at the metal creature like a tantrum toddler, and it turned and toiled back up the sliding mountain with Franco cradled like a captured newborn, a bearded infant, and Franco shot point-blank into the Psi.copath's face but his shells had no effect. The Psi.copath's face was an engine.

The Psi.copath walked to the body of Kuminyana. It knelt, and placed Franco by her side. He glanced uneasily at the corpse, and realised... "Hot damn," he whispered. She was still alive. Breathing, raggedly, quickly, but still alive.

What had Pippa said? *It has Psi powers – can read your mind. But it can only read one mind at once... we need a decoy, something to distract the fucker.* Franco looked up at the towering monstrosity above him. He coughed, and spat on the ground. Shit, he thought. I'm *dead...*

"Wait." Pippa was walking across metal rubble, and the Psi.copath orientated on her. It settled back, with a hiss and ejection of steam. Slowly, in an exaggerated gesture, Pippa threw down her weapons. The Psi.copath shifted, watching her, and Franco lay at its feet like a sacrificial lamb. He made frantic gestures to Pippa. *Shoot it!* he screamed in military sign. *Shoot the bugger!* She ignored him. Pippa held up her hands, to show she was now unarmed; zero threat. The Psi.copath made no move...

Time seemed to freeze. Franco was sure he was about to die. His past life rushed before him; and he realised it was a lurid cacophony of brothels, bars, fights and fucking. He grinned inanely. It had been a *good life*, he realised.

"I understand," said Pippa, reaching the Psi.copath. Behind her, engines roared, and Keenan piloted the stricken Klasp Fighter into the air; it banked, jets glowing purple, and hovered for a moment with huge guns orientating on the bizarre metal AI. If he wanted, he could blast it into eternity. "You're in love, aren't you?" said Pippa.

Franco stared, agog. Pippa was, in his opinion, hardly the intuitive type. A psychopathic man-slaughterer, yes, but not, ergo, a woman who noticed the finer aspects of emotional relationships – especially in a mangled war-scrap AI.

Franco waited for the machine to blast Pippa into oblivion…

Instead, it lowered mini-guns and settled further back. There came several groans and clanks. Pippa smiled.

"Read my mind," she said.

Minutes passed. Eventually, Franco climbed to his knees and crawled across the scrap, face elongated in a vulpine scowl, until he reached Pippa and hid behind her.

Pippa's eyes were closed. She could feel the intrusion; but it was gentle. Like a breeze passing over her soul.

Eventually, she said, "Yes. I will."

Her eyes opened. She kicked Franco on the shin. "Ow," he said.

Pippa moved to the fast-breathing Princess Kuminyana. She stooped, and picked the woman up in her arms, gazing down into her unconscious face. She moved away from the Psi.copath and Keenan touched down, engines roaring, ramp unfolding, and Pippa strode up into the craft's belly. Franco scampered after her like a wounded spaniel. The ramp lifted, the Klasp banked, and shot off high into a bruised and mocking sky. Within seconds, it was a blip. Within minutes, it had left orbit.

Franco stared out at blackness, and winced as a MedBot dabbed his cuts with iodine. "Ow. Ow. Ouch!"

"SOR REE," said the MedBot.

"Dickhead!"

"SOR REE." It hummed, dropping, and jabbed his arse with a needle.

"OUCH!"

"SOR REE."

"So then," scowled Franco, turning to Pippa. "Explain what happened."

"It was in love with her. Rather than destroy us, it recognised we could help her. Help repair the damage we caused. *I* caused."

"Yeah, reet, but we caused it *because* of her!"

"Maybe so. The fact still remains – it was a simple case of eloping. The W'hore religion wouldn't allow her to marry an AI; they came up with a deception to side-step primitive ways, and it would have worked if we hadn't blundered into the web."

Franco thought about this. "That Psi.copath," he said.

"Yeah?"

"It could have killed us at any time, right?"

"Well done," smiled Pippa. "You catch on fast. It wasn't just a robot AI you witnessed."

"What was it, then?"

"The Psi.copath was the city," said Pippa, softly.

"Say again?"

"The Psi.copath was the remains of Shenza City *in its entirety*. We saw an avatar; an intermediate construct with a single purpose: to scare us off. It played to our own specific nightmares."

Franco thought about this. "It didn't play to *my* nightmares," he said. "*My* nightmares consist of buxom naked men with whips."

Pippa frowned, but said nothing. She was too busy programming the console.

"What happens next?" said Franco.

"We fix her up, then bring her back." Keenan slumped into a comfort-couch and lit a cigarette. Pippa coughed in annoyance. Keenan ignored her.

"Erm, isn't that, like, kind of, like, illegal?"

Keenan and Pippa stared at him.

Franco coughed. "Well, you know, I'm a kickass hardcore squaddie who laughs in the face of legality, blows bubbles down the wobbling man-tits of donut-scoffing police; but hell, we've kinda been given a mission here, and…"

"We're bringing her back," said Pippa, voice hard. "No arguments, and damn the consequences. Quad Gal Military can kiss my arse with their missions." She sighed. "Franco?"

"Yeah babe?" He beamed.

"Go and put the coffee on. There's a good lad."

The Maker's Mark

Michael Cobley

1. Ancient Eyes

Cornelius Jamal, only son of Sophia and Ibrahim Jamal, first encountered the Grand Gestator Udroom while visiting Teqavra Zoo. It had ancient eyes. The glowing plate read, 'GRAWF, gender indeterminate; semi-sentient; said to have once been used as food animals by the Shyntanil', but Cornelius knew that the huge mound of a creature was a Grand Gestator. The old tablet book in their Suzerain's library had detailed the species' origins and appearance, as well as their fecundation/incubation process. The book also highlighted the degrading effect of great age on conscious intellect, while claiming that the gestation faculty remained unimpaired almost until death.

Cornelius was 19 e-years old, preciously intelligent and expected to follow his father's lead by taking up an advisorhood to one of the Suzerains of Notamur, as did most of the Human descendants of the crew of the *Morphia*. The Grand Gestator Udroom was, by Human reckoning, 7,385 years old and had the persona of a dissociative child.

2. Entropy's Witness

(Excerpt from '*Early Human Settlements In Hyperspace*' by Saro128)
Prior to the upheavals of the Darien Crisis, Humans were a rarity in the tiers of hyperspace, limited to a scattering of stranded groups. They ranged from a nine-strong team of scientists from Tharsis University to the 230 wealthy passengers aboard the advanced but doomed hyperliner, *Joyous Spirit*. The former wound up in the polyhedral, zero-gravity glass burghs of Ollenaita, a Hodralog city on Tier 24, while the latter found themselves down on Tier 58 and adrift on the Great Ring Sea, harried by Keklir raider clans. The scientists were made welcome and given comfortable homes, while the passengers were forced to adopt a warlike posture to avoid enslavement or worse.

All in all, drone surveys of habitable tiers in the Uppers and Mids documented evidence of nineteen Human communities. A number had encountered strange intelligent species and adapted, some withdrew into paranoid enclaves, while the rest either died out or were slain. But few had stories as bold and colourful as the odyssey of Cornelius Jamal.

3. The Art of Persuasion

"Hello, my name is Cornelius. Who are you?"

"… I am…. Udroom. Are you here to feed me? You don't look like my feeder."

"I'm just a friend, Udroom, but I can get you some of your favourite food if you tell me something."

"Chelgo beans are my favourite. Have you got some?"

"Yes, and you can have them all if you answer a little question."

"What's that?"

"Can you make things? With your body?"

"… oh….Oh!... that's the bad secret! I promised not to say…"

"Promised who? Your feeder?"

"Promised Ithnor in the Long-Ago, promised not to talk about the bad secret…"

"Was Ithnor your friend?"

"Yes."

"Well, I'm your friend too, so you can tell me anything, even why you can't make things anymore."

"No, I can still make things, if I want!"

"Really? That's amazing – here, have some chelgo beans…."

The Grand Gestator lumbered off into a grassy corner of its enclosure, small hands tightly grasping the bag of beans. Cornelius smiled thoughtfully as he slipped the translator back inside his longcoat. It would take several more visits, and a lot of chelgo beans, to fully gain the gestator's trust. And by then he planned to be on the aerobarge pilot roster and to have amassed a stockpile of provisions…although he also had to devise a test to ensure that Udroom could indeed gestate at will. Then with that fabulous creature safely aboard an aerobarge, he could leap away from Notamur, from the stifling, ritual-shackled future which had been laid down for him. Instead, he would be free to explore the full immensity of the Shylgandic Lacuna, the mysterious ice-bound peninsular shelves, jutting hundreds of miles out into the lacuna, and the penduline cities hanging from their undersides, free to chase down rumours, myths and legends, and perhaps to start a few of his own.

4. Divine Fragment

A week later he was on the snow-choked plateau-shelf of Taribul, parked outside a temple-village, and negotiating with the local prelate. Seated in the aerobarge's cramped mess, the prelate eyed the array of flickering readouts that filled one wall, then introduced himself as Yasorn.

"Master Jamal, you are certain that your device can produce a convincing relic?"

"Most assuredly, your reverence," Cornelius said. "I have

supplied it with images of your holy symbol but the main source of information will be yourself. So please, lie back on the hinged table, then I'll swing your head down between the scanning nodes, just....so. Now, picture the relic in your mind, imagine the texture, how it feels to the touch, how large it is and how heavy…"

Two hours later the task was done. While Yasorn curled up to pray, Cornelius went behind the control-panel façade and found the finished item laid out neatly on a linen-lined tray, dry and shiny. Udroom had withdrawn to the woolly, tent-like bower Cornelius had built for him at the other end of the hold, resting from his exertions.

When he brought the object out, the prelate gaped and hissed in amazement.

"Just as I imagined - *exactly* as I saw it in my visions of Trekale!"

After handing over a significant sum in urexpins, the prelate Yasorn hurried off through the snow with the relic, a four foot-long metal spider's limb, wrapped in cloth. From their earlier discussion, it was likely that quite soon the spider leg would by chance be uncovered beneath the Trekalian temple, thus leading to the prelate's recognition and advancement. Cornelius chuckled as he mused on the improbability of spider deity worship, especially by the Agarib, the reptiloid species that dominated the Taribul plateau. That, and the fact that Udroom's mind-reading faculty appeared to be working perfectly.

Time for something a little more adventurous, he thought.

5. Guns On Ice

It was during a visit to the penduline city of Brophoskel that a lack of caution almost led to disaster. Posing as a wholesale buyer seeking a source of contraband Izlertech webs, a Vikantan assassin inveigled his way aboard the aerobarge then produced a silvery needlegun. Directed towards a chair, Cornelius sat down and laid his still hands on his knees.

"Firstly," said the assassin, "no begging, no shouting, no threatening or weeping, although you may say final prayers to the supreme being of your choice. And no attempts at bribery – my contract already amply compensates me and I have no wish to hear any distasteful offers to buy it."

"I would not presume to insult you with such a commonplace prize as money," Cornelius said. "You are clearly an individual of considerable taste and expertise, as evinced by that superb handweapon. It's a Bonraki Family piece, is it not?"

The silver needlegun was an antique, finely chased with intricate, stylised circuit patterns. Its polished gleam and patches of wear showed that it was both well-maintained and in regular use.

The assassin nodded his gaunt head. "As made by the grandfather. Secondly, the reason for this regrettable encounter is the illegal disruptors that you have been supplying to the Abijar Clan."

"I see. So it's the Shondal who hired you – not the kind who would appreciate your artistry. Charmless thugs, in essence."

"Appreciation," said the assassin, "is not a contractual requirement."

"And yet I am forced to admit such. I have a request – since my demise is inevitable I would rather that it was carried out with grace, majesty and elegance. To your mind, what is the most exquisite and superlative weapon in the entire Shylgandic Lacuna?"

"The Moamas Spiner," the assassin said without hesitation. "It has an enclosed, gas-pressured firing mechanism that delivers a long needle via a silenced, stalk barrel which is integral to its white para-composite casing."

"You appear well-acquainted with this Spiner," Cornelius said.

"I was once honoured to hold it in my hands," the Vikantan said. "But since it is still in the possession of the Archregal of

Deytrovan this exchange is purely academic."

Cornelius rocked his head judiciously, outwardly composed, inwardly a fevered whirl of concocted jargon. "Except that my nano-apparatus here can actually create functioning artefacts from thought-images, which is how I came up with those disruptors. It assembles a detailed synthegraph from mind scans then proceeds to build it. Thus you may complete your assignment with matchless elegance. What do you say?"

6. Nine Droplets

"Well, here you sit before me, Master Jamal," said the Concubiness Semmry. "Therefore, the assassin did not fulfill his contract. How did you evade your doom?"

Cornelius shrugged. "In the end the Vikantan came to the conclusion that by replicating such a perfect object I had more than made up for the disruptor consignments. After encouraging me to vow to cease my dealings with the Abijar, and never to produce another Moamas Spiner, he rescinded the kill then left. With the weapon as my gift to him, of course."

"Of course," said the Concubiness Semmry, sipping her drink.

Cornelius smiled. The Concubiness was astonishing beautiful, with a slender neck, pale yet vital skin, a full not quite voluptuous figure, and a delicately-featured, captivating face. Cornelius had to remind himself frequently that she was not Human but Egetsi, despite the fact that she was over eight feet tall. They were seated in a muffled booth in the Damned Poet, a tavern-college located high-up on the tenth span section of the Black Bridge of Runktor. The Black Bridge was a prodigious engineering feat, linking the shelf-plateaus of Orvegruth and Tagisk, and thus the penduline cities suspended from them. Its 212 mile steel and airstone length incorporated a variety of antigravity devices and kept a maintenance army perpetually busy. From his seat in the booth Cornelius had a view of the triframe substructures receding into the white haze of snow and mist.

"I have the items," he said, voice pitched low as he produced two small packages from his pocket. The dark blue sivelvin folds of one were parted to reveal the original black filigree-set shift jewel, then the sun-gold brosheen wrappings of the other were parted to show the copy, exact in every detail, right down to the red-blue-red-blue hues that pulsed slowly through the crystal. The Concubiness Semmry leaned in close, peering through a brass-rimmed lenser for some moments. Then she let out a faint sigh and nodded.

"Excellent – Master Jamal, you have earned your fee. I have one further request, however."

"Please, name it."

"Make me another eight and your fee shall increase ten-fold."

His smile widened. "It shall be done, lady."

7. New Ghosts

It took a lengthy walk through Gylophar City's extensive market deck before he found some chelgo beans. The vendor was an avuncular, one-eyed Gomedran and as he measured out the bags with laborious precision, he chuntered on about the highlights of his week.

"Lots of strange types go through here, good sir, brainlace dealers, slavers, liberators, god-sellers, bounty hunters, and just this morning an Aprati bulletiniser passed by here. Looked skinny and ill, like they all do, but he was rattling off the headlines clear as you like till he said something about a coup on the Black Bridge…"

"A coup, you say…"

"Well, I paid him a couple of pins and he told me. Seems like the High Directors, all nine of them, were murdered simultaneously in the middle of the nightspell, that were three nights ago. No clue who the killers were but the largest faction, the Hammers, accused their enemies, the Hooks, of doing the deed, then they took over the nine great offices. So of course, now the hot words are flying while the banner-toughs fight it out on the gantries."

"By any chance are there any lesser factions on the sidelines?"

"The bulletiniser said that if the Dancers and the Harvesters ally with the Hooks they could force the Hammers out. Could come to that."

"Ah, the dance of politics, eh? How much is that?"

"That'll be 87 urexpins, if you please."

With a cheery farewell, Cornelius hefted the two large sacks and sauntered off whistling. Once out of sight, he picked up the pace. Back on the aerobarge he stowed the beans, started the engines and was aloft in a matter of minutes. Next port of call – Pazpaz City where he would use some of his new-found wealth to effect some fundamental changes; a new ship, a new appearance and a new name. Anyone looking for Cornelius Jamal would be left hunting for a ghost.

8. Trackers And Stalkers

Waved through by the outer custodian, the Hodralog investigator entered the office of the Fourth High Director of the Black Bridge of Runktor, and approached the elevated desk.

"I have news, High Director," he said, producing a list.

"Proceed."

"Investigations have shown the following to be definitely related to our quarry – twenty-seven ceremonial sword-limbs for the bodyguard of the Benign Placator of Whorleye Citadel, a duplicate of the Mask of Vandaris for the private collection of a Kormolite financier, and five glass puzzle boxes for a Henkayan traveller, this being the most recent. We are also certain that he has switched vessels and is now operating under a new name, Carmine Jezzail."

"Will you be able to find him before the Hammers' agents do?"

"With the distance involved, communications are inconstant," the Hodralog said. "But our people are closing in."

The Concubiness Semmry leaned forward to fix him with an icy gaze. "Be sure that Cornelius Jamal understands the choices open to him – work for us or die at the hands of the Hammers."

"It shall be made abundantly clear," the Hodralog said and left.

9. Puzzle Piece Permutations

Behind the sound-proofed façade of readouts, screens and controls, he studied the contents of the linen-lined tray. Another of Meleyag's thought-sculptures lay there, a semi-transparent, seated figure with smaller, multicoloured figures floating around inside it, and a crest of golden spikes that ran down its spine. What got his attention was the grey, metallic object sitting next to it, another mystery component to add to the seven Udroom had already created, apparently unconsciously, over the last year or more. No two were alike and scans revealed fine, enigmatic structures going deep within, but clues as to the function or how they fitted together were absent.

"My inside-shaper made another piece for you," Udroom said. "Do you like it, Cawneelyus?"

"It's very interesting, Udroom, thank you. You are doing so well and shaping the gifts perfectly – we wouldn't have this new ship without you."

The aircruiser boasted a capacious hold, refurbished for the gestator's comfort, but more importantly it was faster by far than either the fanfreighter or the aerobarge. And business was brisk. Knowledge of his unique services passed by word of mouth between wealthy, influential patrons up and down the Shylgandic Lacuna. Unfortunately, that same conduit provided a trail for those less well-disposed towards him.

Cornelius took the piece over to a locker, and the box containing the rest. Opening it, he paused for a startled moment before picking out a large piece he had never seen before…then realised that it was really two pieces joined together. He held the new one up next to it, turning both this way and that. Then an urgent alarm began chiming throughout the ship.

"Is it the bad people, Cawneelyus?" said Udroom, burrowing deeper into its mound of cushions.

"Stay calm," he said as he hurried off to the bridge.

Sure enough, the sensors had picked up a craft heading straight for his mooring point atop the frozen Adwaliger Plateau, where he set down after Meleyag had given his thought patterns to the gestator Udroom via the fake scanner. Cornelius disembedded the servoanchors, revved the already-hot engines, and readied his fore and aft guns. As he sent the aircruiser roaring off into the yawning, blizzard-whitened emptiness, he wondered how they got Meleyag to betray him.

10. **Thundering Future**

By chance, the route to his next possible contract took him close to the plateau-shelf of Taribul. Setting down near one of the major towns, he went for a stroll and discovered that, after his revelation and discovery of the limb of Trekale, Yasorn had risen rapidly and was now Paramount Salvationer and Voice of Trekale, the spider-god. Cornelius toyed with the notion of paying Yasorn a visit but discounted this as too risky. However, risk and chance were already in play; Temple guards were waiting when he returned to his ship and an hour later he was shackled and confined to a stone cell. A day later, Yasorn himself came to see him.

"An unfortunate encounter, Master Jamal," said the Paramount Salvationer. "I am told that thus far you have said nothing, yet I recall you to be the most voluble of charlatans."

"Meaningful words are a precious commodity," he said. "I held onto them in anticipation of this very moment."

"Good, then understand that I will have access to your marvellous device, Master Jamal," Yasorn said. "Otherwise, you will experience suffering."

Cornelius smiled. "My ship will obey only my spoken commands, oh Paramount one. You will have to take me to the berths."

Which is where they took him, with Yasorn following, both enclosed in a swaddling of reptiloid guards. As soon as he was in visual contact with the aircruiser (and its short-range sensors) he mouthed commands to activate specific emergency procedures. But before the crowd-control stunners could target his guards, several blackclad figures leaped in amongst them as smoke billowed up from the ground. Yasorn shouted in panic, suddenly hidden by a grey, swirling veil. Hands grabbed Cornelius and hustled him out of the choking clouds to the walkway near his ship. A tall figure pulled aside a featureless black mask to reveal the sublimely beautiful features of the Concubiness Semmry.

"Quick, Cornelius, open the hatch so we can make an escape…"

… Was all she said before the ship's defences stunned her into oblivion. Carefully, he lowered her willowy form to the ground, placed a light kiss on her forehead, then quickly boarded the aircruiser which, moments later, lifted amid the confusion and smoke and swept away into the pale.

11. Mutable Descent

It took nearly a year but they finally caught up with him on Twilight City. Hanging from the Dihamu plateau-shelf, it was a half-wrecked penduline metropolis given over to both organised and disorganised crime. Working under the name Calvin Jago, Cornelius had concluded some business with one of the gambling oligarchs, supplying copies of delicate mechanisms, and was returning to his ship, garbed in hooded robes. The aircruiser had been berthed in a gaping hollow in the side of the city and he had to pass through several charred, stripped-out decks on the way. He had just climbed out of the Oligarch's territory and was moving along burnt-out corridors when he glimpsed dark figures watching him with shadowy faces. Unhurriedly he doubled back to another stairwell, pausing long enough for a cheery wave before plunging down the steps, with the hunters rushing after him.

When the villainous denizens below saw strangers intruding on their territory with weapons drawn, armed response was inevitable. A deadly and deafening havoc erupted behind Cornelius as he tried to find a way to his ship. Half an hour later, after a twisty route full of dead-ends, he reached his aircruiser. With the ship sealing the externals and auto-prepping for take-off, he had just reached the bridge when he heard a deep, dull boom from outside. A second later the bridge and the aircruiser lurched to one side. Thuds and clangs reverberated through the bulkheads and exterior monitors showed debris falling all about, girders, spars and plating hemming the ship in on all sides. A terrifying possibility leaped full fledged into his thoughts – his pursuers were hell-bent on stopping him but would they go as far as attacking the great hawsers from which the city itself hung?

12. **Wild Hunters**

The *Zanak* was a 10-fan pursuit vessel on loan from the Hammer Faction to the RQL mercenary division. Their leader, the Techmeld Gomedran, Jekahaka, stood out on the freezing starboard balcony, observing the dark, suspended mass of Twilight City from the superior elevation maintained by the *Zanak*. Even though the criminal Cornelius Jamal was known to be down there, and a squad of veterans were hunting for him, there were no guarantees. The Human's guile and luck were legendary. In addition, Jekahaka was all too aware that he himself was merely the latest in a long line of hirelings contracted to deal with this fugitive. Which was why he intended to ignore the latter part of his 'kill or capture' orders.

A door slid open and his aide stepped out into the icy wind.

"They've lost him, haven't they?" he said, pre-empting the

news.

"Yes, sir. Target has evaded neutralisation. Our operatives are under fire and disengaging from brigand territory."

"And no sign of the coalition's agents?"

"None, sir."

"Right – evacuate the squad then implement Plan B. That should put an end to this chase."

Shivering, his aide assented and went back inside. The Techmeld Jekahaka, armoured in furs and steelskin grafts, smiled and waited for the spectacle to commence.

13. The Obsession Attrition

"Cawneelyus!" came a wavering, fearful voice over the bridge communicator. "The puzzle! – the puzzle!"

"Udroom….please, do not be upset…."

But still the gestator called out to him. Trying to ignore the creature, Cornelius began flicking the switches which disembedded the anchors and wound them back into the hull. And between three and four, power in the bridge suddenly died. The boards went dead in the abrupt gloom for a moment, then the backup brought some of the lights and lamps flickering on again. The fourth anchor switch, however, was unresponsive and the anchor barbs failed to retract. Then the status monitor blinked and updated to show a huge power drain taking place in the cargo hold, the Grand Gestator Udroom's quarters….

When he reached the hold, Udroom, now grown huge, was sprawled across the hold deck, scared eyes tiny in that neckless head.

"The puzzle, Cawneelyus – I made another piece, a good piece. You have to do it, get them to fit…"

The puzzle pieces from the locker lay strewn on the deck, and they were all glowing as if from some inner energy. The new piece sat on the tray and was shining too. And from the moment Cornelius laid eyes on them all he knew that he had to put them together, knew this was vital, knew he could get them to fit. Part of his mind was distraught and practically bellowing at him to deal with the crisis, even as the aircruiser jolted massively again. But he patiently brought all the pieces together in their box and began gauging, aligning, testing them against each other. Occasionally his eyes glanced at the auxiliary command station over in the forward bulkhead, but otherwise he was utterly engrossed by the puzzle.

Then one piece slid into place on another, giving off a musical ping and a pulse of radiance. He grinned, Udroom chuckled in delight, and the ship jerked, quivered, and suddenly Cornelius felt the drop, the moment when the hawsers parted and the ruined city of Twilight began to fall.

But the puzzle, he had to finish it, just had to. As the plummeting city accelerated, freefall took over and unattached things, Cornelius, the Grand Gestator, the puzzle pieces in the box, began to drift and float gently upwards. Ping, another joined piece, another bloom of light, while Udroom clapped happily. The voice at the back of Cornelius' mind was now shrieking with fear, imagining what would happen when the plunging city impacted one of the plateau-shelves that had to lie directly beneath, at some depth. But the puzzle was the thing, the whole thing, the only thing he was interested in. And finally, nine minutes and 43 seconds into the descent, the last piece pinged into place, and in quite a different voice the Grand Gestator said, "Well done, Cornelius! Well done!"

14. By An Invisible Road

On board her deep-range flier, parked near the edge of the plateau-shelf of Dihamu, the Concubiness Semmry stared in horror at the transmitted image of the falling city.

"These mercenaries have gone too far!" she said. "Remoter Lisho – have you found the ship yet?"

"Still searching. The debris and freefall conditions are proving hazardous to the probe."

The remoter was in her own tiny craft, tethered to the edge of the plateau and hovering out in the turbulent air, thus maintaining contact with her covey of probes. She had managed to get one inside Twilight City before the hawsers were severed, while the other three fell with the doomed ruin, tracking its descent.

On the flier's bridge, the Concubiness Semmry regarded the various views of the plunging city as the minutes ticked by. Periodic explosions ripped through some of the decks, sending clouds of wreckage spewing out, starting fires that raged through the corridors and chambers, driven to incinerating fury by the rushing air that blasted through the city. Flames grew and merged into great tongues and sheets, trailing like burning banners.

"Found it!" came the remoter's voice, triumphant.

One screen showed a tangle of spars and girders, shaking, jostling and shuddering, with the outlines of a vessel visible beyond them. The probe ducked through to where Jamal's aircruiser hung amid debris, drifting and bumping against larger pieces and restrained by a cable fixed to the deck.

"So that is why he has not left," the Concubiness said. "Can you use the probe to cut that line?"

"Possibly," said the remoter.

The probe slipped through the larger gaps in the debris but before it could get close to the taut cable, the ship itself seemed to quiver like a plucked string then vanish. An instant later the image was blotted out by static. The remoter was apologising profusely over the link but the Concubiness just laughed.

"Call back your probes, Lisho," she said. "Our assistance was not required after all."

On the screen the burning wreck of Twilight City fell away through ice storms and snow-dense wavefronts like a dwindling ember.

15. Time's Devouring Hand

Beneath a purpling sky, inverted mountains drifted, trees sprouting from dark, uneven crags, bushes, grass and moss cloaking their upper ledges. The aircruiser sat on rocky ground near the edge of a small lake, its cargo hold gaping while two figures, one prodigiously larger than the other, sat at the top of the loading ramp.

"A cunning device," Cornelius said. "Reached by an astonishingly indirect route."

"Self-preservation usually makes its provision," said the Grand Gestator.

Cornelius held up the assembled puzzle, eye searching for the seamless joins. "So this is – I hesitate to say it – your brain and a propulsive engine permitting travel between the tiers, all in one." He gave Udroom a baffled look. "Why do such a thing?"

"Ah, Cornelius Jamal, I am so very, very old. Boredom leads one down some odd sidetracks in search of the extraordinary!" The Grand Gestator gave a deep, rumbling laugh. "I have undertaken the forgetful sidetrack five times now and this has been the most fun by far!" The great creature's eyes, aglint with a ferocious intellect, stared out across the placid waters and a sad weariness crept into them. "To know much is to be surprised by little. It is our curse." The Gestator glanced at Cornelius. "I have a gift for you, a reward for all your hard work, and something to help you understand the value of things. Firstly, I must sleep."

So saying, the ancient being shambled back into the shadows of the hold, leaving Cornelius to the breathtaking view and his own rising tide of yawns. Ten hours of solid sleep later he came down to the hold to retrieve the jacket that he'd left there....and was startled out of his wits when a slender woman stepped unannounced out of the dimness.

"... by the Abyss!" he gasped. "Who are you? How did you get on board..."

Then two things forcibly caught his attention – first, she was wearing his jacket and the linen cloth from the duplicates tray, and little else. Second, while she was about his height, she was facially identical to the Concubiness Semmry.

"Well, my name is Natira," she said. "Don't know how I got here or where I came from. But I do know that your friend over there is hungry."

Cornelius turned up the lights, revealing a greatly reduced gestator Udroom, looking much as it did during that first fateful visit to Teqavra Zoo.

"Chelgo beans, Cawneelyus? Do you have some for me?"

16. Mystagogic Logic

At first he thought that the puzzle was gone, until he found two pieces of it fixed to the auxiliary command station in the hold. Pressing either one brought up a screen interface querying the required destination tier – it was the hypertier engine, another gift left behind by Udroom before his descent from intellect's pinnacle.

Two years later, as Natira went into labour with their first child, Cornelius finally understood 'the value of things'. Looking down at the bright, open eyes of their new-born son, he realised what it meant to pass on the mark of a maker, the consequences, the responsibility, the possibilities. Later on, he went down to give Udroom an extra portion of chelgo beans then sat and listened to the Grand Gestator's happy gurglings, just in case a glint of that fabulous mind revealed itself.

Sussed

Keith Brooke

I walk up Central High, head tucked down, collar turned up against the drizzle, face hidden as far as possible from the cams and the goons. All around, people jostle and harry, places to go, things to do, while the streetsellers hawk noodles and innoculations, and cars and bikes cut paths through the bustle.

I reach the Slash, the crowds thinner here. To left and right there's a clear swathe bisecting the city, buildings cut clean through, the ground burnt to black glass. Kids ride boards among the ruins, and cars use the Slash as a throughway as if it had been part of some radical act of urban planning and not a war wound, a vast particle-beam burn from the heavens.

I head left, the Slash offering the most direct route towards the transit depot. I have a ticket out of here, a settler's permit for some backwater planet something like fifty light-years away from the war zone, a fresh start.

All I have to do is reach the depot in one piece.

I dip my head. The gel-refits have rewritten my facial geometry enough to fool any pattern-matching programs scanning the cam feeds, but I don't have anything that would get me past one of Geno's goons with a DNA sniffer.

I pass a four-storey office block sliced in half by the Reps' beam strike. Teenagers sit on the cut-off floors, legs dangling, watching. It feels as if everyone is watching out for me.

I keep walking.

I stand in line. The depot is a big hangar of a building, thrown up overnight about a month ago to process the exodus. The lines of emigrants rank deep across the departures hall, maybe fifty queues in all.

The man ahead of me wears Jensen shades and a sharp tailored suit. Like everyone else, he has no luggage. We will leave this world naked, our only possessions those that can be liquidated and wired ahead in a data-feed. The air is heavy with cologne and perfume, and mingled scents of fear and relief.

Two queues up, voices suddenly rise. An arm flaps, hands point, and security goons close in.

"But it's clean!" cries the woman, as one of the guards takes her arm. "I'm in the feed, man. I tell you, I'm in the feed!"

Maybe. Maybe not. She could be trying to scam her way on. It could be that she had been on the feed but then someone with better credit and more favours to pull in had knocked her out of the queue.

Two goons haul her away, still protesting, even though she must know that no matter how good her case she could never get back on the feed by arguing with two meat-head security guards.

It takes about an hour, and then Jensen-shades is at the desk, submitting himself to ret-scan, DNA sniffing, voice check. He removes his wraparounds for the scan and leaves them on the desk. He won't be taking them with him. The transit clerk takes the shades, pockets them, smiles, waves the guy through.

Now it's me. I nod, smile. I don't have any bribes with me, I'm just a guy in a stolen Swank suit. A cam profiles me. I've removed the gel-refits for this: now I have to pass as me to match the ticket credentials. It's a risk, but by now I have to trust that

I'm so far ahead of Geno that I'm safe.

The clerk smiles back, indicates the reader and so I swipe my wristchip across it as I lean into the ret-scan, let it ID me as a pin-prick probe samples DNA from the skin on my temple.

This is where it could all go wrong. This is where you could really begin to see the consequences of crossing the guy who owns half of this fucking planet and then having the balls to un-glue his network and use his own credentials to buy your ticket out of here.

The clerk looks bored, reading columns of check-lists being fed to him via a retinal projector. Yeah yeah yeah. Check check check. My booking is clean, my credit good, my itinerary standard. I made sure it would look that way. I am good at what I do.

At the next desk a guy in baggy joggers and a feathered fleece says, "But that can't be right... No, really, it can't..."

I glance across at him, but dodge eye contact. Someone, somewhere isn't going to get out of here because I am. Is it him, maybe?

"My wife... My kids... They've gone ahead. We're all on the feed. There's been a mistake."

Outside there's gunfire, but nobody reacts. There's a war going on. Attacks from the Republic above, all kinds of factions fighting here on the planet, including rumoured Rep infiltration units and sympathisers.

My clerk is talking, gesturing. "All clear, Mr Chan. Please proceed to Processing."

I nod. I smile. I walk past the desk, and away from the only world I have ever known.

I follow my arrow as it flashes on the floor a stride ahead of me, while others follow theirs. It takes me along a corridor to a side-room containing maybe a hundred suspods, each sensuously curved coffin-like pod moulded from some bulbous pearlescent material. A dozen or so people mill about in here, mostly travellers with a couple of techs.

Once filled, the pods will be transported to the voidships and loaded like blobby frogspawn into the ships' holds for their journeys to the stars.

My arrow takes me to a suspod halfway along the far wall and then vanishes. The pod's screen displays my name. Following the screen's instructions, I place my palm on the reader and the pod's lid gives with a slight sigh of escaping gases.

I step back and the lid lifts, flipping sideways to reveal its fleshy interior.

A tech approaches, nods towards me and the pod. "Time to get naked," she says.

I shrug, pull at my Swanks and feel the fabric relaxing away from my body. I step out of the collapsed suit and kick my pumps off my feet.

The tech appraises me, then stoops to gather my discarded clothes. She'll get a few bucks for them. One of the perks.

I turn back towards the suspod.

"You sussed before, mister?" the tech asks.

I shake my head, aware of her eyes on my skinny backside.

"Just climb in, okay? Relax into it. You good?"

I step up, gingerly place a foot in the pod, feel warm flesh closing over my toes.

"It's *wet*," I say, suddenly nervous.

"Keeps your skin good," says the tech.

I put my weight on the half-enwrapped foot, feel the pod's interior give a little, and then step in, both feet.

I sit, feel moist flesh sliding around my legs, my balls, my waist.

"Go on."

I lie back.

The sensation of flesh growing up around me is unlike anything I've ever known or imagined. The physical sensations of warmth, skin on skin, moisture, the salty, meaty scents... like a primal womb-memory, like sex, like a child's self-discovery. The swirling mix of sensuous envelopment, of *wrongness*, of fear – being smothered, immersed, drowned...

The tech swings the suspod's lid over me, and it hangs just short of closing. I'm suddenly in semi-darkness, and the feelings of panic surge to the fore.

And then... subside.

The lid closes softly, and I am in a pearly half-light, my body enwrapped, my face not quite touching the lid's interior.

Calm.

I know the pod is doing this. Passing soporifics through my skin and into my blood, soothing me with the mix of the air that I breathe.

Flesh touches my cheeks, the bridge of my nose, my forehead. Moistness spreads up my nostrils, as fleshy tendrils probe me. I experience a sudden tightening as something slides down my trachea.

I stop breathing.

I am fully enclosed, at one with my pod... drifting... suspended.

Everything would have carried on being fine with Geno if his sister Elsa hadn't come back from Earth, and if Elsa didn't have a bit of a thing going on for Chinese code monkeys.

I'd been with Geno's organisation for five years, head-hunted from a gang running a banking scam on the back of stolen wristchips. I'm not so much a coder as a code-fixer: I understand other people's code. I see what needs fixing, and I see the holes left if things aren't fixed. Geno needs people like me: we can either protect or attack, depending on circumstances.

When the war with the Reps came close enough that our planet was exposed to occasional raids, Geno needed people like me even more. In my time with Geno I've worked with state military programmers on safety-netting our orbiting defence sats, I've bred bidding agents to help reshape the global economy, I've run security bit-checks on the surgeons hired to give Geno his latest lift or tuck. Often all before lunch.

And, of course, I fell for his knockout baby sister with her Earth-sophisticated ways and her smooth skin and her soft spot for geeky Chinks.

It all came to a head six days before my departure.

I was working with Joni Garval, leader of a gang of street vigilantes, sowing stories in the media feeds about one of the rival gangs, the Fraternity of Zeal. The Fratz had been gaining the upper hand in some territorial run-ins with Joni's mob, but it turned out Joni had some favours to call in with Geno, which is how I became involved.

My role was to design some spin agents to plant stories that the Fratz were being armed by Republican infiltrators. The attack that left the capital marked with the Slash was still fresh in people's minds, so any taint of the Rep was about as damaging in terms of brand management as you could get.

And so it was that I was waiting in one of Joni's safe-houses for a quiet little rendezvous with Elsa when instead of my girl with a suck like a thirsty camel I saw Geno standing alone in the doorway. Geno doesn't need to be lined by goons to be intimidating. He has presence. And even when he appears to be alone, you just know that a single wrong move and his goons will be all over you in a blink.

"Geno," I said.

"Cozy," he replied. "Very cozy, Chan. It'll never last. You hear? You think you're in love? You think *she* is?"

I stood facing him, my hands spread. "We're just having some fun, Geno," I told him, trying to keep the pleading out of my tone.

"So you *don't* love her?" Geno asked now. He waved a hand across the room. "All this, and you don't love her?"

"I..." I didn't know what to say. I didn't know what I felt and I didn't know how to handle this situation. The one thing I did know is that Geno would have me trapped whatever line I took.

"I make her smile, Geno. I like that I do that."

For a moment, I thought he was going to soften, but then he said, "You touch her again, Chan. You so much as look at her. You do that and you're atoms. You hear? You've seen what happens to people who try to cross me, haven't you? Don't ever cross me, you hear?"

I heard. I nodded. I watched Geno go, and then, quietly, I got my coat and walked out into the street.

Five days before my departure, I walked back up to my apartment with its view out over the harbour. I palmed the door and walked through into the living room and Elsa was there, stretched back in the love seat, tall glass of fizz cradled in her hands, and a snatch-your-breath-away smile across her face.

"Hey, C," she said, and I just stood staring.

You expect me to have some kind of self-restraint when she looks at me like that? You expect me to make the rational decision that, actually, my boss and the man who runs half of this planet is not a person to cross? Really?

Four days before, I cracked the departure feed and slipped a trojan into the roster for some faraway planet nobody's heard of. I set it with a timed release: I didn't want my credentials appearing on that roster until the last possible minute. So even as I stood in line on the day of departure, my name was only just being slipped into the list. Even as I stood in line in the departures hall, I'd set an agent to mimic my own behaviour patterns so that it would appear to any online snoops that I was working on a reconn project from my apartment. I am good at this kind of thing, which is why Geno hired me, and which is why finally I ended up using his own account to buy myself off-planet for a fresh start, on my own, no baggage, nothing.

I would learn to grow cabbages or rear sheep or whatever the fuck they farmed in my new home. I would sweep streets or learn a trade. I was out of here.

Like being turned inside out... The lining of my throat is being ripped out... And then, with a soft popping sound, the suspod's tendrils pull out of my nose and I'm breathing air again.

I move, for the first time in I don't know how long, and feel the meaty interior of the pod yielding. I feel at peace. It all seems so far away now.

The dim light penetrating the suspod gives my gaze a pink glow, like staring at candy-fog, no features visible, just the soft light.

The pod's lid lifts with a soft sigh. I feel a sudden draught tickling across my skin, and I hear the deep rumble of the voidship. The lid swings open and I sit, pulling free of my fleshy embrace with a series of squelching sounds. I climb out, and stand by the pod. Around me, others are climbing out, looking disoriented. The mucoid coating on my skin dries quickly to nothing in the air.

I have never seen so many naked bodies in such a small place. There is something, I don't know, *institutional* about it. The other striking thing is that everyone is young and well-muscled. I had not anticipated that the other émigrés would be so well-honed. For the first time I wonder what is really in store for me, just how much of a wild frontier I have chosen.

They are pulling on grey jumpsuits. I look around, find one by my pod and step into it.

"Moving *out!*" yells one of them from the far side of the hall, and I think, Fuck, but I've ended up in some kind of boot-camp.

We walk... we march... out into a gangway, squeezed two abreast in the narrow space. I hang back and then tag on at the end, trying to fall into step with my fellows.

It is soon clear that we are still on the voidship. I guess we're heading for a shuttle down to the surface, although it would probably have been simpler just to transport us down while we were still suspodded.

We file into another hall, one wall of which is a viewscreen showing a moon with networks of encampments scrawled across its surface.

I feel a tingle in my wristchip. Something is trying to access it, triggering a sentinel routine to warn me. The others around me have paused in what they were doing, clearly absorbing some kind of datafeed, but mine is just a jab of the sentinel and nothing more. I'm clearly not set up to receive whatever is being sent.

There is a hush now, and two men approach, both wearing military greys, one with some kind of hand-weapon drawn but not raised.

They stop before me.

The older man with more stripes on his shoulder stares at me for a long time before saying, "Just who the fuck are you?"

My cell is long enough to lie down in, so narrow that you can touch both walls simply by raising one arm. The only domestic comfort is a slops bucket. I have been here for more than twelve hours.

They must be running checks, trying to find out who I am and how I got here.

I could tell them that.

It's Geno. Fucking Geno.

I'm not the only shit-hot code monkey he has head-hunted over the years. One of them... one of them must have deciphered my trail, tracked me down to the émigré roster, and told Geno. And Geno must have had his monkey reallocate me: no longer on a one-way ticket to a cozy new colony-world. No. Instead they put me on a military ticket into the middle of the war zone. Right now, Geno is probably drinking a toast to me, picturing me waking up with a squad of sweaty grunts and wondering what in hell is happening. Right now, Geno is laughing.

Lukacs, the commanding officer of the assault squad comes back in and stands across from me. One of his goons stands at the door.

"So tell me," he says, "just what is one of Gene Bateman's lead information specialists doing on a class A military voidship preparing for an assault on a Republic staging post?"

I smile. "Geno has a sense of humour," I tell him. "I crossed him, I went on the run and thought I'd escaped, and he thinks it's funny to divert my suspod so that it gets added to a military consignment."

"You're here as a joke...?"

I nod. "I hate to tell you this, but Geno must have it on good authority that this assault is going to fail, because I'm sure he doesn't expect me to emerge alive at the end of it."

"Come on," says Lukacs, "come for a walk with me. Stretch your legs."

We pause a few minutes later in an operations room, three military analysts talking into jaw-mikes, fingers dancing over virtual keypads, staring at a bank of screens showing the target: aerial views of one or more military bases set out like maps; street-level views from within domes, army vehicles on the streets, Republic soldiers all around; ground-level moonscapes of no apparent significance.

"You know what I think?" says Lukacs.

I shake my head.

"I think you're one hell of a surprise, and believe me, when I plan an operation on this scale for this length of time I don't like surprises. I ask myself what Gene Bateman has to gain by planting someone like you out here."

"You think I'm a spy? You think he sent me here?"

Lukacs shakes his head. "That was my first thought," he says. "But then my second was, if Bateman wants someone out here then he wouldn't do it in such a dumb-ass way as this. He'd just make sure one of his people was part of the op. He isn't stupid."

"So you believe me?"

"Well nobody's come up with a better explanation. Sensible thing for me to do now is to have you locked up for the duration, keep you out of the way, just to make sure you're no risk. But then... what you said about Bateman has been nagging at me: he must be pretty damned sure this operation is doomed if he sent you out here."

I stare at the screens. It seems odd to just be seeing Reps out on their streets like that. Just humans like any of us.

"Like I say, you're a surprise," says Lukacs. "So maybe we can use that. Maybe you're a wildcard. You've worked on military systems before, haven't you?"

I nod. He knows that. He's had me checked out.

"You want to sit down here and see what you can make of the Reps' set-up? See if you can find any holes?"

I never set out to be a fucking soldier. Military fatigues just aren't my thing. The real soldiers can tell that I'm not one of their kind. They can see I don't fit. They don't know my story, but they clearly don't trust me. None of them likes surprises.

I sit at my screens, picking up feeds through my wristchip, planting agents and routines in captured Rep datastreams, trying to find my way in. Their codebases diverged from ours maybe a hundred years ago. A long time in dataspace. They use biological models a lot more than we do; they seem to base everything on wetware and neural processing. But it's still data, and I recognise the architectures and patterns – information is self-organising, after all, common patterns always an emergent phenomenon. But how to make sense of it all!

War, I learn, is ninety-nine percent tedium and one percent sheer terror. Trouble is, you never know when that one percent terror is going to rear up, so you're always on the edge.

We're something like 75,000 kilometres from the planetary surface, mostly out of reach of the Reps' defences, but they know we're here and every so often they find a way to lash out.

The first time, I was walking to the mess after a ten-hour shift when all of a sudden the lights dimmed and a deep rumble shook through the ship like an earthquake. I crumbled to my knees, and could feel the vibrations still ringing from the deck and up through my bones like ringing crystal.

"What the...?" I gasped.

A young black soldier who looked about twelve crouched just ahead of me, hanging onto a handrail. She glanced back and said in conversational tones, "Reps buzzing us with a beam."

At that moment, the lights went altogether and the ship rattled with another assault. A couple of seconds later the lights came back up and I said, "But... I thought we were shielded?"

She grinned. "Sure we're shielded. If we weren't shielded we wouldn't be passing the time of day like this – we'd be fried!"

We've had two more assaults like that since then, each time as terrifying as the first even though I know what's happening. Understanding doesn't cut down the fear that they might just find a weak spot and we'll all be burned to hell and back.

So I sit here, bored stiff, fighting code that doesn't mean much to me, just waiting to be vaporised in a war I don't even really understand.

I never asked to be a soldier.

Elsa. Do you still think about me, Elsa, or have you found somewhere else to get your kicks? I'm not even sure what it was we had, or what we might have had.

I didn't love you Elsa. I hadn't got that far. But to say it was just fun, like I told Geno, is too dismissive.

We had good times, didn't we, Elsa? Good times that could have become more.

All that... to me it's only a few days ago that I was back

home, having fun with Elsa and living the life. But I asked around here and found out that I spent nearly six months in that suspod, while this ship jumped the void.

You've had six months to move on, six months to get over me.

When I decided to get away from there I thought I'd get over you quickly, Elsa. I thought it was for the best.

What did we have, Elsa? What might we have had?

I'm lost in a data-dream when they strike, drifting in a near-Zen state in the flow, following shapes and patterns, finally starting to understand some of the noise.

Alarms flash me back to the real world and I feel that ship-quake once again, only this time it lasts for longer and is accompanied by a deep metallic groan. I heard a sound like that down in Malberg when I was a teenager: the sound that glaciers make as they shift. It's not the kind of sound you want to hear your voidship making.

Another quake, another primal groan. Voices in the gangway outside our ops room. I look across at Bilby and he's gone white as one of those icebergs and is crossing himself as if that's going to make any fucking difference.

The lights have dimmed again, and now arrows flash on the floor.

"Come on, Bilby," I say, pulling at his arm. "Just another drill."

We vacate the room, follow the arrows, and soon we've joined a steady flow of troopers heading towards the evac bays.

I'm still with Bilby, still half-walking half-running. We pass through a bulkhead and there's another strike and we're thrown into the air, as if the whole ship has been swiped a few metres sideways from under our feet. I find myself on the ground, the wind knocked out of me. My leg is throbbing and when I look down I see that my coverall is ripped, my knee bleeding. Alarms are klaxoning all around now. I feel dizzy, think I've hit my head from the dull throb in it, and then I realise that the reason I'm struggling to breathe isn't that I was winded but that the air seems to have thinned.

I remember the drills, reach back to my shoulder, find a breather mask and slap it over my face. And breathe.

Bilby's there, a few metres back. I crawl over to him, fumble at his shoulder for his mask. I yank it free and make to slap it onto his face but then stop as finally I take in his bloated, purple features and staring eyes.

I push up to my feet, ignoring the dull throbbing of my damaged knee. I struggle to get my bearings, then look down and see an arrow patiently flashing me This Way.

Somehow I make it to the evac bay, my head dizzy and hot, the breath ragged in my lungs. I pause, and the ship groans again.

I find a pod, strip off and stow my coveralls, then climb in.

Warm flesh folds around me as the lid sighs shut. With my wristchip I signal the all clear and I feel a judder as the pod primes itself for launch.

Acceleration. Release.

I am in space, free of the ship. Fleshy tendrils probe, drive into my nose, my trachea, my lungs. Darkness takes me.

I wake to whiteness. So white it's hard to make out any features, any detail. Just white.

I look down at myself and it's as if suddenly my eyes have learnt to see again, to focus.

I am naked.

And I have healed. The bloody mess of my knee has gone, the skin flawless, smooth. More... the scar on my shin from a biking accident is gone. I feel healthy and strong. I feel renewed.

I sleep.

Whiteness, still.

Finally, they come. Two of them. Tall. Human, I think. Or at least, at some point they or their ancestors were human.

They sit before me, although I cannot make out the form of their seats from the white.

They have golden hair, mid-brown skin, blue eyes. They wear cloaks of silver, tight bodysuits. They remain silent, although I have the distinct impression that they are communicating somehow.

"We found you," says the one of them to my left. "Adrift. We found your vehicle's signal."

"We have reconstructed your language so that we may communicate," says the other. "It is an ancient tongue."

I was lying but now I sit, and support materialises at my back. "Ancient?" I ask.

"We study your time," says the first. "We are honoured."

"We would wish to understand," says the second.

I think of you, Elsa. My first thought. How long have I drifted into your future? For how long have I been in suspension until these beings detected my escape pod's signal?

I realise that I am still naked, but these two do not seem bothered.

"Clothes," I said, covering myself. "Can I have some clothes?"

"Of course," says the first. "We still have much to learn about the norms of your period."

I sit in the love-chair, while one of them stands by the balcony door. They have shaped this space so that it resembles my apartment, based on what I have told them. They have paid a lot of attention to detail. They want to get it right.

"This war," says my examiner, as she turns back to face me. "What caused it?"

I shrug. "The Reps. Or at least that's what they always taught us. Started before I was born. Politics, ideologies, religion, territory... All most of us know or care is that there's – or there *was* – a war." I pause, look into her eyes. "Tell me... do you know who won? Who won the war?"

"It was a long time ago," she says. "The archives are not well preserved that far back. This is why you are so fascinating to us. You are a direct connection."

"You won, didn't you?" The Reps. Their mastery of healing, their direct communication with each other, some of the things they said... The Reps had always been far more advanced in the biological sciences. My examiner... she was a Rep.

"We live in the Republic," she says evenly. "So does that mean we won? I do not know. Does it really matter?"

I should feel like some kind of time-delayed prisoner of war. They keep me here, study me, try to understand me.

But I don't. Not really. I am alive. That is all that should matter. I try not to think too much of the future, or of the past.

"So tell us," says the examiner who was the first to visit me, "what was it that you did for Geno and his organisation? He was not a political figure and yet he wielded great power. He was a criminal and yet he worked with the government and the military in the effort against the Republic."

"He was all of these, yes," I say. "He pretty much ran the place, and he used people like me to do that. If the planet needed protecting from the Reps then it was in his interests to make that happen."

"So what did you do? What was your role?"

"I did all kinds of things. As far as defence goes, I worked with the sat network people to sharpen the Shield's reflexes to protect against attack. The Reps broke through occasionally—" I think of the Slash here "—but not nearly as easily as they would have if we'd kept out of it."

"Tell me more..."

Patterns in data are an emergent phenomenon of the data itself.

You surf the feeds and you can see those shapes jumping out at you if you know where to look, *how* to look.

My examiners started to let me out to walk with them through the corridors of the complex where I was being kept, and later, out into the gardens. At first I marvelled at the act of walking under another sun, at plant-forms and animals that looked familiar and yet were alien, all mixed in with the ubiquitous sparrows and starlings and squirrels that had spread with humankind to probably every settled planet.

But then... well, the more you explore, the more you come across oddities, anomalies. The white room had been so alien to me and yet out here it was just another set of buildings. I could have been anywhere. Anytime.

Not far from my room there is a common area, with seats that fold around you as you descend. Always accompanied by my examiners, occasionally here I will see others, but there is no chance to talk with them.

There are datafeeds here, though. My wristchip sentinels tingle: feeds that are alien, in a language I could not parse. At first, I thought nothing of this: of course they have feeds in unintelligible code-forms and protocols – this is the future.

I captured feed snippets, though, and later, when I was alone, I started to explore.

Now, I lie back in my room, my head reeling.

My wristchip is seeing those emergent patterns in the feeds, just as I was starting to do with the Rep code-streams back on the voidship. The same patterns. In my own time, the Rep codebases diverged from ours maybe a hundred years earlier, but languages evolve. Now, thousands of years on... why is it that my examiners' code-streams have made no progress at all? Why have they frozen in time?

I lie here and lose myself in data-dream, following the shapes and patterns of my captors' code, wandering through a now-familiar architecture.

I am not a time-delayed prisoner-of-war after all.

I am just a prisoner-of-war.

"So tell us, help us to understand your time, your war..."

"It wasn't my war," I snap. "It was never my war."

I swallow, then plunge on. "It was a job. It was the world I grew up with. I never had anything at stake except a living and saving my skin from Rep attacks. Hell, what did I have against the Reps? For all I know they were the good guys. The closest I've ever come to meeting one of them is now, with you guys. You find me in space, you fix me up, you try to understand me and my time. Hell, if you guys won, then maybe that was the best thing after all. I don't know much of your world, but if it's all like this..."

They call it the Stockholm Syndrome. Keep someone captive for long enough and they become psychologically and emotionally attached to their captors. They switch sides, often with an intense zeal. It is a phenomenon that has been established since the twentieth century.

Another time...

"Geno... he was never a public figure because he had far more power if he stayed behind the scenes. There wasn't a single government that took office without Geno yanking their chains. If the Reps had taken him out the planet would have been theirs within months and then it'd have been like dominoes."

My examiner nodded. "So how would they have done that? Despite the rumours, they never had anyone planet-side – look at us: our kind would have been detected immediately. Our difference goes beneath the skin. We are hard-wired *different*."

I shrug. "Long-range strike like they did with the Slash," I say. "Get someone who's not so obviously a Rep to either take him out or target the strike. I don't know. I'm not a military strategist, I just write and remix code."

Another time...

"Geno... he destroyed people. You either went with what he wanted, became the person he needed, or you ended up getting wiped out. People were disposable to Geno. He had no conscience, no ethics other than that he should only ever look out for himself."

"Himself and his sister."

"And Elsa," I agree bitterly. I have already told them all about Elsa. "He thought he was protecting her, but he was stifling her, smothering her. He dragged her back from Earth so he could keep a tighter rein. She could barely breathe without his say so."

"You worked for Geno for twelve years. You were loyal."

"But he would have squashed me under his heel," I say. "Hell, he *did*, or at least he nearly did."

"You did not like Geno."

"I hated him," I say. "I'd gladly have killed him, given the chance..."

Another time...

"If you could take revenge against Geno, would you do so?"

I nod.

"There may be a way..."

I save them the trouble.

"We're not in the far future, are we? We're not way on forwards, looking back and trying to understand the war. We're here and now and the war is still going on and you've been trying to trick me into spilling everything to give you an inside view of the people you're fighting."

Silence.

"It'd have been far easier if you'd just told me," I say. "This isn't my war. I just wanted to live a life. It was never my war."

After a long silence in which my examiner communes with others, he says, "Everyone has a war."

I shrug.

77

"So which war is yours?" he continues.

I pause. Then, "Geno," I say. "Geno is my war."

They change me.

They change me so that no one will recognise me. Elsa: you will not know me. I am no longer your geeky Chinaman. I am taller, my features diluted to that cosmopolitan mix – still a little oriental around the eye, but my skin is dark, my hair thick black. My facial geometry has changed, my voice lowered, my gait been reprofiled... all the identifiers modified. They cannot change my DNA, but they can mask it so that any DNA tests will give me a different graph.

It is only what is in my head that remains, and what is in my heart.

I am going home, with my own war to fight.

I am coming back, Elsa.

Will you still know me? Will you still care?

The Cuisinart Effect

Neal Asher

The ruined city sat incongruously surrounded by thick forest and tangled jungle, open on its east side to the plains. On top of a crumbling skyscraper an eerie light appeared and strange gravitic effects tossed about rubble amidst a tangle of girders to the rear of a floor once inside the building. Out of this light appeared a mantisal: a spherical, vaguely geodesic structure formed of glassy struts ranging in thickness from that of a human finger to a man's leg. Within the substance of this thing veins and capillaries pulsed, and the thicker areas were occupied by half-seen complex structures that sometimes looked like living organs and sometimes tangled masses of circuitry. From the outer structure, curving members grew inwards to intersect below two smaller spheres that were only a little larger than human heads. They appeared to be huge multifaceted eyes positioned above fused-together glassy feeding mandibles, a spread-thin thorax, and the beginning of legs that blended into the curving outer members, and thence into the surrounding sphere. It looked like some insane glassmaker's representation of a giant praying mantis turned inside out.

The mantisal settled on the floor and Kyril, a Heliothane man, removed his hands from the control spheres of the two mantisal eyes, then reached down to haul up his pack. His three companions, the man Thrax and the two women, Jelada and Coney, also took up their equipment, which included a large selection of weapons.

"That was surprisingly accurate," said Coney, looking at Kyril with obvious dislike. Typically for a Heliothane woman she was tall, beautiful, and perfectly capable of tearing the head off anyone from the earlier weaker ages of the Earth. "This place is a long way down the probability slope."

Hoisting the strap of his assault rifle over his shoulder, Kyril gazed up at the sky where birdlike creatures could be seen circling. He nodded to himself then pointed towards the back of the floor the mantisal had come down on, where a large generator, red lights winking over its surface, rested canted amidst the girders, a perfectly spherical hole cut all about it. "That's because we were supplied with energy from this end. We threw over fifty generators at this parallel before we got the right location."

"So what's the story?" asked Thrax, a massive man who was the only one of them capable of easily wielding the huge portable cannon he held.

"Quite simple," Kyril replied. "An Umbrathane sabotage unit occupied this place, but their mere presence here pushed this past Earth down the probability slope and they abandoned it."

"And we are here why?" Thrax was contemplating the bird-things in the sky, whose raucous cawing had grown loud now they were much lower.

"Their fusion reactor is still here, still connected to their time-snatcher." Kyril held up a detector, studying its screen, then nodded across the city. "Over there. It's still causing disruptions on mainline time and we have to knock it out."

"But why are *we* here?" asked Jelada, standing with the butt of her assault rifle resting on her hip.

Kyril stepped outside of the mantisal. "Come on." He began heading for the tangle of girders amidst which stairs could be seen leading down into the building. As the others followed him, shadows fell across them and a webbed and clawed foot slammed against Thrax's shoulder sending him sprawling. Coney swung her assault rifle up and fired, and with a shriek a massive pterosaur crashed into the girder tangle. Then more of the monsters were attacking. Jelada hauled Thrax to his feet, while firing up into a great flock of creatures. They ran for the cover of the girders, but as they reached the near edge one of the pterosaurs landed and lumbered straight at Coney.

"Fucker," said Coney, going down on one knee, her squat assault rifle up against her shoulder. The pterosaur reared, shrieking and spreading its wings. Coney pumped her weapon like a shotgun and fired. The explosive bullet detonated in the creature's chest, opening out its keel bone and ribs and blowing it backwards towards the building edge. It tottered there for a moment then fell out of sight.

Passing under where the first pterosaur had fallen, its ugly head dangling through the girders and dripping blood, they finally reached the stairs.

"They were nothing," said Kyril gesturing back to the dead pterosaur. "The Umbrathane were collecting here some of the deadliest predators from Earth's prehistory, which they intended to transport into our cities. Those creatures are still here and the mechanisms used to feed them broke down some time ago."

"You could have warned us," Coney spat.

"I shouldn't need to warn you," Kyril replied. "You are Heliothane, not some weakling from the old ages of Earth."

As he descended into the darkness of the stairwell, Thrax turned to Coney. "Y'know, one day I'm gonna have a friendly fire incident with that shit."

Coney nodded, obviously still annoyed. Jelada slapped Thrax on the shoulder.

"Not a problem," she said. "He believes the only cause of violent death is stupidity."

The pterosaur fell down the face of the building and crashed onto the roof of a rusting car, its blood trickling down the metal. From the nearby entrance to an underground garage came an excited chittering, then out sped a small dinosaur, to stop between the entrance and the car like a pointer dog. After a moment it scanned about itself before stalking forwards. It leapt up onto the car bonnet and began tugging at a chunk of gory intestine hanging from the pterosaur's body cavity. Suddenly a whole flock of these dinosaurs rushed out after it and began feasting.

The first one continued tugging at its prize, growling like a dog with a bone. The others began to tear the pterosaur apart, squabbling amongst themselves as they did so. Then, except for the gut tugger, they ceased all movement and turned to look in one direction, before abruptly fleeing. The first little dinosaur continued tugging at its prize and growling until a shadow fell across it. It paused and looked up, then cringed. A troodon, a dinosaur three times its size, slammed its jaws closed on the creature, wrenched it up and shook it like a dog with a rat, then proceeded to try and swallow it whole. Another troodon appeared and attempted to pull the snack from its mouth. A tug-of-war ensued, resulting in the little dinosaur being torn in half. Gobbling down their bloody prizes, the two troodon then turned to the dead pterosaur.

One of them began worrying at an overhanging wing whilst the other leapt onto the car to feed on the contents of the body cavity. With its head down it wasn't watching its surroundings too closely, so did not see the massive pterosaur that simply snatched it, while in flight, from the car roof. Seeing this, the other troodon released its hold on the wing, turned and ran, straight into the underground car park. After much shrieking racket it then shot out again with the whole horde of little dinosaurs in pursuit, straight into the jaws of an allosaurus which slammed it to the ground with one claw and proceeded to eat it alive

Meanwhile, another allosaurus had arrived at the car and was disputing ownership of the dead pterosaur with a pack of utahraptors, and from the surrounding streets even more carnivorous dinosaurs from disparate ages of Earth were heading in. Soon the street was filled with brawling dinosaurs, scattered body parts and pools of blood.

Thrax thrust his shoulder against the heavy metal door and it crashed open, admitting bright sunlight and the sight of a rearing troodon. He raised his weapon, but even before he could fire an allosaurus crunched its jaws closed on the troodon's neck. The troodon scrabbled at its attacker with its back legs, like a cat, but the allosaurus shook it, cracking bones, then carted it off.

The other three Heliothane moved up beside Thrax and peered out the door at the carnage.

"Fuck," said Thrax. "Aren't there any vegetarians here?"

Kyril pointed down the street at two advancing triceratops. One of them, confronted by an allosaurus just turning from its latest victim, swung its huge armored head and gored the creature, swung its head again sending the allosaurus crashing through a plate glass window.

"I don't understand," said Coney. "Why are they here? There's nothing they'd want to eat." She gestured at the street which was now beginning to look like the interior of an abattoir.

"Of course you don't understand," said Kyril snootily. "Look behind their head shields."

As they tramped on in, one of the triceratopses swung its head to one side. Some sort of device was surgically affixed to the back of its head behind its head shield.

"What is that?" Coney asked.

"The Umbrathane wanted aggressive killers and, let's face it, some herbivorous dinosaurs are bigger and more dangerous than some of the predators," Kyril explained. "Those little machines alter the brain chemistry, so even the vegetarians here are looking for a fight rather than being intent on defending themselves."

"Sweet," Thrax observed.

Kyril glanced at him with a moue of annoyance then started inspecting his screen.

"Is there any way round this?" Coney asked.

Kyril pointed to his right. "Down there, but we still have to cross the street."

Thrax swung the door shut and they moved through the gloomy interior of the building until reaching another door. Opening this, they stepped out onto the street. To their right the triceratopses were roaring and beginning to charge and to their left lay the main carnage.

"Let's go." Kyril led the way.

Even though the mayhem was not so intense where they were crossing, it was impossible for them to avoid the notice of hungry predators. An allosaurus bore down on Thrax, who raised his portable cannon and fired. The creature's head disappeared in an explosion of brains and blood yet, like a headless chicken, it ran on past him, then, tilting over, began running round in circles. One of the triceratopses reached the hapless beast, gored it, then began stamping it to slurry. Kyril and Coney faced up and down the street, hitting with automatic fire anything that drew too close. And grinning all the while, Jelada calmly took down anything else with short bursts of deadly accurate fire into their heads.

"Keep moving," Kyril instructed coldly.

Jelada shot a dwarf allosaurus in the head, but that seemed to stop it not at all. She shot it twice more, still to no effect, but then Thrax stepped in, blowing out its side with one cannon shot.

"Hey, thanks!"

"Jelada!" Thrax shouted, just as a triceratops horn punched through her back and out between her breasts. It lifted her struggling form high, tossed her to one side. Where she landed, troodon and other mid-size dinosaurs sped in and, before any of the other three could react, tore her apart as they fought over her.

"Jelada," said Thrax, his voice dead.

"Thrax, keep moving!" Kyril ordered.

Ignoring him, Thrax turned on the triceratops and began firing, blowing massive holes in its body and bringing it down to its knees. He circled round and fired once more, the shot hitting behind its head, tearing the boney shield forward. The beast collapsed completely.

"Fucker," said Thrax, staring at the creature.

"Thrax! Move it!"

Kyril and Coney had reached the kerb and were heading along to the corner. Thrax abruptly snapped out of it, looked around to see the other triceratops charging towards him, then turned and ran after his companions.

There were fewer dinosaurs along the new street Kyril and Coney headed down, but still, every so often something threw itself at them. They passed a couple of alleyways and, reaching another street corner, Kyril went down on one knee to inspect his screen while Coney covered him.

"Get a move on!" she shouted to Thrax, who was struggling to catch up with them.

Thrax raised a hand in acknowledgement, paused to hoist his cannon onto his shoulder, then picked up his pace. The tyrannosaurus had obviously been lurking in the alleyway. It snapped Thrax up like a gharial taking up a fish. As it crunched him to position him just right in its mouth, body parts slopped to the ground and his cannon clattered into the alleyway, useless, then it swallowed him whole.

"Oh hell." Coney raised her assault rifle as the tyrannosaurus swung its head here and there, tracking the progress of other dinosaurs in the street. Kyril rested a hand on the rifle barrel and pushed it down.

"Don't waste ammunition," he said. "Let's go."

She turned on him, and spoke through gritted teeth. "You're a cold bastard aren't you?"

"Thrax and Jelada forgot they are Heliothane, and that's why they are dead," he said. "I haven't forgotten, and I hope you haven't either."

She lowered her weapon and nodded, then followed as he led off, staring at his back with concentrated hatred.

"They just keep coming," said Coney, eyeing a couple of allosauruses that had a stegosaurus backed into a space between two buildings on the far side of the street. She glanced up the street and observed the triceratops charging into view, making plaintive noises and swinging its head from side to side as if in search of something

"The smell of blood will be drifting out of this city like a fog," said Kyril. He was standing at double steel doors rigging explosives. "Five seconds."

They quickly moved away from the doors, crouching in adjacent doorways. The explosives detonated, the sound stunningly loud and stilling all the calls and shrieks of the dinosaurs in the surrounding city. They ducked back towards the doors.

"Damnation," said Kyril.

The doors, though badly dented, were still in place.

"I think you need to get that rigged again, and quickly," said Coney, noting the two allosauruses swinging away from the stegosaur and now stalking towards them. She glanced towards the triceratops and saw it had now turned and was gazing directly towards them. "Shit, I think we've attracted a bit too much attention." When there was no response from Kyril she glanced round and saw he was just standing, hands on hips, gazing at the door. "Problem?"

"The door…" He gestured towards it, seemingly at a loss.

"Fuckit! Rig it again!" shrieked Coney. She aimed at the nearest allosaurus as it broke into a loping run, and opened fire. The creature went down head first, somersaulting and crashing on its back. The second allosaurus now noticed the stegosaurus escaping from confinement between the two buildings. It turned towards the creature, but the stegosaurus was an entirely different matter now with freedom to move its tail. As the predator attacked it turned, honking noisily, and swung the mace of its tail straight up underneath the allosaurus's head, tearing off the lower jaw. The predator crashed to the ground and, still honking, the stegosaurus sped away, came face to face with the triceratops, then abruptly turned into a side street and disappeared.

"We must try a different approach," said Kyril.

Coney whirled on him and studied him for a long moment.

"You piece of shit," she said. "Thrax and Jelada dead because, according to you, they weren't Heliothane enough, and all for nothing?"

Kyril just gazed at her.

"You didn't bring enough explosive," she spat. "Did you?"

"It is Thrax's fault. If he hadn't lost the cannon…"

"Screw you." Coney turned away and fired down the street, her shots zinging and raising dust around the triceratops, which reared on its hind legs and roared.

"You shouldn't waste ammunition," Kyril berated her.

"What about the reactor?"

"Shutting that down is not a problem – we just need to set it to maximum and hole the cooling jacket."

Coney fired again, raising more dust around the triceratops. It roared again, came down on all fours and charged towards them.

"I will not tell you again," said Kyril, trying to reassert himself.

Coney turned and hit him with her rifle butt and he went down. She stooped and dragged him to one side before moving back out to the middle of the doors.

"Come on baby," she said, firing again at the approaching monster.

The triceratops lowered its head, bearing down on her fast. With a yell she ran forwards to meet it, jumping high at the last moment. Her right foot came down on the top of its head, her left on its back, where she slipped and tumbled off the side of it, hitting the ground and rolling, her rifle gripped across her stomach. The triceratops, unable to halt its charge very quickly, slammed straight into the doors. It backed up, tearing both doors out of their frame, one of them crashing to one side, one of them still impaled on its horns. It tried shaking the door free, eventually hurling it clattering down the street.

Up on one knee, Coney took careful aim at the mechanism attached to the back of its head. She fired and the thing exploded, miniature lightnings spreading from the point of impact. The monster convulsed and collapsed in a cloud of dust. She stood and walked past the triceratops, glanced once at Kyril, who now seemed to be recovering, and stepped inside the building.

The fusion reactor lay to one side beside a dais: a sphere from which spread a jungle of pipes and ducts. On the dais stood the time sampler, its cylindrical field flickering to reveal a dinosaur skeleton lying within. Shouldering the strap of her weapon, Coney advanced to a pedestal-mounted control panel and inspected it. After a moment she tapped two or three icons on a reactive screen then slid her fingers up a virtual slide switch. Immediately the hum of power in the room rose and the snatch field grew steadily brighter. Stepping past the console, Coney unshouldered her rifle, and released bursts of fire at the pipes leading into either side of the reactor. Steam and coolant began to scream out. Swinging her aim to one side, she targeted a device covered with cooling fins, loaded an explosive shell and fired at the mechanism, blowing a hole in its side. Smoke and wisps of fire began pouring from the hole and the hum in the room became intermittent. The main lights dimmed and numerous emergency lights began to flash. A warning klaxon began to sound, then a voice spoke calmly: "Reactor overheat. Emergency shutdown required. Estimated time to containment breach is eighteen minutes."

Coney turned and headed for the door.

Kyril was leaning against the door frame.

"Well done," he said.

She ignored him and stepped past, moving on down the street.

"You see," said Kyril, hurrying to catch up with her. "If you are Heliothane, there is always a way."

Almost casually Coney shot a dwarf allosaurus and moved on. Others came to feed on the body and ignored the two Heliothane. Ahead of Kyril, she reached a corner and paused to peer around it.

"Unfortunately," said Kyril from behind her, "there will be no way for you – no way back home that is."

Coney froze, then slowly nodded her head, a sneer twisting her features. "No witnesses to how you fucked up this mission?"

"I'm sorry," said Kyril flatly.

"Yeah, sure you are."

Coney tried to get around the corner but a shot slammed into her shoulder, twisting her and flinging the rifle from her hands. Further shots whipped past her, but she managed to dive from view. Rolling, she came up onto her feet and staggered for a little way then paused, recognizing Thrax's helmet lying on the ground, and nearby the man's hand.

"I can always just leave you here," said Kyril, rounding the corner. "I've no problem with that."

He raised his rifle and Coney threw herself into the alleyway the tyrannosaurus had attacked from, then slumped against the wall clutching her shoulder. Only after a moment did she become aware of a noisy digestive bubbling and a rumbling sound and then see the massive clawed foot just inches away from her. She tracked the leg up to see the tyrannosaurus standing over her, asleep – it was snoring. Then lowering her gaze she saw Thrax's cannon lying on the other side of the alley.

"Of course," Kyril called cheerfully. "if I leave you here I wonder how you'll die: eaten alive or fried when that reactor blows."

The tyrannosaurus opened its eyes, shrugged, parted its jaws a little to drop some threads of drool. Kyril stepped round the corner into the alley, first focusing on Coney then, after a moment, his gaze straying upwards.

"Fuck."

The tyrannosaurus roared and charged. Kyril opened fire, his bullets tearing holes in the creature, but to little effect. He turned to run but it ducked down, its jaws crunching shut about his legs. It lifted him screaming into the air, and began eating him legs first.

Coney crawled across to Thrax's cannon, awkwardly heaved it round and aimed it up at the mouth of the alleyway in time to see Kyril, still screaming, disappearing down the monster's gullet. It paused for a moment, dipped its head as if in contemplation, then abruptly coughed, spitting out Kyril's rifle, before striding out of sight.

With an absorbent dressing held up against her shoulder, Coney pressed her hand against a control sphere of the mantisal. The organic time machine lifted from the concrete, weird effects propagating around it, then it winked out of existence.

A moment later the mantisal reappeared high in the sky at a fair distance from the city. Coney checked her watch, nodded to herself and donned protective goggles, before settling down in the craft's glass bones to observe. An eye of fire ignited deep in the city, spreading into a massive fusion explosion, incinerating all. Coney reached up to a control sphere and before the shockwave could reach it, the mantisal disappeared.

Harmony in my Head

Rosanne Rabinowitz

The noise starts in my left ear again, hissing and whistling like a pressure cooker.

Antony's late. As I think about him the hissing in my ear gets louder. Maybe it's just that damn cappuccino machine setting off the tinnitus, so I go outside with my coffee.

Like most of central London, Russell Square seems badly hung over after a big party. I'm sure I can see bits of red white and blue trampled in the grass and gutter, confetti dragged in from yesterday's Olympic bid celebrations. Given the weather few people sit on the benches, let alone sprawl or snog under the trees. Even the "G8 – shut it down" banners on the squat down the other side of the square hang bedraggled and limp.

I go for my usual seat where I have a good view of the squat. For several months it's been like having my very own episode of *The Bill* for entertainment as I drink my coffee and watch shuffling congregations of coppers search and photograph people going in and out of the building.

But only two plods stand sentinel today, and they look bored now all their mates have followed the activists to their protests at the summit in Scotland.

I take a table facing the street instead, giving two seats a wipe with a serviette before sitting down. I open my newspaper to the inevitable Olympic bid bravado, but I don't get too far before a skinny black lurcher hops onto the seat next to me, tail thumping a greeting against the plastic chair. She puts a paw on my knee and looks at me with big beseeching eyes.

"What do you want from me, dog? I'm only drinking coffee," I tell her. "It's not even a latté, if you're the kind of dog that likes milk."

The dog only looks more mournful and lets out a tentative whimper. Then she licks my hand.

"So what are you trying to say? Have you been stood up too?"

Perhaps it serves me right, the way I dragged my feet when Antony first rang me.

I finally said yes to breakfast. It seemed safe. It could work out like this: after we have a chat, he'll go on to his work in Camden. And I'll go to the library and read and try to order my thoughts about infinity and harmonics, resonance and decoherence.

But maybe I'd still spend too much time staring out the window as I try to understand more about what happened the night – the only night – I'd been with Antony two weeks ago. Could I call it an experiment in sensual resonance?

The pressure-cooker effects in my ear go up a notch. I'm not so sure whether it's beans or brains getting cooked in there. In any case, whatever it is feels as if it's about to go off and spatter onto the washed-out sky.

Like music, the siren in my ear has different layers. First there's the hiss, then the winding-up screech, and then it lets loose with a wail. And something else may chime in from way in the back. I hear the hiss in the day when I wake up. When I'm working in the library. When I'm watching TV. When I'm trying to sleep.

I've been listening to it for two weeks. I woke up around mid-day after Antony had left. I heard this noise from outside. So who was the dickhead with the annoying car alarm going off again? Then I realised the ringing came from inside my head.

"Briony, perhaps your tinnitus is trying to tell you something," said the health counsellor at the audiology clinic. They'd passed me on to her after my MRI scan came back negative.

She clasped her hands together as if she wanted to lead me in prayer, and stretched her smile out a few more inches. "Why don't you make friends with it?"

Fuck off. I can't say I've been feeling very friendly.

But now I listen closely as the noise gets softer and subsides into static. Voices and strains of near-melody move in and out. There's a booming sound like a pulse, as if it comes from a distance and *would* be very loud if I ever came close enough. It feels like I'm eavesdropping on something I'm not supposed to hear, or trying to tune in to a distant radio station.

What else is on the air? A quick explosive breath. A sigh.

The lurcher is barking and pawing at me.

I relent and scratch the animal behind her ears. "Hey, what's wrong? Where's yer mum?"

The sound in my right ear goes from static level to siren – and back again.

"Leila! Leila!" I hear a hoarse voice from across the road. "Leila! Leila!" The call rises above the traffic. A bus moves past and then I see her. A thin woman with wild multicoloured hair, a loose dog lead trailing from her hand.

I wave to the woman. "Here! Here! Your dog is here!"

So I've done my good deed for the day. Now I'll be left in peace until Antony makes his appearance. But, as the woman crosses the street and approaches my table, I start to have doubts about that.

I expect the woman to be relieved to find her pet safe. I expect a smile. But she is frowning, her eyes intent and probing. She is not only thin, but close to skeletal. Her jeans fall loose around her hips, revealing jutting bones and a concave belly.

Leila sits upright and alert at her mistress's approach. Her tail gives a welcoming twitch, but she seems more apprehensive than anything else.

That makes me apprehensive too.

Now the woman smiles, her make-up cracking with the motion of her lips and eyes. "Thanks for looking after her. Leila, you naughty dog! Why'd you run off?"

The dog shrinks back and her tail quivers as the woman attaches the lead onto the collar.

"I don't know what's got into her. I was taking her out and she just ran! It's the noise, you see. I live down the Brunswick Centre, got me own flat and all with the council. But they're doing all sorts of building, and closed down Safeway so I come to Tesco's till they open that new Waitrose. And who can afford shopping at Waitrose? They think we're in Bloomsbury when it's still sodding Kings Cross! But there's something funny down Kings Cross. There were sirens, like."

The left ear is revving up again. I try to ignore it. "Your dog was no problem at all," I say. "Bet she's looking forward to her walk now."

I rustle my newspaper and turn a page to show that further conversation isn't desired. But the woman pushes her dog off the seat, sits down and looks at my paper. "Good news about us winning the bid. When I was a girl I *loved* the Olympics, watching that Olga Korbut doing her back-flips on the telly. She was lovely!"

"I don't follow sport myself," I say, flipping past Olympic-bid fanfare to a photo of a huge black helicopter discharging a stream of riot police into a field.

"Oooh, that looks heavy. Where's that then? Iraq?"

"No, it's *not* Iraq. It's in Scotland." I close the paper with a sigh.

"Name's Ellie," the woman says. She thrusts her hand towards me and I give it a quick shake. Feels like chicken bones wrapped in parchment. "Are you waiting for someone?"

"Yes, I am in fact."

"Is it yer feller?"

"Maybe."

"Oh I know what that's like, love. Is he messing you about?"

Who wants to know?

But I pause, and think before replying. "It's more like *I've* been messing *him* about. Maybe I'm too involved in my work to be in a relationship. Now, I might even get on with some work while I wait for him."

Ellie frowns. "Work? What work is that?"

"If you really want to know, I'm a mathematician. I've just about finished my doctorate, and I'm branching out a bit. I'm interested in infinity."

Now that should do it. Saying I'm a mathematician can be a real conversation-stopper in some quarters. After all, it came close to putting Antony off. Not what you say when you're chatting up a guy who tells you he has 'dyscalculia' and suffers palpitations when faced with the editorial budget at work.

"Oh I *say*," Ellie exclaims. "That sounds bleedin' serious, don't it? Infinity! Well, there's a lot of *that* about."

"Too right!" I let loose a laugh at this accidental maths humour, the sort of joke you groan at when you're knocking back a few pints with the boys from the department in the uni bar. "There's certainly a lot of it about," I agree. "All kinds. Lower and higher infinities, and infinities of space and time. Even an infinity of worlds."

Ellie raises her over-plucked eyebrows as if she thinks I'm even madder than her, and she just might leave me alone.

Then she tilts her head as if trying to see me from another

angle. There's something familiar in that gesture, in the line of her neck and shoulder. That intent look, those sharp features. Have I ever known her? This makes me curious, perhaps even nosier than she is.

Ellie sighs. "If I try to think about something that just goes on and on… Christ, it gives me a headache, know what I mean?"

"Yeah, don't I!" I rub my temples, remembering what it's like when I've been studying too long. "But I've learned you can't understand by only *thinking*. You'll find the skeleton of a solution, but where's the flesh? What enters the mind comes in through the eyes, nose, ears and *skin*."

Ellie crosses her arms and huddles as if she doesn't like the idea of anything touching her own skin at all. But she also gives a sharp nod as if she is interested and wants to hear more.

It may just be a shift in the clouds above us, but Ellie's eyes have taken on an unusual colour, a mixed-up murky blue. There's green too, as if fragments of an old bottle are contained there. Their colour makes me think of the pieces of glass you sometimes find on a beach, stuff that's been floating in the sea and pounded on the sand.

On a rare trip to the seaside when I was a kid, I found some old glass and peered through two pieces as if they were a pair of spectacles. Everything looked tinted and altered through time and the places that glass must have been.

The colour I'm seeing reminds me of that. And it's like the colour I saw in the space that surrounded me and Antony two weeks ago.

As we walked up the hill to my block, Antony took the piss a lot. I didn't mind. That was only fair enough after I had my go in the pub. He was tall and lean, taller than me even. As I stalked up the hill he kept pace while gazing into the foliage-filled bay windows of the blocks lining the road. I liked the way he moved, and the grace of his long strides.

Among other things, he teased me about my living in Hampstead. Even though it's a council flat and it's *Highgate* I live in – these South London dwellers don't know their arse from their elbow, let alone the finer distinctions of northwest London.

But when we arrived he took off his shoes and stepped with care into my home. I opened the window and we stopped to listen to the trickle from a fountain in the artificial pond outside, the croaking of frogs that live there. A breeze brought the scent of roses and flowers from the woods that fringe the garden.

My flat's only a tiny bedsit without proper heating, but it's on a Georgian estate some rich do-gooder bequeathed to Camden Council to house single ladies of slender means. I moved in after years in dodgy student accommodation, squats or worse. Immediately this was a sanctuary. It didn't feel like it was in London, or the kind of place where I usually live. I've been there for two years, but Antony was the first bloke I took home for the night – normally I'm the one who visits.

I'd painted the flat white, except for the Tree of Life I made on the wall. I'm no artist but I enjoyed slapping down layers of paint to clothe the naked geometry of the figure with fractal leaves, buds and shoots. They thickened over the months in a profusion of forms and colours, combinations of blue, green, yellow; inner layers of rust-red. I gave them the colours of all the seasons at once. I added the moss-green vine winding up the tree, twisting in Moebius loops turned slippery with a coating of metallic Hammerite paint.

The Tree helps me concentrate. And Antony was entranced by it.

I showed him the numbers for each branch, for the trunk, the other clusters and the crown where the leaves were thickest. I showed him the colours that went with each number. I told him I didn't have a number for the vine yet.

He stroked the slickness of the vine with his long fingers. "These leaves look poisonous, but they're beautiful too. I expect something to look out from those clusters of leaves… some weird animal or a face from a dream. That vine's fine the way it is, though. Why do you need to stick a number on everything? Numbers are a trap, a prison. You can't turn around without some part of you getting counted and quantified."

But I wanted to show how their realm of logic offered me an escape from superstition and poverty. I wanted to prove that he didn't have to be afraid. And if he saw that my Tree was beautiful, numbers could be too. I realised he loved words as much as I loved numbers, and we could discover a common ground there. Aren't words full of metre, and colours formed from beats of light?

I described curves and points that never meet and others that meet when they shouldn't. Ideas leapt from the background, connections sizzled as I spoke. Everything became clearer. I pushed past what had blocked my vision. I showed him vibration and waves of light, but how do you ride those waves? Sound – and sensation of the deepest kind.

When we began kissing, I stretched against the painted Tree. His mouth tasted of the Guinness we'd been drinking and a flavour entirely his. I had to tilt my head back to see more of him. His eyes were grey like mine, but slate instead of silver. I felt the uneven layers of paint against my back and the vine growing up the tree seemed to wind around us both. As we moved, the lower branches of the tree shook and fractal leaves wafted and swirled around us. His thick hair brushed my skin as he kissed me everywhere.

I told him: "My skin's surface never stops. Keep touching it. There'll always be more."

A new colour filled the air. It had no name but made a sound like the sea that I remembered, a constant flow and swell. I was swimming in that colour: the pearl-grey light of a northern seaside shot with green. Yet it changed beyond any known grey or green as with each touch from Antony I travelled further beyond it.

The colour marked a boundary and everything changed as I passed through. The room *opened* just as I opened to Antony. The Tree on the wall became many trees, and multiplied into an endless forest. Each tree was a universe, with its own languages and laws. Their branches reached towards each other to create corridors, and I entered one.

I gripped Antony and he looked into my eyes with a question. I was still with him, yet he wasn't with me. The sadness of that separation had a ring, a drawn-out ring that turned shrill. Perhaps other notes should go with it. If I found them, perhaps those new notes would change the ringing to a harmony that would stop the sadness. I heard hints of the harmony in the rustle of leaves, a murmur of moving branches, a soft rainfall with a rhythm that matched the flow of blood in my veins.

The corridor of branches led to a wooden house that stood on its own. Its paint was weathered and peeling. Inside the house I saw myself looking out the window.

The other Briony was my age, but much thinner. She was rosy and languid as if she'd been making love. But where was her lover?

She drew her white terry dressing gown around her, and stared out that window with longing, such a longing to be somewhere else and see what couldn't be seen.

The shrill ring of sadness swelled to become a siren, keening and blasting through several octaves.

I moved closer, closer still to the other Briony until I saw through her eyes. This made me itch, I wasn't quite fitting in her skin. I was cold and I was hot, still flushed with Antony's hands upon me.

I stood astride two worlds, and they filled my head with a dreadful clanging. And everywhere else became full of that elusive colour until I saw nothing, nothing at all.

Is it only a play of light that hints at that colour in Ellie's eyes, or did she ever see something that brought her close to it? Then Ellie moves, and the impression's gone.

"But what about your feller?" she asks. "You're just not sure about him, are you? Oh, I've been there too. But if he gives me a good time in bed, I'll give him the benefit of the doubt!"

"A good time?" I can't help laughing again. "It was so good... I kind of lost consciousness. Or perhaps it was like a computer crashing and something got lost."

"Oh dear..." Ellie pushes her hand through her nest of hair. Even Leila looks concerned and rests her head on my knee.

Then Ellie brightens. "I don't know nothing about computers. Tell you what though, if you don't want this guy you can give *me* his number!" She lets loose a loud cackle. "But you oughtta give him a chance," she urges. "Remember what Janis Joplin said... Get it while you can!"

"And look what happened to her."

"But you don't take drugs, do you? I can tell you don't. So that won't happen to you. Or me. Not now. The only drugs I take are what the doctor tells me to. But when I was in the band... I was in a band once. In 1978. We almost got to be famous. We made this album called *Threshold*, see. And there was this song, it was called..."

She looks beyond me while trying to retrieve the information and tilts her head as she shades her eyes, though there's no sun out. Then I know what is familiar about her. Now I remember a much younger Ellie on a record cover, an LP made a decade before I heard it. It was very rare, my old boyfriend assured me. A band part punk, part folk, and another part something never defined before. When he played that LP for me I heard a soaring voice, crystalline in quality. The songs were strange, melancholic and full of the same striving to *see* that I felt all the time.

That boyfriend went off travelling. I never heard from him again, he just disappeared. He'd asked me to go with him, but I stayed in London. If I'd gone with him, would I have disappeared too? But that album… I loved listening to it as we lay together, watching dusk change the sky in the attic window above us.

"So tell me more about your feller," demands Ellie. "He wants to see you again?"

Now that I know who she is, I don't mind telling more. I also wonder what could have happened to her. I don't like to think that Ellie was once like me – or worse, that I could become like her. But I try to put preconceptions aside. That's how I got to know Antony, after all.

"Well, the next day he rang to see how I was. He'd seen I was sleeping OK when he left, but he was worried. He wanted to come over, but I still wanted to be alone. We've talked on the phone a couple of times. And he sent me a card."

"So what're you waiting for? He sounds *sweet*. He must really like you. And he knows how you are, with your work and all."

"Yeah, he didn't mind that. In some ways we clashed, but it made me see new things. Maybe I did the same for him."

I feel a rush of affection for Antony. I see him tucking that duvet around me, putting a pillow under my head. Hovering, worrying, but also leaving me be because I'd told him not to interfere. Ringing me, checking up but not pushing.

As I think more about Antony, the tinnitus gets louder. Another layer of sound in my ear begins, starting with a mess of minor chords.

"So where'd you meet him then?"

Ellie's rasp pushes the inner noise to the background again. Keep talking, it'll turn the noise down.

"On the tube," I tell her. "I was on my way home from some celebrating – I'd finished my dissertation. And he was on way to his way to work and someone pissed him off so he was quietly singing a song that… well, it has my favourite number in it. I take chances on clues like that. It's how I find things. And we got to talking."

Ellie is nodding.

"Then I met him for a drink. He's some kind of writer, he works on a website and he hates maths. So I wanted to explain things to him…"

"And?"

"He came back to my place. And I told him about my research. He said he hates anything to do with numbers, but infinity is *not* just a number. There's a geometrical concept, an artistic concept. There's infinite sets, infinities that are larger than others – even infinities of infinities. Can understanding one aspect lead you to the others, or help access an infinite multiverse? And what's the role of perception? My approach to the problem is a bit more DIY than my colleagues. You have to use *every* sense…"

"Oh yeah, I bet. And you showed him yer etchings!" Ellie cackles again.

"Well, I did show him a special one, called the Tree of Life, my version of it. It's a tree and every branch is a symbol. It's a beautiful geometrical figure…"

"And I bet he had his mind on another kind of figure, coming home with a bonny girl like you."

"The two aren't unrelated! I experiment with *every* sense, including touch."

"I think I'm with you. And what about music? When I was in my band…"

Sirens are ringing again, real ones this time. Maybe they come from Kings Cross. Or closer. There's a *whoosh* in my ear, and that drawn-out chime. It makes me think of a wolf howling.

"What's up? You look worried. Sorry… I don't even know your name."

"Briony. My name's Briony."

The chiming in my head now assumes a haunting regularity and a crunch sounds between its blasts. But what about the notes that belong with it, the rest of the harmony?

"You alright Briony?"

"Yes, I'm alright. Maybe a little nervous. Don't know why."

"I'm sure he'll come."

Then my phone is ringing too.

"Briony? Sorry I'm late."

Yes, it's Antony. The relief must have shown on my face because Ellie grins and gives me a thumbs-up.

Though I've got my phone pressed against my ear, his voice is almost lost amid the noise in my ears, the noise in the street, the static surrounding Antony on the phone.

"I'm outside Kings Cross station. I was changing to the Piccadilly line and they told us to get out. Something about a power surge and they're closing the station…" Antony stops talking for a moment, garbled voices come into the foreground.

"No one knows what's going on. It's chaos here, lots of cops."

"Sounds dodgy… just get here soon as possible. If you're at Kings Cross you can walk, it's not more than ten minutes."

"There's loads of cops," he says as if he hasn't heard me. "They're cordoning off part of Euston Road, Hope we won't be stuck here. But there's a bus… Dunno what a 30's doing here, but it's going in the right direction. It'll get me outta here, see you soon."

He hangs up before I have the chance to say that I look forward to seeing him.

Ellie is grinning. "So he's coming? Your feller's coming?"

"Yeah, he is."

A soft boom-boom increases in my right ear, adding a bass note to the ringing. I'm really *not* in the mood for this. I tap the palm of my hand over my ear as if trying to get water out, though I know that does no good.

Ellie's face lights up with recognition. "Do you hear voices? I do too!"

She leans closer. I can smell the stale tobacco on her breath.

"What do they say to you? My voices used to tell me a lot of things. They gave me the words to my songs when I was in the band. But now my voices don't want to help so much."

"I *don't* hear voices. I just have tinnitus. Started a couple of weeks ago, so I'm not used to it."

"What is your tinnitus trying to tell you? Why don't you listen to it instead of fearing it?"

Okay, okay, I'm listening.

The ringing swells and recedes. Within it there is static and fuzz, and spaces between. There's that hint of melody again, an anguished minor chord. A beating sound, then I realise it's just a helicopter overhead. A normal helicopter, not the military helicopter in that picture from Scotland.

The street is full of people now. Everyone has a mobile in their hand or pressed to their ear, faces bereft as if nothing's coming through. An extra-large contingent of confused people with wheelie suitcases and maps wander about.

"We did a song that went like this…" As Ellie opens her mouth, her eyes widen. But her voice is scratchy, like chalk on a board or a gramophone in an old film. It comes out in a thin whine, with no words yet available.

Then a bang sends the pigeons flying in a cloud from the square. It is deep and thudding as if its full force is trapped inside a shell, but ready to crack out. I feel the thud kick in my stomach as a pall of smoke spreads from up the street. There's a shriek of rending metal, the shattering of glass. My hand is wet. I've knocked over the remains of my coffee.

Human screams from the street mingle with Leila's yelps as she cowers, releasing a stream of doggy urine. Ellie is shaking, but she hooks her fingers into Leila's collar and draws her close.

People rush towards us, some run into the café. A man in a hotel security uniform is shouting that a bus exploded. Someone is crying.

Ellie pulls at my arm with her free hand. "Come on Briony.

Let's go inside."

I pull away. "No, he's coming from there. On a bus! I have to find him!"

Ellie won't let go. Her grip is hard and pincer-like for such a frail-looking woman. "We have to get off the street!"

"Let go of me!" I finally pull free and run against the eddies of frightened people. More sirens join the siren in my ears in a crescendo that pushes me forward, left on Tavistock Road towards Euston.

"Hey, don't go there lady! There's a bomb!"

The air stinks of smoke. It smells of burning… something burning.

Pieces of twisted red metal lie in the road. A grey clot of smoke rises from a roofless #30 bus, its sides falling outwards like broken wings. On one side I make out the remains of an advert for a film called *The Descent*: "Outright Terror!"

The wall behind the bus is spattered with blood. People still stand on the upper deck, dazed and uncomprehending. One man slumps over the side. Is he throwing up? Or maybe he's dead. Some jump down off the top of the bus, others stagger away. There are bus seats and shattered glass and papers everywhere.

Two women stumble towards me with blood on their faces and pieces of glass in their hair. Another woman lies curled in a foetal position in the road. She doesn't move. There are other people in the road. I should help them. But I have to find Antony. Maybe he needs help too.

Is he still on the bus? Has he run from the blast or is he… I can't see who's in the road. I must get closer.

"Where's my husband?"

"I've lost my friend!"

The ringing in my ears winds up, going up and down a scale. The sequence isn't complete. Where's the rest of it? And a new noise starts, and when it meets the other notes the combination is unaccountably sweet in the midst of the pain and panic. It swells to a harmony in my head, to the music I almost heard when I was with Antony. I try to reach for it, and reach for the place it comes from.

Then I hear him, his voice coming and going through the music. "Briony, I'm glad to see you again…" he starts. "I enjoyed being with you. I also enjoyed arguing with you." Likewise Antony, but where the hell are you?

I feel like I'm eavesdropping again. This is something I'm not meant to hear, even though he's talking to me. "I did the budget…" Now he's only chit-chatting about work, but that's fine. His small-talk comes from somewhere better than here.

"… so if I see a number as a word or colour it helps." His voice is untouched by blood and glass and metal. He speaks as if he didn't get on that bus, as if a lot of things hadn't happened. He sounds as if he's talking to me in the pub, or in bed, or next to the pond just outside my block. "I'm writing my own stuff again… You helped me. I'm not afraid of numbers anymore – but they still bore me to tears." There's the beginning of a laugh, then his voice is receding again.

Do I hear something about "Guinness"?

"Antony, where are you?" I raise my own voice like I'm shouting into a mobile with bad reception.

But there's no answer from him, and the music is gone. There's only static, only sirens and screams, the crunch of glass underfoot. Fire engines and ambulances squeal to a stop. Police are starting to clear the street, their vans flashing blue and orange lights over the wreckage.

And reflected in the shattered glass, glancing off the surface of blasted metal… I see a different colour, transformed by time and distance. If I walk towards it, maybe I'll pass the barrier it marks between where I am – and the world of what never happened.

Then the colour fades.

"Antony, you should have walked! You should have fucking

walked," I sob and whisper as a cop pushes me back towards the pavement.

Our Land

Chris Beckett

"The Romans sir," said a girl with pebble glasses at the front of the class.

"Yes. Yes, that's right, Jessica, the Romans," agreed Thomas Turner.

He was a history teacher, and he was teaching history to class 7G.

"Well done, Jenny," said Thomas belatedly, remembering that Jenny was not very bright and needed encouragement.

He was feeling rather strange, rather distant, as if he were looking out at the world from the end of a long tunnel.

"The Romans. Exactly so, Jenny. And who lived in these parts *before* the Romans?"

It was a hot day, he supposed, a hot stuffy day and he was tired. From outside the open window he heard, with pleasure and some surprise (for they were not so very common in these parts), the lovely song of a skylark.

"The Brythons," said a boy at the back called Edward – and for some reason everyone hissed.

Thomas was puzzled. He hadn't noticed before that Edward had a speech impediment. And why the animosity?

He really was feeling *very* peculiar. Perhaps he was unwell. Perhaps he was anaemic or something?

"The *Britons*, Edward" he corrected. "The ancient *Britons*." But to his surprise this sounded all wrong. So now, having corrected Edward, he corrected himself: "The Brythons, rather. That's right, Edward. Well done. The Brythonic Celts."

There was a leak in the ceiling in the middle of the classroom and rust-coloured water was dripping into a grimy plastic bucket. Somehow he'd never noticed it before. Nor had he ever seen that large piece of lino that was missing from the middle of the floor, with the rough boards showing beneath, nor the paint that was flaking off the metal window frames...

He cleared his throat.

"And of course in 300 AD or thereabouts," he said, "the Romans expelled the Brythons. Most of them made their homes in Gaul and Iberia, in the countries we now call France and Catalonia and Spain, from where they spread out into the New World."

Catalonia *and* Spain?

It was *hot*. Outside the window the skylark went twittering on.

"... and many of them assimilated into the local population which at that time was Celtic-speaking like the Brythons themselves. But a small number held onto to their own Brythonic faith, in spite of persecution, maintaining that the Brythons were the chosen people of God – y *pobl Duw* - and that their lost homeland of Logres – *Lloegr* as they called it – remained their birthright, given to them by God himself when Joseph of Arimathea planted his staff at Avalon, cut from the same tree as Christ's crown of thorns. Or so they believe, anyway."

The odd thing was that, though his own voice was saying it, all of this was news to Thomas the teacher. He had never referred to the Ancient Britons as Brythons before. He had never heard before of them being expelled by the Romans. He had never heard of the Brythonic *faith*.

"A century or so ago, Brythons from the Americas and from mainland Europe began to settle in this country, believing that, even after seventeen hundred years, it was still theirs, although we English had been living here all this time and the country itself was called England after us…"

He had never heard of any of this before. He had no idea where it was coming from. It was all very eerie and odd, and yet there was something familiar about this feeling all the same. He had a vague memory of there having been another time like this. It resembled the memories we have in dreams of other dreams long since forgotten in waking life. He knew that this wasn't the first time that he had stood in front of the class intending to tell one story and another completely different one had come out of his mouth.

In fact, now he thought about it, he realised there had actually been a whole string of these moments. And now, quite suddenly, he could see them quite clearly, stretching back through time. He found he could contemplate them while his mouth continued to teach its unfamiliar lesson on its own. It was as if he had.emerged from the mist onto a hilltop from which he was able to see other peaks all round him that were normally hidden from view.

And he knew too that soon they would all be hidden again. He would forget. He would forget all the histories except one. He would believe that it was the only history there was…

"Excuse me sir. Do we need to write all this down?" asked Belinda Dewsbury.

"Oh for goodness sake girl, not *now*," Thomas snapped. "Can't you see I'm trying to remember something."

Belinda looked as if he had struck her across the face. There were tears forming in her eyes. Oh God, what was he doing? Everyone knew that poor Belinda had been having dreadful problems at home. The whole class was staring at him, appalled.

"Sorry," he said. "Sorry Belinda. Sorry everyone. Distracted for a moment there. No, no need to write all this down. All this is just by way of a general introduction."

Oh dear. Something had distracted him and you couldn't afford to let that happen when you were standing in front of thirty teenagers. But what had it been? What had he been thinking about? There'd been something important, something he had badly wanted not to forget...

He looked down at the textbook on his desk, hoping for clues. *English History* it was called, tattered and threadbare like the classroom itself, and at least twenty years old. It seemed familiar, and yet simultaneously it seemed strange. He felt pretty sure that it wasn't the same book that he'd laid there at the beginning of the class. For surely that had been a new book, recently published, with a shiny blue and white cover?

"Now where was I?" he said, playing for time, in as hearty a voice as he could manage.

And then the bell went. As the children rushed out he turned from habit to wipe clean the whiteboard and then remembered that the school had never had whiteboards.

"It's as if I'm in two places at once."

The book of English history fell into three pieces when he picked it up. So he stacked them together again and placed the battered volume carefully back into his briefcase. It was a hot and humid day. His head was aching, and he felt a faint twinge of nausea. He felt he had been travelling for miles and miles. Yet this was just Ely and he had only driven the few miles in from Sutton as he did every morning.

What was I thinking about back then? he asked himself. *What was it that I remembered?*

As he stepped out of the classroom a Logrian helicopter gunship was passing low overheard.

A *Logrian* helicopter?

He was momentarily surprised by the age and shabbiness of his car, but by the time he'd got inside and started it up, he was no longer asking himself questions. It didn't seem unusual to him that the roads of this Fenland city were crumbling, nor that a pervasive smell of burnt rubber hung over the place. He didn't wonder why the famous cathedral tower was pockmarked with bullet holes. It didn't strike him as odd that from time to time he passed a heap of rubble where a house had once stood or that a tank squatted by the road out of town with its gun trained on the passing cars. And he knew without thinking about it that the initials "BCL" stencilled on the tank's turret stood for *Byddin Cenedlaethol Lloegr*, the National Army of Logres.

Under the bored eye of two Logrian soldiers lounging against the tank – a tall black man and a Latin-looking woman – he pulled over outside a house on the outskirts of town, honked his horn and got out of the car. The black soldier ran his tongue over his lips and put his hand to his gun strap.

"Just letting my friend know I'm here," Thomas called out to him in Brythonic, without wondering how or when he'd learnt this Celtic tongue.

It's always best to let the soldiers know what's going on, he said to himself. When people were edgy and jumpy and trigger-happy, it was best not to keep them guessing or to spring things on them.

He took a square of rag out of his pocket and wiped his face. His wife had cut up the rags, he suddenly remembered with a complicated mixture of painful emotions. He had a wife called Jenny and a son called William who was twenty-one. Jenny had weary, bitter eyes and she filled her time up with repetitive money-saving tasks. William mostly sat in the living room and watched TV.

"*What* you said?" called out the black soldier in broken English.

"It's my friend Richard," Thomas called back in Brythonic. "I'm just honking my horn to let him know I'm here. I'm giving him a lift home."

The soldier just perceptibly nodded.

"Ah here he is!" called out Thomas again, as Richard Duckett emerged from the house where he'd been working all day, a big, sturdy man with a round, open face.

Richard lived in Sutton too. He had a son called Harry who was a friend of Williams, and a wife... Thomas felt a stab of grief... *Richard had a wife called Liz who was Thomas' first and only love.*

Richard was accompanied by a stocky stranger with close-cropped hair.

"Hey Tom!" he called, giving a quick angry glance at the BCL. "Mind if Jack here comes too? He's been helping me out today."

"No that's fine," Tom said. "How do you do Jack?"

"Hello mate," Jack said. His accent immediately identified him as one of the refugees from Birmingham who lived in the Churchill Camp. "Thanks for the lift. Appreciate it, mate."

The two of them climbed into the car in a hot blast of plaster dust and sweat, Jack in the back and Richard in the front. Characteristically, Richard reached forward at once for the knob of the car radio.

"It's no good, Richard," Thomas told him as he started up the car. "It doesn't work anymore."

"Damn," Richard said. "Well get home quickly, will you, so we can listen to the news there."

"What news?"

"What do you mean 'what news'? Haven't you heard? Blair has just cut a deal with the Brythons. He's conceded the lost land."

"How do you mean he's conceded it?"

"He's agreed to accept the existence of the State of Logres."

"What... He's.... Are you sure? On what terms?"

"On the basis that they'll let him return and set up a government of sorts here in part of the occupied area."

"And the Brythons have *agreed* to that?" Thomas asked. "To Blair coming back out of exile?"

"Yup. They've agreed he can return and set up an administration in Ipswich."

"Blair back in England. I can't believe it."

"I don't know what he thinks he's playing at," said Richard, "but I bet the Brythons can't believe their luck."

"He's bloody sold out," Jack said.

Thomas thought privately that Blair had probably struck the best deal they were going to get, but he would have found it hard to say this even to Richard, let alone to Richard's friend. All the inhabitants of Churchill Camp had lost their homes - and pretty much everything else - when Birmingham was taken by the Brythonic militias and renamed Dinas Emrys, 'City of Ambrosius'. Virtually all its English population had been driven out at gun point. A few had been killed.

There was a BCL checkpoint just beyond Wilburton. Three young Logrian soldiers stood beside the barrier, guns over their shoulders and an armoured car parked beside them. The flag of Logres - the thorn bush on its golden field – fluttered over their heads.

Thomas pulled up and leant out of the window:

"*Sut dych chi heddiw?*" he asked the soldier who came to check his papers.

The soldier was surprised to have an Englishman ask him how he was in any language, let along in Brythonic.

"*Da iawn,*" he muttered uncomfortably, looking at Thomas's identity documents and then at Richard's and Jack's and passing them back through the window.

"Okay, you could go now." he said in heavily accented English.

He gestured to one of his companions to lift the barrier.

"I wish you wouldn't talk their language to them," muttered

Richard, as they passed through. "This is England. We're English. Why should we change the way we talk for people who came here from outside?"

Thomas shrugged.

"It gets me through the checkpoints quicker."

And it invariably winds you up, he silently added.

"I speak Brythonic better than a lot of them do actually," Thomas said. "I reckon that chap there would have been a lot happier talking in Spanish."

Richard snorted with disgust.

"Well they're not really Brythons at all are they? They're Spaniards and Frenchmen and Africans and Christ knows what, who've persuaded themselves that claiming to have a distant ancestor from these parts entitles them to live here."

Thomas said nothing. Not that he disagreed. It was just that he felt there were only so many times that it was useful to repeat the same point over and over again.

"Want me to fix that radio of yours?" Richard asked after a while.

He was good with electrical things. He had once, in more prosperous times, been the technical director of a large electronics company down in Cambridge.

"It's probably not worth bothering," Thomas said, swerving to avoid a pothole. "It's as old as the car. Fifteen years. I'm surprised it lasted as long as it did."

"Well we've got to make things last nowadays haven't we?" observed the Brummie Jack in the back.

And then the radio came unexpectedly to life.

"Of course we must have the historic centre of London," Chairman Blair was saying in his disarming bloke-next-door way, "including, you know, the Houses of Parliament..."

"Oh," said Thomas. "It must just have been a loose connection."

"Ssssh!" Richard commanded.

"… London is the capital of England, after all," said Blair, though the Brythons had always insisted that Llundain was a Celtic name and that Londinium had been a Romano-Brythonic city long before the first Anglo-Saxon ever set foot there.

"… and of course, while we are prepared to recognise, you know, the State of Logres, our people must have the right to return to their own homes if they want to."

"I want to go back to *Birmingham*," said Jack the Brummie. "I don't want to go back to Dinas bloody Emrys."

"But, look, we must be realistic," Blair said. "Logres is here to stay. We are going to have to make peace with our Brythonic neighbours."

The radio was tuned to Radio England, a Flanders-based station set up by the exiled Free England Committee of which Blair was the chairman. Now it played extracts of statements from the President of France, the Chancellor of Prussia and the Foreign Minister of Spain, all praising Mr Blair for the statesmanlike thing that he had done and saying how wonderful it was that the English might now have a nation of their own again and rejoin the European family, alongside the new Brythonic nation of Logres.

"Jesus," murmured Richard softly.

It took a bit of getting used to. Blair was not only the chair of the Free England Committee but the leader of the Labour Party of England, an organisation which had spent the last fifty years fighting for the restoration of England as a single unified state, spilling not a little blood. But now, in exchange for being allowed to return and set up some sort of semi-autonomous government, he had settled for this – not the whole country, not even half of it, but the twenty-odd percent of it which had not to date been formally annexed by the Brythonic state.

"It's going to be a rolling programme," Blair said. "To start with, the Logrian Army will withdraw from Ipswich and I'm going to set up an administration there. Once we get that established and thrash out some more of the details, the Logrians will gradually withdraw from more land. Of course I don't pretend it's going to be easy, but the idea is to agree the final border sometime in the next five years. There are some difficult questions to sort out first, of course, such as the status of London, and the return of refugees - and what to do about all the Brythonic settlements we've got in the occupied area. But I want to say this: we are working towards a solution, the best solution that can be achieved. The time for armed struggle is over."

Thomas turned off the potholed surface of the main road onto the dirt track that led into Churchill Camp. It was called a camp but actually it was really a small town of five thousand people, bigger than Sutton itself. Little Brummie children and Brummie dogs were playing in narrow alleys between the corrugated iron huts.

"Just along here mate," Jack said. "This will do fine."

Richard lived across the road from Thomas, on the edge of the Sutton ridge with the wide Fens below.

"Come in and look at the news on TV, why don't you Tom?" he said. "You can translate for me. I'd really like to know what they're saying about this on the Brythonic stations."

"I don't know Richard. I think maybe I should go straight home."

"Just for a bit," his friend pleaded. "I do really want to know what they're saying."

Thomas glanced guiltily across the road at his own house. He couldn't say he was particularly looking forward to going back to Jenny. She was *so* weary and flat and empty these days, and she was prone to a certain kind of thin, angry weeping which refused to be comforted or shared.

And of course he always looked forward to seeing Richard's Liz.

"Okay, ten minutes then."

Richard led the way straight into the front room where his son Harry sat at a table tinkering with the dismantled parts of a computer.

"Alright, Tom?" Harry grunted, bending down further over his task.

Richard turned on the TV, switching through several channels. On the main Logrian news channel as well-known Brythonic politician was holding forth. A big dark Argentinian, Ieuan Ffranceg (nee Juan Franco) was the powerful leader of the settlers' bloc. Now he was denouncing the new agreement in a fractious Logrian parliament.

"The counties of Eastern Logres," he bawled, as if explaining something very simple to an exceptionally unintelligent and recalcitrant child, "are every bit as much the sacred birthright of our people as are Western Logres, Northern Logres, Llundain and Dinas Emrys. The final frontier of Logres must include the *whole* of the historic kingdom of Arthur and Ambrosius. It must include not only the present State of Logres and the so-called occupied areas but also Scotland as far North as the Antonine Wall. To accept less would be to betray the legacy bequeathed to us by God."

He made an exasperated gesture.

"I really can't understand what these Saxons keep whinging about!" he exclaimed. "They already have a country. It's called Saxony. The clue is in the name. Why don't they go back to where they first came from?"

"These people talk as if the last seventeen centuries were *nothing!*" Thomas said wonderingly, after translating this for Richard. "I couldn't even say exactly where Saxony is."

"Self-centred bastards," Richard growled, "they nurture grievances from two thousand years ago, but expect us to forget ours when they've still in living memory."

"They don't really see us as people, that's the difficulty," Thomas said. "Their history and faith has made their destiny seem so self-evidently important to them that anyone who gets in their way is simply a *problem.*"

"Why must you always try and *understand* them?" Richard grumbled. "Why should we *care* about their motives?"

"Hello, Tom!"

It was Richard's wife Liz, a pretty woman with bright restless merry eyes, who Thomas had secretly loved since he was fifteen. As ever, a knife blade twisted in his heart. Oh God, how different she was from his own wife Jenny, across the road there, pale and colourless and flat, at the bottom of her grey sea of misery.

"Coffee anyone?" Liz asked, quickly averting her eyes from Thomas's.

"For Christ's sake, Liz," Richard growled, "never mind coffee. Come and watch this. Your own country being sold."

"Oh Richard leave it!" she said. "It's not good for you, all this anger. You know the news now. We all know it. You can't do anything about it. Turn off the TV and talk about something else."

But their son Harry, who'd been sitting quietly in a corner, backed his father up.

"You should be *more* angry, Mum, not Dad less. Where's your pride? Think what we could have been if it wasn't for the invaders!"

Since Richard had lost his job in Cambridge, things had been very hard for the Ducketts financially. He had once briefly tried to make money by doing factory work in the State of Logres itself (first in Llundain, then eighty miles away in the city of Rhydychen, which the English had once called "Oxford"). But then came the first violent English uprising against Logrian rule, and all work permits for English people had been cancelled. Richard now had to eke out a living locally as a general purpose handyman. It wasn't easy when no one had money to spare.

"I'm not saying we shouldn't be angry," Liz said. "I just think being angry shouldn't become the *only* thing we are."

Which is what Thomas thought too.

But he knew he ought to go.

"Look," he said, "I'm sorry but I really must be getting home. Jenny will be worrying about the news as well. And wondering if I'm okay."

As he crossed the road back to his house a BCL jeep was going by. He didn't pay it any attention at first but it stopped right beside him. Thomas tensed, as any English person would have done, expecting some humiliating demand.

But the voice that called out to him was entirely friendly.

"Good news, Mr Turner, don't you agree? Peace! Peace in prospect at last!"

"Colonel Rhys."

Thomas reluctantly acknowledged the Logrian, conscious of the inquisition that would face him if any member of Richard's family were to see him talking in an amiable way to a BCL officer. But actually the two men met quite regularly at work, Thomas having a community liaison role at school and Colonel Rhys being the BCL civil liaison officer for the East Cambridgeshire military district.

"I've always thought if it had been down to people like you and I, we would have reached a solution long ago," said Colonel Rhys in his bad, French-accented English.

A stocky, balding man with prominent eyebrows and a quick but slightly mocking smile, the colonel had grown up in Paris. In civilian life he was an academic chemist and, as a strictly secular Brython, he had always made a point of differentiating himself from the religious Brythons and their talk of the holy destiny of the Brythonic Celts. Thomas actually rather liked him.

"Maybe," he said with an awkward laugh.

Colonel Rhys reached out from his jeep to shake Richard's hand.

"Maybe one of these days you and I will be able to sit in a

pub with a pint of English beer and laugh about all this nonsense. We Brythons and you English have so much in common really don't we? We are all Northern Europeans after all!"

Thomas looked anxiously over the Colonel's shoulder at the Duckett's house.

On Saturday morning, Thomas went over to see his mother Doreen in her bungalow on the far side of the village. It was a depressing errand. There was so little that he could share with her and so little she could share with him. She was eighty-two and suffered not only from emphysema but from Alzheimer's disease. In her mind she was back in the days of her adolescence when England was England, Logres did not exist and the Brythonic immigration had only just begun.

"I really think the government ought to do more for us old people," she grumbled at one point. "We built this country up, we paid taxes, and look at the thanks we get!"

On the way back home, Thomas heard the angry shouting of young men ahead of him.

A small crowd had gathered outside the church, consisting of a group of young English youths from the village and from Churchill Camp, and a group of young Logrians up from the fortified Brythonic settlement of Tre Morfa. The young settlers were armed with automatic rifles, and they had unrolled banners protesting against the deal between their government and Chairman Tony Blair.

GOD GAVE EASTERN LOGRES TO US!
THERE IS NO SUCH PEOPLE AS 'THE ENGLISH'
SAXONS BELONG IN SAXONY

About three hundred Logrians lived in the Tre Morfa settlement. Surrounded by a high razor wire fence and CCTV cameras, it was on the opposite side of the village to the five thousand Brummies in the Churchill Camp and it occupied about the same amount of land.

"Fuck off Logrian scum!" the English crowd shouted. "This is England! We'll bury you! We'll fucking bomb you into the sea!"

The Logrians, outnumbered but made confident by their guns, shouted back:

"England? What's 'England'? This is Logres! *You* belong in Saxony! That's *why* you're called Saxons. Duh!"

"We're *not* called Saxons. We're English. And we were born here."

Thomas sighed. Soon some English idiot would start throwing stones and then another idiot on the Logrian side would point a gun and then…

Richard's son Harry was at the front of the English crowd:

"Convenient how your God tells you to steal land from other people," he called out.

"How can we steal what is already ours?" one of the settlers shouted back in strongly French-accented English (the Tre Morfa settlers came from Montreal and still spoke French among themselves.)

"How can it be yours when *we've* lived here for a thousand years?" called out Thomas' own son William from the back of the crowd. "And you lot were living in Canada until a few years ago."

"Because God gave it to *us*, scumbag, and *you* had no right to take it."

Thomas broke in before anyone else could reply.

"Leave it, all of you," he told the English group. "You're giving them exactly what they want. Ignore them and walk away."

Being a schoolmaster gave him a certain authority. The English kids reluctantly began to disperse.

"Scared are you, Saxons?" the settlers jeered after them.

"Keep walking away!" Thomas told his compatriots.

But he couldn't resist one small jibe at the Logrians himself: "If you're so brave," he said in Brythonic, "why don't you leave your guns behind next time?"

"I thought you said to ignore them," said Harry Duckett

afterwards, but Thomas could see he had risen a little in his young neighbour's estimation.

A couple of days later Thomas had to take his mother Doreen for an appointment at Addenbrooke's hospital down in Cambridge. She needed to have the fluid drained from her lungs. Jenny came too to help. The appointment was at one o'clock but, although it was only about fifteen miles down to Cambridge, they set out at seven with the aim of getting through the BCL checkpoint at Cottenham before the queues grew too long.

At first Jenny and Thomas congratulated themselves on their plan. There were only ten vehicles ahead of them in the queue at the checkpoint and they thought they'd get through in thirty minutes or so and maybe have time to look round a few shops and grab a cup of coffee somewhere before it was time to get to the hospital.

Jenny, by her standards, was almost cheerful.

"Not that there's much *in* the shops these days, mind you," she said.

But even if the shops were bare, things seemed a little more normal in Cambridge than they did out in Sutton, sandwiched as Sutton was between the two sets of incomers in Churchill Camp and Tre Morfa. In Cambridge you could almost imagine that you were in a place called England, and not in something called the Eastern Occupied Territories.

Four cars passed slowly through the checkpoint. Three young Logrian soldiers were there as usual with an armoured personnel carrier. They asked for papers, peered into the vehicles, looked at luggage, asked people what their business was. This was slow and tedious but no special problems cropped up until the fifth car reached the front. Perhaps the driver was known to them, perhaps he was deliberately provocative, perhaps the soldiers simply felt in the mood for a change of routine, but for whatever reason suddenly the mood changed. The soldiers shouted at the young red-headed driver and his girlfriend to get out – "Now! Now! Let's go, Saxons!" - and proceeded to empty his suitcases onto the road and poke through the contents with their rifle barrels. The man protested loudly. His girlfriend began to weep.

Thomas looked at Jenny and saw the little spark of humour and hope fading once again in his wife's eyes.

"We should have started earlier," she said flatly. "We should have known things would be slow just now."

She clenched and unclenched her hands.

"Damn, damn, *damn!*" she hissed. "We're *so* stupid. Stupid, stupid, stupid. We should have *known*."

Things had been tense since the deal between the Logrian government and Blair. Rejectionists on both sides had accused their leaders of selling out and had begun to react with violence. It was obvious, at least with hindsight, that the soldiers would be on edge.

The day was warming fast.

"Why aren't we at the hospital yet, Andrew?" whimpered Doreen in the back of the car. "I'm so hot. And I'm going to need the toilet soon."

Then the red-headed owner of the suitcase made the mistake of shoving one of the soldiers. The soldier, a Spanish-looking boy ablaze with the full bloom of adolescent acne, rammed him back against the personnel carrier. The man's girlfriend screamed and the soldier backed off a little. The woman went to pick up the contents of the suitcase that were strewn over the road, only to be ordered to stop. When she ignored this, another soldier came forward and very roughly pushed her away so she stumbled and fell. At this drivers and passengers emerged protesting from their cars.

"What do you think you're doing?"

"Leave the girl alone!"

"What's happening, Tom?" Doreen called out. "Why can't

we go now? What's all this waiting for?"

"It's alright, mum," Thomas said, "It's just the soldiers…"

"What soldiers? Why are there soldiers here? Are we having a war?"

It was no good trying to explain to her. She lived her life at a time before the occupation began, when the country called Logres didn't even exist except in storybooks.

"It's just… the police. Just the police, Mum, that's all."

The soldiers were badly rattled by all the people emerging from their cars. For a moment Thomas actually felt sorry for them. They were only boys, after all, younger than Jenny and Thomas's own son William, and only three of them there, alone in a hostile land where many people would cheerfully kill them.

Suddenly one of the soldiers fired some shots in the air.

"All of you, back in your cars and wait!" he shouted. "Do you understand? In your cars *now!*"

Another half-hour went by. Eventually the owner of the suitcase and his girlfriend jumped into their car, did a U-turn and roared back the way they had come with much squealing of brakes and grinding of gears. The next car crawled forward. Three more cars waited in front of Thomas and Jenny, and the soldiers looked set to deal with each one very slowly and thoroughly indeed. Even with all the windows wound down it was now very hot indeed.

"I need the toilet," Doreen whimpered, "I can't wait any more."

Thomas got out of the car and called to the soldiers in Brythonic.

"Excuse me. It's my mother. She's eighty-two. She needs to go to the toilet. Could we just…"

"Are you deaf or something Saxon? I said stay in your fucking car."

He got back in. After a few minutes a spreading stench told him his mother hadn't been able to hold on.

128

It was nearly ten thirty by the time they reached to the front of the queue and Thomas and Jenny, nauseated by the stink, had both vomited out of the windows. The spotty-faced soldier ordered all three of them out so they could be searched.

"Holy Joseph!" he exclaimed in Brythonic as Doreen climbed unsteadily out. "The old bag has shit herself!"

The other Logrians laughed.

Thomas knew the best thing for everyone would be if he could contain himself – Doreen didn't understand Brythonic after all and had no idea what had been said about her - but his nerves were at breaking point.

"That's my mother you're talking about, you silly rude little boy!"

Immediately the soldier swung up his rifle and hit Thomas across the head with the barrel.

"Who are you calling a boy you Saxon arsehole!"

Thomas was momentarily dazed. Everything moved in slow motion and seemed very far away... and he remembered the strange sensation that he'd had in the classroom a few days previously.

This particular world, he realised, this particular England, this particular history, was just one of many that he'd passed through. It wasn't real, or not real in the sense that all these people around him, English and Logrian, thought it was. Even the people weren't real in the way they thought they were.

A spotty young boy from one imaginary nation had just struck a cautious old school teacher from another imaginary nation that happened to occupy the same space. The schoolteacher was Thomas Turner, aged 52 and born a few miles away in Sutton, Cambridgeshire. The soldier (Thomas didn't ask himself how he knew) was Private Salvador Gallego, aged 19, born in Madrid to a schoolteacher mother and a father who was a minister in the Spanish Brythonic Church.

"Tom?" Jenny called to him, fearful and yet somehow

resentful too. "What are you doing?"

The little bird's strange, rapid, angular little song went on and on. Thomas laughed cheerfully, peering upward, trying to find the bird. But it was hiding in the white hot heart of the sun.

"Yes, I'm fine. As a matter of fact I'm just trying to spot the lark."

Salvador Galego, the acne-faced soldier, didn't have enough English to understand what Thomas was saying, but he was unnerved by Thomas's apparent indifference to the situation in hand. It seemed to him subversive.

"Get back in the car, Saxon!" he shouted at Thomas. "And take that stinking old woman away from here."

The lark went on singing in the sun. Thomas considered the anger of the Logrian soldier with interest. Then his attention became drawn to a certain loud high-pitched sound coming from nearby. It was a frail old woman called Doreen who had no idea where she was or who the foreigners with guns were that had just hit her son round the face. After a moment he remembered that she was his mother and that the poor grey creature with her was his wife.

"It's alright, Mum," he said, smiling at her. "It's all alright. Get back in the car and we'll have you sorted out in no time."

He noticed a chill on his cheek, touched it and looked down in surprise at the redness on his hand.

When Jenny and Thomas pulled up outside their house that night, their son William was in the front room playing video games with Harry Duckett. Doreen was to stay the night with them and Thomas helped Jenny to bathe her, calm her down and tuck her up in bed. Then he went to the kitchen and heated up the pasta that William had made for them two hours previously. Harry followed him.

"How did you get that mark on your face?" he demanded.

He was like his father. In any other area of life the Ducketts would be the first to forgive a wrong done to them. But when it came to the Brythons, they were implacable. They never let it rest.

"It was the soldiers, wasn't it?" Harry persisted. "One of them at the checkpoint hit you."

"It was my own fault really."

"What do you mean your own fault?"

"Well, I…"

"Did you attack him?"

"No, but I called him a silly boy."

"Good for you. This is *our* land. You've lived here all your life. So did your father and your grandfather before you."

Thomas laid cutlery on the table for Jenny and himself.

"I'm rather tired, Harry. I'm sure you're right. But I'd prefer just to forget it now if you don't mind."

"But that's all wrong! You can't just forget it or they'll have beaten us. You might as well emigrate and let them help themselves to everything."

Actually, Thomas had been increasingly tempted to do just that. He could get a job abroad as a teacher, with better pay and a life free of checkpoints and curfews and daily humiliations. He was getting tired of the struggle to hold onto the idea of England. He couldn't help thinking that perhaps England had had its day.

"So what happened?" Harry pressed him.

"If I tell you will you let it drop?"

"Okay. For now."

So Thomas told him: about being forced to stay in the car, about Doreen soiling herself, about the insulting comment and his reaction.

Harry exploded; "The callous *bastards*! An old woman of eighty-two! In the country where she was born! How *dare* they?"

"You said you'd let it drop."

"Yes, but…" Harry checked himself with difficulty. "Well alright. But just for the moment."

Jenny came down. She and Thomas ate their pasta. William and Harry sat with them for a bit, William trying to make conversation, Harry dark and glowering in the background, saying nothing at all. Later on Harry went out to meet someone and William and Thomas watched TV. Then Jenny went off to the kitchen and had one of her solitary little cries.

Thomas kept thinking about a lark twittering in the sun and wondering what it was that it seemed to remind him of.

In the middle of the night there was a series of explosions out on the Fen. Thomas jumped out of bed and ran to the window. He couldn't see anything at first but he heard gunfire, then silence.

"What is it, Tom?" Jenny wanted to know.

He shrugged and got back into bed. Neither slept.

Half an hour later they heard the throbbing of helicopters low overhead, not just one of them passing over, but five or six going to and fro, their spotlights sweeping the village and from time to time flooding the bedroom with a spurious icy daylight that disappeared as quickly as it came. Some time later tanks and armoured troop carriers came clanking and rumbling into Sutton and there were more spotlights, more icy, comfortless false dawns.

"... By order of the Eastern Logres Command," crackled a megaphone on a BCL jeep on the road outside, "this district is under indefinite curfew...."

"Remain in your homes," replied another megaphone over in the direction of the church. "Any Saxon found in the street is liable to arrest and detention. We will shoot if necessary..."

The first jeep came back: "Sutton village and Churchill camp are now subject to curfew under the Prevention of Terror regulations. Do not come out of your houses. Our orders are to shoot to kill if this is necessary to maintain order..."

The phones were still working at first. Villagers called one another. The story went round that someone had managed to get some sort of homemade rocket launcher in through the outer wire of the Tre Morfa settlement. It had been set to fire at 1 a.m. Two settlers had been injured. Some said that a small child in there had been killed.

So of course there'll be hell to pay, Thomas thought.

The phones were cut off half way through the morning and then, at about 2 p.m., five Logrian soldiers with flak jackets and automatic rifles arrived at the Turners' house. They made Thomas and Jenny pull out every drawer and empty the contents over the floor. They made them empty their food cupboards onto the table and their coal bunker over the back lawn. They even slashed open bags of sugar and flour with bayonets and pulled up the fitted carpet in the hallway…

An hour later the soldiers returned. Thomas, Jenny and William were still scooping up the sugar and the coal (which they could ill afford to lose) and trying to get the torn carpet back into place. The soldiers said they were looking for Harry Duckett. Some informer in the village had told them that William was his closest friend.

"I don't know where he is," William said. "I really don't."

They arrested him and took him away.

Jenny and Thomas didn't sleep at all that next night. Jenny sat clenching and unclenching her fists at the kitchen table, rocking to and fro, while Thomas patted her shoulder and told her stories about young men he'd heard of who'd been arrested and then returned to their parents unharmed.

As it turned out they were lucky. William did come back the next day. A jeep pulled up and dumped him outside. He had a black eye but was otherwise outwardly uninjured.

Jenny hugged him. Thomas hugged him. William pulled away in distaste.

"I'm alright. Don't make a fuss."

"I'll put the kettle on," Thomas said. "I'll make us a pot of tea."

(They were English after all. This was the whole problem. They couldn't be anything other than English.)

When Thomas brought the pot over the table, William was staring distractedly at the window while Jenny stroked the back of his hand.

"I'm worried about Harry," William burst out. "That's why they've let me go, isn't it? They've found Harry somewhere, or they know where he is. That's how they know he wasn't with me and that I wasn't lying. Otherwise…"

He put his hands over his face and began to cry in a strangled, lonely, distant way that was very like his mother.

"They were about to start on me," he said. "I was stuck in this interrogation room with them and they were going to start on me."

"But they didn't, did they?" Thomas said.

"No, but…"

"Whatever they were going to do to you. I suppose you're thinking that's what they're now doing to Harry."

"Well it is, isn't it? It is. It's happening to him now."

William nodded. This was an appalling thought for all three of them. They'd all known Harry since he was a funny reckless indomitable little toddler.

"The thing is, Dad, I actually think he did it. I think it was him that went through the fence with those rockets."

"Stupid Harry," said Thomas, "*Stupid, stupid* Harry."

Jenny began to sob. None of them thought even for a moment about the dead child over in the Brythonic settlement of Tre Morfa.

On TV the Logrian politicians came over like weary grownups pushed to the edge of their patience by foolish and ungrateful children.

"The Saxons are going to have to learn that if they want a

state they must behave like decent human beings," said the Prime Minister of Logres.

One of his coalition partners - Emrys Llewellyn, the leader of the *Gwlad y Greal* religious party - said that this incident confirmed the need for the Logrian state to retain control in perpetuity over *all* of the country formerly known as England:

"This appalling terrorist attack has exposed the folly of handing over even the smallest part of our land to a people who have always refused our offers of peace. Little Angharad was an innocent child who had done no harm to anyone. She must *not* be allowed to have died in vain! We must bury, once and for all, the dangerous, the lunatic, the *criminal* notion of a separate so-called English state. If the Saxons want their own country, they should return to Saxony."

Later a news bulletin confirmed that two terrorist suspects had been arrested: Harry Duckett and John Fison. The Fisons lived just two doors down from the Ducketts. They had once owned a farm on the site of the Tre Morfa settlement. According to the bulletin both Harry and John were members of the English Young Socialists, the youth wing of Chairman Blair's organisation, the Labour Party of England. But Blair himself denied any involvement in the attack.

Late that afternoon a military bulldozer arrived, accompanied by two tanks and a platoon of soldiers. Colonel Rhys was with them, the BCL civil liaison officer for the Cambridgeshire military district, his face taut, his gaze fixed on the soldiers and the job in hand.

They knocked down the Fisons' house first. Then the bulldozer pulled back from the wreckage with a bit of the Fisons' blue curtains still dangling from its great blade, turned awkwardly on its tracks, and rolled along the road towards the Ducketts', crushing the tarmac as it went.

Richard, Liz and Harry's younger brother Ned stood watching, under the eye of two Logrian soldiers.

"Where were you born, eh?" Richard demanded of them. "France? America? Spain? This is our land and you won't make it yours even if you knock down *everyone's* house."

But they didn't answer him. Perhaps they didn't even understand. The bulldozer rolled forward. In about twenty-five minutes all of Richard's and Liz's extensions and improvements were reduced to a heap of rubble. The Ducketts themselves were so completely covered in the dust of their own pulverised home that they looked like statues, like plaster-cast corpses from the ruins of Pompeii.

Thomas called down from the window, "Liz! Richard! Ned! Come over here and let us look after you!"

Liz looked round with a blank plaster-cast face, but she was in a state of shock, unable to act or speak or feel.

Next day the BCL lifted the curfew from 10 a.m. to midday to allow the people of Sutton and Churchill Camp to hurry out for supplies.

Thomas walked down to a farm on the Fen just outside the village for some eggs and potatoes. On the way back he met Colonel Rhys driving up from the Tre Morfa settlement. It was very different from the previous encounter when the Frenchman had embarrassed Thomas with his friendliness and volubility. This time Colonel Rhys tried to pretend he hadn't seen Thomas at all, but Thomas stepped out in front of the car so the Logrian officer had no choice but to stop.

"How can you live with yourself?" Thomas demanded. "How can you come across from Paris to a place you have never seen before and be party to the destruction of the home of a family whose people have lived here for generations and generations?"

After all, Colonel Rhys wasn't religious. He wasn't one of those Brythons who believed that God gave Britain to them in perpetuity when he sent Joseph to plant that damned thorn tree at Avalon. In all of their meetings, Rhys had made a particular point of differentiating himself from those people. In fact he often expressed the view that rational people on the Logrian and English sides had more in common with one another than they did with the fanatics of either variety.

But now the Colonel's manner was distant and cold.

"It was the home of a child-killer," he said. "Do you expect us to pat you people on the back when your sons murder our kids?"

"It was the home of a young man who attacked a fortified colony of invaders who have deliberately dispossessed and humiliated him for many years."

The colonel shrugged.

"I'm angry now and maybe I will feel differently when I've had time to think," he said, "but right now what I feel is that you people are just going to have to find somewhere else to live. We've tried to be reasonable but look how you repay us!"

"The English must leave *England*?" Thomas began to say. "What kind of sense does…"

He broke off. He felt strange, as if he was looking into the world from the far end of a long tunnel.

"I'm sorry?" asked Colonel Rhys.

Thomas noticed a sky-lark twittering far above them.

"The English…" he began, and stopped.

On and on went the lark's song, like the song of sunlight itself.

There was no chosen race, there was no them and no us. There was no England, no Logres, not deep down at the core of things. There was nothing like that, just the world itself endlessly upwelling from non-existence.

"We should try and remember," Thomas said.

"Remember what?"

Rhys looked troubled. He was watching Thomas with a puzzled expression on his face, wondering why his neighbour had made him stop in the middle of his morning run.

"Oh I... I just..."

Thomas broke off. *Why on earth am I angry with this man?* he wondered.

All he could remember about Rhys was that he was a Welshman, a research chemist from Aberystwyth, and that he'd moved to the area a few months previously to take up a post at Cambridge University. Thomas had always thought he seemed quite interesting and nice. He'd told himself more than once that he really ought to make the effort to befriend the clever Welshman. What could he and Rhys have possibly have found to quarrel about?

He shrugged, and stepped aside. Rhys nodded, gave him a puzzled but not unfriendly smile, and set off on his run again. The lark kept on singing.

Thomas was standing on the wide flat empty Fens, but once again he had the feeling, though only very fleetingly, that he was on some kind of hilltop, looking out at the other hills that were normally hidden from view. Then the feeling was gone.

Thomas remembered that he had a lesson to prepare about 1066 and the famous victory of Harold the Great over the Normans (the last time, of course, that a foreign enemy had ever set foot on English soil.) And he remembered too that when he got home Liz would be there, his dear wife of twenty years, whom he loved with all his heart.

For some reason he found both these thoughts immensely reassuring.

Fallout

Gareth L Powell

1.

Despite what was to come, the day started well. An hour before sunrise they landed the rented jet at a decommissioned RAF base in Wiltshire, near Swindon. It was a cold morning and frost glittered on the grass at the edge of the runway.

Leaving the pilot and cabin crew to look after the plane, they pulled four motorbikes from its hold and clipped dosimeters to their lapels. Then they donned helmets and drove their bikes downhill, through dark and empty villages, to the army check point at the M4 motorway junction. Rusty, concrete-filled oil drums blocked the westbound slip road and a tired sergeant blew into his hands. He wore a long coat and a fur hat with khaki earflaps. The men behind him cradled standard-issue SA80 assault rifles.

"We were told to expect you," he said through his moustache. His breath steamed in their headlights. He glanced at their papers, then back over his shoulder at the unlit, empty carriageway stretching away behind him, into the dead zone. He shivered.

"Rather you than me," he said.

On the lead bike, Ann Szkatula pushed up her visor. She had silver eye shadow and a matching silk scarf. Behind her, the three other riders each had a foot on the ground, engines running, eager for the off.

"Thanks," she said.

Some of the soldiers wanted autographs. Ann sat patiently as the three American boys signed iPod cases and posed for photographs. Then, with the barrier open and the empty road stretching ahead, she led them out onto the carriageway, and up to a steady 110 kilometres an hour. Travelling at that speed, they soon passed the derelict service area at Leigh Delamere, and the Bath junction.

On both sides of the road the countryside was dark. The farms they passed were deserted. There were no crops in the fields and the cattle were long-gone. On the motorway verges, abandoned vehicles rusted, their tires flat and windows broken; and until the white sun rose behind them, the only lights Ann saw were their own.

"Welcome to the West Country," she said over the bike-to-bike intercom. No one answered. They were all too caught up in the desolate splendour of the cold dawn, and the creeping fear of the invisible radiation sleeting through their bodies from the crash site ahead. Beside her, she saw Dustin leaning forward on his bike, his chin almost touching the Honda's handlebars. The other two members of the band were weaving around on their yellow Kawasakis – trailer park kids still adjusting to their new-found wealth.

Dustin was the cute one. With his blue eyes and floppy fringe, he was the face of the group. He sang lead. The other two, Kent and Brad, danced and did backing vocals. Today, all three were wrapped in brand-new matching black leathers.

Together, they swept down to the junction with the M32. It was the main turn-off for Bristol. Ann pulled over and the boys slithered to a halt beside her. Dustin was the closest. He flipped up his visor.

"How much further is it, Ann?"

Ann looked at her dosimeter. This close to ground zero, the ambient radiation levels were more than a hundred times higher than normal – not enough to cause undue concern, but enough to remind her of the need for caution.

"If we carry on for a couple of miles, we'll be able to see the crater. We can't go any further than that, so from there we'll take the A38 right into the heart of the city, where there'll be plenty of empty streets for you to race around."

Four-abreast, they rolled up to the Almondsbury interchange, where the M4 crossed the cracked and shattered surface of the M5. From there, the Severn Valley stretched out before them, a patchwork of overgrown fields and industrial ruin.

Ann turned her engine off and leaned the bike on its stand. They could go no further. A barricade of charred and rusting cars blocked the carriageway. Below, through the morning haze, the irradiated waters of the Severn smouldered like molten bronze. The ruined power stations of Oldbury and Berkeley lay to the north, and directly ahead, the twin Severn bridges stood, their towers partially collapsed and their sagging steel cables slowly unravelling...

The boys took off their helmets and Dustin ruffled his trademark fringe into shape. Brad shook out his white dreadlocks. Ann took a pair of binoculars and climbed up onto the bonnet of a burned-out Volvo. It was hard to make out the crash site itself from this angle, lying as it did in the mud at the water's edge.

"There's some wreckage over there," she said. She handed the glasses to Dustin, guiding him to where the nose of the crashed alien craft lay in the thick estuary mud like a dropped eggshell. Smaller fragments littered the grass for miles around, like twisted tinfoil. As she moved her head, some of them caught the morning sun.

"I heard it was bigger than that," Dustin said.

Ann took the binoculars back and handed them to Brad. "It exploded in the air," she said. "I guess some of it fell in the water."

When they'd all had a look, Dustin gave Ann his mobile camera phone and the three boys posed on the rusted cars as she used it to take pictures of them, with the collapsed bridges and crash site as an apocalyptic backdrop.

Dustin tucked his helmet under his arm and struck a heroic attitude.

"I'm so putting these on MySpace," he said.

They took the A38 down through Filton and Horfield, to the centre of Bristol.

"Watch out for rubble," Ann said as they hit the roundabout by the bus station. The boys ignored her. This was what they'd been waiting for: the chance to go wild. They ripped open their throttles and surged away into the empty streets, dodging potholes and leaning crazily into the bends.

Within seconds, they were gone.

Ann followed them as far as Castle Park before giving up. It was where they planned to regroup. She pulled her bike off the road, rumbling through the unkempt grass to the ruined church. Her front wheel wobbled over the uncertain, frosty ground. When she turned the engine off, all she could hear was the wind in the bare trees and, far away between the buildings, the distant roar of the other bikes.

The church had been gutted by the Luftwaffe in 1940 and then left as a memorial to that distant conflict. There were empty birds' nests in its eaves, strands of ivy scaling its walls. Beyond it, the waters of the old dock were thick with weeds. The few remaining pleasure boats wallowed half-submerged, their sides green with accumulated scum.

Ann stretched the stiffness in her back. After two decades of neglect, the city didn't look as bad as she'd been expecting; the shops and office buildings appeared almost untouched, if she discounted the fire damage and broken windows.

She unpacked her portable gas stove and put a pan of coffee on to heat. She checked her dosimeter: they'd be okay for another hour or so, as long as the boys didn't try anything stupid, like trying to bust their way into one of the shops, where the seriously contaminated dust still lay undisturbed.

She blew into her hands and bent down to stir the coffee. At heart, they were good, all-American boys. But they were young and, like all young people, they thought they were immortal. As the person responsible for keeping them out of trouble, she'd be much happier once they were all safely on the jet this evening. She hadn't wanted to come here and, now they had, she couldn't wait to get away.

She'd been eighteen years old when the alien ship exploded above the Severn mudflats, damaging the nuclear reactors at Berkeley and Oldbury. At the time, she was living near Oxford with her parents, both Polish immigrants. Like so many other families, they fled for the continent when they heard the news. They panicked at the thought of the radiation. Spurred on by memories of Chernobyl, they packed their lives into suitcases and crossed the English Channel at night, crammed onto a dangerously overcrowded car ferry.

Two days later, dirty and hungry, they made it to her paternal grandparents' apartment in Warsaw, where they stayed for the next six months.

There were only two bedrooms. In order to escape, Ann joined the army as a trainee chef. She did two tours in the Middle

East. After that, she went into business for herself on the streets of Krakow; selling hamburgers containing vat-grown meat cloned directly from pop stars and celebrities. She nearly got rich. But when her patties turned out to be ordinary pork instead of vat-grown human flesh, she wound up in jail.

When she got out, two months later, she drifted down through Slovakia and Hungary to the pebbly beaches of Croatia. There were British refugees everywhere she went. She'd lived for a while as a busker in Budapest. She drove a cab in Zagreb, and then worked the door at a music club in Rijeka, where she drank Ouzo with the roadies.

Then, at the age of thirty-three, she woke on a tour bus in the unreal light of a wet Italian dawn to find she'd blagged her way into the music business. Now, years later, here she was: babysitting this boy band from an American TV talent show, chaperoning them through their first (and probably last) European tour.

Her job was to keep them clean and sober, and show them the sights. When they were finished here, she'd lead them across country to Stonehenge, and then back to the plane. Tonight, they'd be in Helsinki for two shows, then on to Copenhagen, Prague, Belgrade, and Bucharest.

She wrapped her arms around herself and stamped her feet on the cold, shattered concrete. After all these years, and sandwiched into such an itinerary, being back in the UK, the land of her birth, didn't feel like coming home. In fact, it didn't feel much like anything at all.

Half an hour later, the other bikes rejoined her. Dustin, Kent and Brad were laughing, bubbly with adrenalin, their mid-west accents loud in the stillness of the abandoned city. She poured them coffee and broke out the sandwiches. There were apples in the lunch box. She took out her penknife and sliced them into quarters.

As she handed them around, she heard the echo of another engine. Brad met her eyes. "What's that?" he said, cocking his head, his dreadlocks swinging. Ann shrugged. They were supposed to have the city to themselves. As far as she knew, the army hadn't granted permits to anyone else. She turned in the direction of the sound. As she did so, a tattered Land Rover lurched into view, weaving crazily. It roared along the road toward them, then bumped over the kerb, through the trees, and ploughed to a halt in the long grass.

Dustin took a step forward: "Is it the paparazzi?"

Ann pulled him behind her. "I don't think so."

A rat-faced man and a woman were sitting in the front of the vehicle. Both had black army fatigues and short blond hair. The woman stepped out, a compact silver pistol in her right hand.

She said: "Hello, Skat."

Ann bristled. She hadn't been called that since school in Oxford. She had a gun of her own in her bike's pannier. She'd packed it to scare wild dogs but now couldn't reach it. Instead, she narrowed her eyes.

"Vic?"

The woman held the heavy door open. She motioned with her gun. "Get in the van, Skat."

2.

Inside, with the doors shut, the Land Rover's cab smelled damp. The plastic foam seats were rotten with mildew.

Vic said: "Buckle up." She still had the middle class Cotswold accent that Ann remembered, and she'd taken the rat-faced man's place at the steering wheel. He now stood out on the grass, his gun trained on the three boys.

"Where are we going?" Ann asked.

Vic ignored her. She had the gun in her lap. She mashed the

gear lever into reverse and backed out onto the road, then crunched it into first and they rolled off in a cloud of blue smoke, rattling through the city centre, past the cathedral, and out onto the road following the river through the Avon Gorge, towards the grey shores of the Severn Estuary.

As she drove, she said: "You remember me then, Skat?"

"It's been a long time." Ann eyed the pistol in the blonde woman's lap. She hadn't seen Victoria O'Neill since they were at secondary school together.

"I heard you went to Spain and joined the army. And now you're managing this boy band, what do they call themselves?"

"One Giant Leap."

"That's it." Vic shifted gear, coaxing a little more speed from the aged engine.

"After school," she continued, "I joined the army as an officer. I was in Afghanistan for a while. And then I had the bad luck to be stationed over *here* when the crash came."

They passed the abandoned coal terminal at Avonmouth, its skeletal cranes and coal dust conveyors rusting in the open air like abandoned Martian tripods.

"I was on one of the first choppers into the crash site. It was dark and there were fires burning on the water from the spilled fuel, and fallout from the cracked reactors."

"It sounds grim."

"I was only nineteen. But to cut a long story short, I found something in the wreckage. Maybe it was a weapon, maybe not. But I stashed it. I dropped it out of the helicopter as we left."

"And now you're looking for it?" Ann had heard rumours of scavengers selling illegally-foraged artefacts to anonymous collectors.

Vic shook her shaven head. "I know *exactly* where it is. That's where we're going. I memorised the GPS coordinates. But when we get there, I want you to get it for me."

"Why me?"

"Because it's probably radioactive as hell and frankly, I'd rather not touch it."

After a few miles, the Land Rover bumped off the road onto the rough windblown grass at the edge of the Estuary, and the engine died. Across the water, the hills of Wales were brown with winter bracken. The sky was a clear eggshell blue at the horizon, shading to navy at the zenith.

Ann waited until the other woman stepped out of the vehicle, and then popped her own seatbelt. She still had her penknife, tucked safely into her zipped jacket pocket, but Vic had the gun.

"There's a metal detector in the back," Vic said.

Ann walked around and pulled it out. It was a lightweight carbon fibre model with a battery at one end and a magnet at the other. There was a lead-lined plastic container sitting next to it, about the size of a shoe box.

Ann took both around to the front of the van, to where Vic was consulting a portable sat nav unit.

"Try over there," she said imperiously, pointing to a thorny clump of bushes beside a reed-clogged drainage ditch. Ann trudged over and turned the detector on. They were a few miles downstream of the main crash site and the grey mud had a clinging, fishy smell. It stuck to her motorcycle boots. A few dozen yards away, it merged into the thick grey water at the shoreline.

"Why are you doing this? I mean, it's been twenty years, why now?"

Vic scowled. "My reasons don't matter." She pushed the sat nav into a shoulder pocket. "All you need to know is that there's a buyer in the Ukraine who'll give me at least a million for this object."

Ann moved the detector around on the scrubby grass. She knew there had to be a good reason why the other woman hadn't come back before this; perhaps a long spell in hospital or even prison. Whatever the truth, Vic clearly had no intention of telling her.

Instead, Ann said: "Meeting you here, now. It's not a coincidence, is it?"

Vic shook her head. "I've been looking for a way to smuggle the object out of the country. When I heard your boy band announce this little trip of theirs, it seemed like too good an opportunity to miss."

She checked her dosimeter and frowned at what she saw. She waved her pistol impatiently. "Now, get on with it. We *really* don't have all day."

Twenty minutes later, Ann found what they were looking for: a short metal tube, about an inch thick at its widest point, tapering to half that at either end. Reluctantly, she scraped it from the mud with her bare hands and placed it in the lead-lined box from the back of the Land Rover. The thought of it being radioactive made her skin crawl.

"What is it?" she said.

Vic still had the sat nav in one hand, the gun in the other. Her combat jacket flapped in the offshore breeze. "There were four bodies at the crash site, and they all had one."

"Do you think it's a weapon?"

"That would be my guess. It's certainly what my buyer in the Ukraine believes."

Ann rubbed her hands together, trying to brush off the sticky mud. "What were they like? The bodies, I mean. What did they look like?"

Vic shivered. "Trust me. You really don't want to know." She shook her head, as if trying to dismiss the memory. Then she straightened up and motioned for Ann to get back into the Land Rover with the box.

"We came up the river last night by boat," she said as she

released the handbrake and eased the vehicle back onto the road. She was trying to change the subject. She looked tired. She was holding the pistol against the steering wheel as she drove, ready to use it if necessary. "Phil's my husband. He found this old heap and got it going." She tapped the Land Rover's steering wheel, as if willing it to keep running. "But tonight, we're flying out of here on your jet."

Ann looked down at the box on her knees. When handling the tube, she'd noticed three touch pads spaced around its waist. Thinking of them now, she wondered what they were for. They were obviously controls of some sort, but there had been no markings or other clues to their purpose.

"You'll never get out of here by road," she said. "The soldiers saw four of us go in, they'll be expecting the same four to come out."

Vic shook her head. "They saw three blokes and a girl go in wearing motorcycle helmets. As long as they see the same number coming out tonight, no one's going to be any the wiser."

When they reached Castle Park, Ann saw Dustin, Brad and Kent sitting miserably around the camping stove on the steps of the ruined church. The blond man — Phil – stood opposite them, his gun held loosely at his side. He looked around in obvious relief as the Land Rover's corroded brakes brought it to a squealing halt.

"You found it?" he said.

Vic jerked a thumb at Ann. "It's in the box."

Walking stiffly, she led Ann over to the stove, where the boys were huddled. Dustin looked up.

"Are you okay, Ann?"

Vic pointed her pistol at him. She made him get to his feet and then shoved him toward Ann. "The two of you get undressed," she said.

Dustin bunched his fists. "No fucking way."

Vic took a step forward and the thin sun caught her blonde

hair, turning it silver. "We need your leathers," she said. "Now, I'm going to count to three." She pointed the gun at his forehead. "One."

Holding the lead-lined box in one hand, Ann slipped the other inside and grasped the alien rod. It felt cold to the touch. Her skin itched at the thought the metal might still be radioactive, but she knew she had to act now. Vic wouldn't leave them alive. She wouldn't take the risk. She'd shoot them as soon as she had their clothes.

"Two," Vic said.

Ann pulled the rod free, letting the box fall to the floor. "Stop it," she said.

Vic looked at her. "What are you doing?"

Ann's thumb found one of the rod's three touch pads. "I'm going to turn this on."

Vic blinked. "Don't be an idiot."

Ann glanced at Brad and Kent, still huddled together on the flagstone steps. She was supposed to be protecting them. If she died now, with Dustin, she knew they wouldn't outlive her for long, and they were just kids. Vic might need them for the moment, to con her way through the army checkpoint, but as soon as she got the jet airborne, en route to the Ukraine, Ann knew they'd be disposed of.

She brushed her thumb over one of the touch pads. It was soft and warm.

"I mean it. Back off or I'm going to press this."

"You don't know what it does."

"Neither do you."

Vic still had her gun aimed at Dustin's head. She puffed her cheeks out in frustration.

"Three," she said.

Everything slowed.

With her thumb pressing the rod's touch pad, Ann saw Vic

fire her gun. The flash and smoke erupted from the barrel at a glacial pace. Subjective seconds later, Dustin jerked as the shot hit him. Ann tried to move but couldn't. Her muscles were encased in something thick and viscous. Straining forward, she saw him twist and fall, the bright spray of blood from his shoulder suspended behind him in the morning air like an angel's wing…

3.

Ann blinked her eyes.

Time had passed. She was lying on the grass, looking up at the clear sky. She sat up carefully and checked herself. She didn't seem to be injured. Beside her, Vic and Dustin lay where they'd fallen. By the church, Brad, Kent and the other man were also on their backs.

Vic stirred. She still had the gun in her hand. Ann walked over and kicked it free, the steel toe cap of her motorcycle boot sending it under the parked Land Rover.

Vic snatched her hand back. Her eyes were wide.

"What the fuck just happened?"

Ann ignored her. She moved over to Phil and took his weapon. Then she shook Kent awake and handed it to him.

"If either one moves, shoot them," she said.

When she got back to Dustin, she saw he was bleeding onto the grass. His shoulder and arm were slathered in it. Carefully, she unfolded her penknife and used it to cut away the sleeve of his leather jacket. His shirt was sodden. The bullet had clipped the outside edge of his shoulder, ripping a deep and ragged tear through the deltoid muscle. As an ex-soldier, Ann had seen worse. Many shoulder injuries were fatal. She knew he was lucky not to have been hit in the ball-and-socket shoulder joint. There were some huge blood vessels and delicate nerves in there, plus the joint itself, which no amount of surgery could repair if smashed.

She unwound her silk scarf, wadded it up and slipped it between the sleeve and the wound.

"Keep pressing this," she said, lifting his right hand onto the improvised dressing.

Dustin clenched his teeth. He looked up at her. "What happened?"

Ann straightened up. "I pressed the button."

She walked over to her bike. Somehow, the blast from the alien rod had disabled their equipment. Their bikes were useless. The radios were dead. Even Dustin's phone had been fried.

"What are we going to do?" Brad said.

Ann looked accusingly at Vic. "You could have killed him."

Vic was on her feet by now, backing off. She was halfway to one of the Land Rover's open doors, her hands clasped in front of her.

Ann took a step towards her. She had the open penknife in her hand.

"Dustin needs medical attention," she said. "We need to get him to a hospital."

Vic was still wide-eyed. "Fuck you, Szkatula."

She opened her hands. She had the rod.

"Put it down," Ann said.

Vic shook her head. "Sorry Skat, I want my million dollars."

Ann glanced at Kent. He was holding Phil's weapon but he looked scared, as if it might bite him. He was a dancer not a soldier, and he didn't know how to use a gun. He was pointing it at Phil as Vic ducked behind the Land Rover, stooping to retrieve the weapon that had been kicked under it. Seconds later she reappeared, head down, running for the shopping mall on the other side of the road, keeping the bulk of the vehicle between herself and any pursuit.

Ann swore under her breath. She unclenched her fists and looked across at Dustin. Her anger with Vic would have to wait.

She pulled some cord from her panniers and used it to tie

Phil's hands behind his back. Then she helped Dustin into a sitting position. She unzipped her jacket and used her penknife to cut strips from her t-shirt, which she then used to clean and bandage his shoulder. Although thankfully the major blood vessels seemed to be intact, it still took her a while to stop the bleeding. When she had, she folded her jacket into a makeshift pillow and did her best to make him comfortable.

"I can't believe that bitch shot me," Dustin said.

Ann brushed his cheek. "Leave her to me."

She walked over and retrieved the gun from her motorcycle pannier. It was a Browning semi-automatic with twelve rounds still in the clip, one in the breach. Holding it, she turned to Phil. The man had a thin, rat-like face with scared green eyes in a web of crow's feet.

"Is there a radio on your boat?" she said.

Phil looked at the gun in her hand and the expression on her face, and then he looked away.

"Yes," he said.

Ann turned to Brad and Kent. She didn't want to leave them but knew they wouldn't be safe as long as Vic remained at large. With a million dollars at stake, her former schoolmate wouldn't want her or the boys to alert the authorities.

"Take Dustin," she said. "Find the boat. I'm going after Vic."

She left the park in the direction Vic had taken, following the Land Rover's tracks back through the trees to the road. On the opposite side, concrete steps led up to the smashed doors of the shopping mall she'd seen Vic running towards.

Keeping the gun ready, Ann stepped through an empty window frame into the mall's unlit hallway. Her heavy motorcycle boots echoed on the tiled floor and there were dried and blown leaves everywhere.

"Vic?"

She inched her way along the hall. Beyond, it opened onto a balcony overlooking the central atrium. A stalled escalator led down to the next level. Pigeons flapped under the glass roof.

"Vic?"

"Don't come any closer."

Vic stood at the far end of the balcony, gun in one hand, alien rod in the other.

"Just tell me which button you pressed."

"No."

Vic scowled and shifted her weight. "Look, there are things you don't know, Szkatula. Things the government has been covering up."

Ann took a step towards her, ready to shoot.

"Such as?"

"The crash in the Severn," Vic said. "It wasn't an accident. After we recovered the bodies, they kept me on the project. And it turns out the ship was shot down."

"Shot down?"

"Yes. There was a second craft, a hostile. They were fighting."

Ann risked a peep over the rail. The atrium was three floors deep, criss-crossed with escalators, and they were on the uppermost level. She gripped her gun. "I need you to stand down, Vic. I have a wounded man and I need to get him to safety."

The other woman rolled her eyes. "Don't you see, Skat? Don't you get it? This was just a skirmish. There's a war going on out there. There are ships fighting and we don't even know what the sides are." She looked up at the dirty glass ceiling and the cold blue sky beyond. "From what I've seen of the photos from the space telescopes, the main action seems to be happening a long way from here. And thank God for that, because we're totally outclassed. We can't match their technology. If and when the fighting comes our way, we're fucked."

Ann squeezed the grip of her pistol. "I still need you to drop the gun," she said.

Vic shook her head. "I can't do that, Skat. I'm going to take the money I get from this and disappear somewhere remote, away from the big cities. Somewhere I'll stand a chance if push comes to shove." She waggled the rod in her other hand. "Now tell me how it works."

Ann took a deep breath. She thought of Dustin injured and hurting, and the other two boys with him, back in the park. "I'm not going to let you stop us from leaving," she said.

Vic curled her lip. "What are you going to do, Skat? Are you going to shoot me?"

Lifting the rod, she moved her thumb onto one of the touch pads ringing its waist.

"Is it this one?" she said.

She pressed the pad. There was a jumping, electrical flash and lightning crackled from the rod. It leapt along her arm. Ann caught the sharp tang of singed cloth. Vic yelped in pain and surprise. Then, engulfed in blue sparks, she staggered back against the balcony rail and began to fall.

"No!"

Ann dropped the gun and lunged, trying to catch her as she went over. But by the time she reached the rail, Vic had gone, spinning down into the darkened lower levels like a falling bonfire spark, disintegrating as she hit the dirty tiled floor; the cooked flesh blowing from her bones like ash...

4.

Some time later, when Ann returned to the park, she found the boys were still there. They were trying to rig up an improvised drag stretcher for Dustin. As she came across the grass, they turned to her.

Brad looked worried. He said: "Did you find her?"

Ann pulled the alien rod from her pocket. She'd walked down three escalators to retrieve it.

"She's gone," she said.

She walked over and dropped the rod back into the lead-lined box, closing the lid.

"Are you okay?" Dustin asked. His voice was thin with pain. With her back to him, she nodded.

"I will be."

She looked up at the clear sky overhead, and took a deep breath. The air was cold in her chest. It smelled clean and helped dispel the charred barbeque stench of Vic's burned body from her nostrils.

Had Vic been telling the truth? Could the crash – whose after-effects had shaped her adult life – really be the result of an alien conflict? Here in the park, were they actually standing in the radioactive fallout of an interstellar war?

She exhaled. Then she looked at Phil – Vic's husband – still sitting with his hands lashed behind his back. "Has he told you where to find the boat?" she said.

Kent still held Phil's gun. He said: "Yes, but we weren't sure what to do with him."

Ann shrugged. All her anger was gone, replaced with unease. How long did the Earth have before the next 'skirmish' came its way?

"Leave him here," she said. "The army can pick him up later."

She turned her back on the man and walked over to where Dustin sat. She crouched beside him.

"Can I take a look?" she said.

The young man pushed his fringe out of his eyes. "Sure."

He held still as she pulled out her penknife and started cutting away the tattered leather of his jacket.

As she pulled the severed sleeve free, he winced. "You know," he said, "there'll be reporters waiting for us. When we tell

156

them what you did... When you hand over that rod... You'll be a hero."

Ann stripped the last of the leather away, exposing her improvised dressings.

"I don't know whether to replace these now or wait for the chopper," she said.

Dustin forced a brave smile. "Leave them."

She made to stand but he put his good hand on her black-clad knee. His eyes were the same colour as the sky.

"You're going to be famous," he said. "How does that feel?"

Ann blinked.

"You're the rock star, you tell me."

Proper Little Soldier

Martin McGrath

Solomon and I had tried to push too far the previous night and so we spent the daylight hours lying in a ditch at the side of the road. This had seemed a comfortable enough spot to start with, a slightly deeper hollow hidden by the branches of a willow and an ancient, overgrown hedge. It was out of the wind and pleasantly shady in the early morning sunshine. But the rain started falling heavily from about midday and the ditch quickly filled, turning the hollow into a freezing pool.

Solomon refused to move on – he was certain there was a pod nearby but the rain and the whipping wind were making it difficult for him to pin them down. So he sat and strained to hear while I just got soaked, too afraid to make a sound and getting colder and more miserable as the day went on.

The rain stopped just before nightfall, the clouds cleared and a sparkling frost began to crisp the grass and spread rainbow crystals across the tops of small pools of rainwater. It was too early, the western sky still a stripe of burnt orange, but we had to move or we were going to freeze.

We took the chance that the cold would have sent any pod back wherever it had come from and clambered out of the ditch.

We stripped off our clothes there on the road, swapping into some of the relatively dry gear we'd hidden under our tarp. I gripped my sides trying to control the shivering that was shaking my ribs. Solomon began to do half-hearted little star-jumps

"Let's not do that again," I said.

"It wasn't my fault," Solomon spat the words at me.

"I didn't say-"

"You picked the stupid place," he said.

"Sol-"

"You know, Maggie, I don't know why I bother." He started to stamp off down the road. "You can be such a bitch."

"Oh for God's sake, Sol!"

And off I plodded after him.

He stayed in a foul mood all evening and we bickered like an old married couple. Not that we *were* a couple. Not like that. Sol was a handsome man, the colour of the darkest chocolate, with high cheekbones and eyes you could melt in. But before things got bad I'd always said that all the good men were either married or gay – and Sol was both. His partner, Patrick, had been in London when it was hit and so with any luck he had been dead for almost eighteen months. I knew sometimes Solomon had nightmares that Patrick was alive and was being hunted in the ruins of the city.

We were aiming to head north, into the cold, but we were staying off the main roads, keeping to country lanes and tracks where we could. Tonight we seemed to be heading more to the east, but the road was old and sunken between deep banks on either side, offering a feeling of comfortable protection. We walked on through the night, our conversation limited to a series of long and sullen silences interrupted by bouts of furious half-whispered bickering.

The arguments were good. They kept us warm and kept us moving when it would have been easier to stop and shiver and feel sorry for ourselves.

We were in the middle of a particularly good row about who was carrying the heaviest pack when Solomon stopped, turned and shoved me hard.

"You bast…"

The crossbow bolt ripped the air where I'd been standing and hit a tree in the hedgerow with a crack.

Solomon dropped to the ground and I followed.

"Don't shoot!" We yelped together.

Another bolt pinged the tarmac between us and tumbled off into the dark.

"Go back!" The voice was a high-pitched squeak. A child.

Solomon and I shared a look.

I stood up, raising my hands.

"Maggie!" Sol made a grab for my ankle but I shook him off. "You silly cow!"

"Go back!" I heard the kid grunt as he snapped the crossbow string back into position.

"We just want to pass through."

I saw his silhouette against the moonlight, peering out from behind a tree where the road turned sharply ahead. He was small – I'd have guessed nine or ten but the past two years had been tough and food could be hard to come by. He might be older and half-starved. The crossbow was big, but he handled it confidently enough.

I tried an experimental smile then realised that in the shadows of the deep-cut roadway it was probably too dark for him to see my face.

"We just want to follow this road and go on our way."

"This road doesn't go anywhere," the boy shouted out. "This is the end of the road."

I looked back at Solomon. He had the map. He shrugged.

"Then we're lost and could use some directions," I said.

"Go back!" He gestured with the crossbow.

"Oh come on, kid," Solomon stood up and took a step

forward. "Just let us past."

A third crossbow bolt flashed by.

"Sod this!" Suddenly Solomon was running, his long legs eating up the distance to the boy.

The boy was struggling with the crossbow, heaving at the string.

Solomon snatched the crossbow and smashed it against the tree.

The boy cowered back. Solomon raised his fist.

"Sol!" I shouted.

"He tried to kill me!"

"He's a scared child!"

"He tried to kill you!"

"Let him be."

I walked up to the pair of them. The boy was crouched at the foot of the tree. Solomon was glaring at him with an impressive impersonation of fury.

I put a hand on Solomon's shoulder, and reached the other one out to the boy.

"We're not going to hurt you."

"I am," Solomon growled.

The boy cowered back further.

I shoved Sol with my shoulder and he turned away, laughing.

"We're not going to hurt you." I knelt down and reached across. "We just want to pass through."

And then he started crying.

Sol's map reading was hopeless; we were miles from where he thought we were. The road we'd been following took one more sharp left turn and opened into a farmyard. The house had been hit hard. You could see where at least two pods had done their best to clean the place out.

The boy, Alf, had abandoned the house when the first attack had taken his parents but had made himself a surprisingly comfortable shelter high up in one of the barns.

It was well camouflaged, we'd never have found it without his help and even then we had a hard time scrambling up after his tiny frame.

The space was big enough for all three of us to lie down, but though Solomon and I were exhausted, the boy just wanted to chat.

He'd been alone for a long time.

After an hour or so of constant interrogation I tried to shush him with the threat that a pod might hear us talking.

"There's no monsters around today," he said, cocking his head, listening. "I can hear them when they come."

I looked at Solomon, who just raised an eyebrow and shrugged. Sol's ears were sharp – his ability to hear the creatures before they heard us had kept us alive for the last six months. Perhaps the boy had the same gift.

"Anyway," the boy said, "we can see from here if they're coming this way."

He showed me where he'd cut out little viewing slits in the roof of the barn then disguised them. From up here he had a panoramic view of the surrounding fields.

The boy was right: nothing was moving out there except the low grey clouds that swept westward.

The boy had plenty of food, too – apples and vegetables from the garden behind the house, and jars of homemade raspberry jam. Solomon sat for over an hour, solemnly dipping his finger into the sugary mush slurping it up, He rolled his eyes and moaned softly with each new mouthful.

"I used to take this for granted," he said once the jar was finally empty.

The day went by slowly. Alf, exhausted at last, fell asleep with his head in my lap.

I stared down at him, feeling totally helpless.

I looked up. Solomon was smiling ruefully, knowing what

was to come but refusing to meet my gaze.

"We can't leave him here," I said.

"He might be safer here," Sol said.

"Nowhere is safe."

Sol nodded.

"I can't leave him on his own."

"What if he doesn't want to come?"

"He will."

Eventually I slept.

And that night the three of us set off. Heading north, to where it was colder and where, rumours said, there were still safe places.

We rarely managed more than four or five miles a night – we were being cautious, finding places to bed down for the day early on, setting out only when we were sure the creatures had retreated. The going was slow, but the first chill of autumn turned the trees gold and lifted our spirits. Dusk was coming earlier, darkness lasted longer and it was getting colder. We felt that the planet was on our side.

After a week we came to a small village and found a shop that was almost intact. We helped ourselves to the stock on the shelves and made a little camp.

We hadn't seen or heard from the creatures for days. We had full bellies and we were feeling good. We were happy.

Solomon shook me awake. The sun was shining straight down through the gaps created by missing slates in the roof, so I guessed it was around noon. I turned to Alf, reaching a hand across to cover his mouth in case he made a sound but he was already awake, staring at me.

He raised a single finger to his lips.

I smiled.

Then we sat and waited. I could hear the scuttling of rats and the steady drip of water into a puddle from a broken pipe. It was hot and I was thirsty and that water, no matter how stale, was very tempting.

The sun moved slowly across the sky, pools of light from the holes in the roof shifting across the floor. We were in an attic that was perched precariously on top of the slumped ruin of a suburban house.

How long passed before I heard the creature's distant screech? It felt like hours but it might have been fifteen minutes, though I never doubted they were coming. Sol's ability to pick out the high-pitched sounds the monsters made had saved our lives often enough. I kept silent and very still.

Alf had heard them too. I felt him shivering next to me, but he jammed his tongue between his teeth to stop them chattering. The day was too warm for him to be cold. I reached my hand across and placed it on his chest. He gripped it tightly.

I hoped they might slip off to the side of our little village. The resistance sometimes baited places like this; a vulnerable little hamlet stuffed full of thermobarics could take out everything for half a mile and was enough to make even the creatures cautious. But these things seemed confident today. We heard their thump and squeal and shriek as they came closer and closer.

The creatures used sound. They used it to communicate, just as we did, though I never met anyone who claimed to understand what they said to each other, constantly chittering and squealing and mewling.

They also used sound to see – echo-location, like bats – even though they had things that looked like eyes. I'd heard people say that you could stand still in front of one and they'd slither right past so long as you didn't make a sound. I never felt the urge to find out whether or not that was true.

And they used sound as a weapon.

The first one was almost right below us when it boomed.

We'd known it was coming. The only time a pod was silent was just before a boom and just after. We'd known it was coming, but still it was like being smashed in the chest by a hammer. We'd known it was coming, but it was still hard not to grunt or moan or gasp.

And that would have been death.

All around us we heard the things pounce. A spear-like tentacle crashed through the floor of our hiding place, impaling a surprised rat through the throat before flashing away again. Across the road we heard a dog yelp and something that, for a horrible instant, sounded like a baby's squeal but was probably only a cat, or maybe a fox. The things snuffled, unhappy with their pickings.

The second boom came quickly, faster than I'd expected. Too soon. We weren't ready.

"Unff!"

Alf? I looked down, gripped with a sudden terror that mixed an almost maternal desire to protect the boy with the shocking awareness he had his arms wrapped tightly around me, making us both a target.

The boy gazed up and I looked into his wide, wise eyes. He shook his head.

Not the boy. I felt relief, then a sudden, cold shower of sickening certainty.

Sol.

I turned my head.

The look of surprise on his face slipped into one of disappointment.

"Ah fu-"

Three spears splintered the slates and wood of the roof. One slammed through Sol's skull, two pinned him in the chest. They whipped back. Sol disappeared, leaving just an after-image of his shredded body and a mist of blood.

The boy and I watched but made not a single sound.

For hours the pod circled our building, warbling their delight at their catch and booming, hoping for more, but the boy and I were still.

As afternoon turned to evening they seemed to move away, though every now and then one would suddenly unleash a boom nearby. The desire to move became an urgent pain and then a constant agony, but we sat motionless and silent. The sun went down and the village became still, but we did not move. Only when it was fully night and the moon was high and clear and frost stung the air did I allow myself to shift.

Alf smiled at me, then gasped, then sobbed and collapsed forward.

His trousers were slashed open across his hip and his leg was soaked with blood. One of the spears that killed Sol must have glanced off him.

"I didn't cry!" He said.

I gave him a kiss on the cheek.

My first instinct was to flee that village as fast as I could, but Alf couldn't walk and we had plenty of supplies.

So that night I ferried our stuff across to another attic, because I couldn't stand to look at the dark stain of Sol's blood on the floor, and then carried the boy across.

In the new attic I washed out the boy's wound and stitched it up as best I could. Through it all the boy bit his lip but never whimpered or cried. No sound left his lips except, when it was over, he whispered "Thank you" before falling asleep.

The creatures didn't return, but Alf developed a fever and the wound on his hip turned red and swollen.

That night I did something I hadn't risked in nearly two years – I lit a fire, just a small one in a metal bin downstairs. The warmth and flickering light were shocking. I boiled some water over the fire and used it to wash out Alf's wound. I'd found some antiseptic cream in the little shop and slathered that thickly onto Alf's hip, then wrapped it in gauze and tape.

Alf's temperature rose. He slept night and day for a week. I tried to feed him and give him sugary drinks but most of it seemed to end up on the floor.

A lot of the time there was nothing I could do but wait and watch.

He never moved. He never cried out. He never made any sound, even when the fever was at its worst. He was silent and still.

And, as his fever broke and he started to come round, I began to realise something.

These creatures, whatever they were, wherever they'd come from, they had the power to wipe us all out. They'd destroyed our cities and our armies and shattered our civilisation and left us scrabbling in the dark.

They could wipe us out.

But they hadn't.

Those of us they left alive survived because they thought we could do them no harm and because they enjoyed having us to hunt.

They believed we were beaten.

But they didn't realise what they were creating.

After ten days Alf opened his eyes and smiled weakly up at me.

"Was I quiet?"

I nodded, and wiped a strand of hair out of his eyes.

"You were a proper little soldier," I said.

They were making us stronger.

They were making the children who would one day defeat them. All over the world children were learning to use silence as a defence and silence as a weapon. One day, it might not be soon, but one day we would become the hunters again and the booming beasts would pay for their mistake.

War Without End

Una McCormack

"As flowers turn toward the sun, by dint of a secret heliotropism the past strives to turn toward that sun which is rising in the sky of history."

Walter Benjamin

For Ika

Liberation +40 years

Roby's sun was behind them. The planet itself gleamed dimly against the black, pocked and marked like a target. The jump here had been swift but pitiless, and Shard had been violently sick. His constitution – his strength – was not what it once had been. Now he sat limp and passive in his seat, his cheek resting clammily against the cold porthole, directing all his will towards heading off the tremors that coursed through his body and threatened him with further indignities.

Beside him, Lowe rattled on about arrival times, departure

times, transportation to the city, agendas... At some point, Shard thought, this trip would end. At some point, by extension, Lowe would stop talking. Shard pointed his fingertips at the world below, aimed, *fired*... The shuttle banked and he missed. Roby was gone from view – but it was still there, he knew. It had always been there. Shard snapped, "I'm not so far gone I can't remember what you've told me three times already."

Lowe stopped, perplexed rather than cowed. He was a careful young man, well-informed and attentive to detail, untroubled by any broader passions, making up in precision what he lacked in perception. Usually Shard preferred it that way; not now.

"On arrival at the port," Shard said, "a car will be waiting to take us to the capital, where accommodation has been arranged for the duration of our stay in the fourth tower. Tomorrow morning – eighth hour, free standard – another car will take us to the Archive. After which –" this said bitterly, "– I'm on my own."

"Exactly so." Lowe, content, returned to his briefings, with no apparent appreciation of Shard's irony. Shard's hatred peaked – then passed, like his nausea, like all things.

It all unfolded much as Lowe had sketched, with the single notable exception of the protest that was waiting for them between the port and the first of the promised cars. Under siege in the arrival hall, Shard looked out to see upwards of fifty people, few of them old enough to remember the war, carrying banners executed with an otherwise uplifting degree of competence and literacy, chanting their complaint with no small grasp of rhythmic structure. Their unifying theme was their hatred of Shard. The local police watched affably from the side and showed no particular interest in moving them. Grimly, Shard said, "Now this wasn't in the itinerary."

Lowe did not reply. He was deep in the grip of that paralysis that overwhelms functionaries when their best-laid plans prove susceptible to simple human irrationality. He was not, Shard saw, going to be any use.

After thorough consideration of the terrain, the nature of the enemy, and the men and materiel at his disposal, Shard was in a position to offer a professional appraisal of their situation. "I suggest, Mr Lowe, that we make a run for it." Seeing Lowe baulk, he hastened to explain. "All we have to do is get through the crowd and across the road."

"That's all?"

"The passenger doors are on this side of the car, see? You make for the front and I'll head for the back. Keep your head down and your forearms up – like this, see? Don't stop. It's me they're after, anyway."

Lowe was not measurably comforted. Shard took hold of his elbow and marshalled him through the doors, into the hard light and cold air of Roby, amongst the signs and voices calling him *evil* and *butcher* and *murderer*.

The doors closed behind them. Shard surveyed the mob and the mob stared back. Then it moved in, with a single purpose.

Battle was joined. Shard lost hold of Lowe within seconds. In the crush and the chaos, he stumbled, falling forwards with a gasp, an old man on his knees. Somebody laughed. Just before he hit the ground, the police intervened, swooping in as if to relieve a falling city. Two of them gathered up the visitors, while the rest formed a barrier to let them pass, calling to the crowd that it was over, that they had had their fun.

They deposited them on the far side of the road and would not accept thanks. In the sanctuary of the car, Lowe inspected the marks on his arm which would shortly become bruises. "I had not anticipated that."

Shard was too busy trying to slow his heart rate to be able to point out that such was Lowe's entire purpose. By the time he had his breath back, the moment had passed, but he was able to communicate enough silent fury to penetrate even Lowe's thick skin. They journeyed to the capital in silence. Shard brooded on his reception. It was the youth of his assailants that troubled him most; how long this hatred had lasted, how deep it must still run, down even to this generation, which had not been born when he was last here and could only know him through the medium of history lessons, propaganda. Was there to be no end?

Full darkness had fallen by the time the car landed at their accommodation. Shard's room was functional but clean. By this point all he cared about was the bed. "Marshal," Lowe said, "we should go through the agenda for tomorrow."

It was too much. Shard – sick in heart and body, wearied almost beyond relief from the journey, from the events of the day, from all that had brought him back here so late in life – snapped. He strode over to the door and threw it open. "Get out! You bloody halfwit! Get the hell out!"

Lowe, bewildered, blinked twice and then withdrew. With peace of a kind restored, Shard could devote himself again to throwing up, in privacy if not in comfort. This done, he drew the curtains, blocking out any sight of the city beyond. Then he lay down on his bed and returned to that solitary contemplation of our mortality which is the nightly pursuit of many, not simply sick old men, and in which we should all on occasion be indulged – even those of Shard's stripe.

Liberation +39.5 years

When the message arrived from the Archive, Shard was raking over the leaves in his garden. Autumn had come early to this part of Mount Pleasant. Soon it would be too wet to work outside on a daily basis, but Shard had a bonfire planned first, an innocent and agreeable pleasure. Shard could be found in his garden most days. He liked the nature of the tasks, which required total attention and absorption, and to which he was entirely committed. His dedication over the years had reaped rewards: his lawn was smooth and uniform, and his flowerbeds triumphant in competition. Moreover, as he liked to say, the exercise kept him fit.

There was a low wall at the far end of the lawn, separating the more cultivated part of the garden from a patch of ground that Shard had left deliberately untouched, for the sake of spring's unruly spread of bright wild flowers. On the wall stood a portable comm: Shard usually brought one out with him to listen to while he worked. All morning, it had been peacefully burbling out news and other nonsense.

A soft chord interrupted the flow, signalling the arrival of a message. With a short puff, Shard stopped work. A few joints cracked. He removed his gardening gloves and wiped his forehead. "Play," he said, and walked over to the comm.

A woman was speaking; an old woman, talking as if from a pre-prepared script. "*Marshal,*" she said. "*My name is Ines de Souza. I am the co-ordinator of the Archive of Public Memory on Roby. Next year will be the fortieth anniversary of the Liberation. Gaps remain in our records – as they always will and always must – and yet I remain curious that you have never given an interview about your time on Roby.*" He heard a rustling of papers, like the crackle of flames, and then the woman sighed. "*We grow old, Marshal. Time passes, not much remains – for us, at least. Whatever contribution the former commander of the Commonwealth's forces would be willing to make, the Archive will most gladly receive it.*"

The message ended. Shard stared down at the comm. His heart had begun to pound and his face was burning. The message began to repeat, as he had it set to do. "*My name is Ines de Souza. I am the co-ordinator of the Archive of Public Memory on Roby –*"

With a roar of untrammelled rage, Shard kicked the comm off the wall. It soared high into the air, free as a bird in flight, coming to land deep, deep into the wilderness he had made. That finished him for the day. He retreated indoors. Mid-afternoon it rained, heavily, and all his plans came to nothing.

Once upon a time, Shard had believed in loyalty. By this point in his life he still believed in discretion, and for this reason he did not reply to de Souza's message. What purpose would it serve? What could he say about Roby that had not been said already, by both sides? Why pick over the corpse? But during the winter he had no work and few distractions. Instead, he looked out at his modest garden and brooded about his place in history. In the spring, his sense of grievance flowered like a cactus. He contacted Forshaw, and was granted an audience.

These days Forshaw lived on Xanadu, in the humid confines of the biodomes. It was not cheap to retire here. Gabriel Forshaw, a veteran of nothing more brutal than the press conference and the lecture circuit, could afford it. Mark Shard, who had kept a loyal silence, could not. Inside the dome, it was lush, protected, secluded. Outside, interminable dust storms screamed across empty land indifferent to human suffering. Yet that is all there is.

Abundance – of wealth, of talent, of connections – was what Shard had chiefly associated with Forshaw. Now all spent. Forshaw was a sick man; shrunken. His skin was grey and papery, and his eyes lacked hope and lustre. Not even gerontotherapy could combat the cancer; cosmetic surgery could no longer conceal the decline. Forshaw was dying – and the sheer extravagance of the environment in which he would spend his last days only served to reinforce how cruelly.

Once, in a busier and more active life than either of them now led, Shard and Forshaw had conferred on an almost daily basis. The whole business of putting down a revolt required the military at least to go through the motions of informing the political arm what it was up to, although Forshaw had been particularly adept at not hearing anything that might incriminate. His fitness for the political life had been boundless: he had been snake clever, capable of aping authenticity, and blessed with the moral compass of a tiger. His genius, his *trick*, had been to make this animal behaviour appear urbane – likeable, even. He was one of a very few from that time to have retired undefeated and all-but-untarnished. Yet this was how it was going to end.

Shard had not liked Forshaw, but he had suffered him as one of the inevitable crosses borne when one chose – as one must – to participate in public life. He had never forgiven him for the end of the war on Roby. Not even the sight of him now could move Shard beyond this. Perhaps there was a moment of tempered compassion – the fearful kind of fellow-feeling that arises from imagining oneself in such a state – but no more than a moment, and then it was gone.

Forshaw's house was filled with literary awards and pictures of him with the other luminaries of his generation. He had Shard brought out onto the terrace, where they sat under the cover of huge, regular green leaves. Life throbbed around them in studied, well-marshalled profligacy. From deep within the foliage, songbirds of the kind designed and kept for pleasure trilled harmoniously. No mention was made of Forshaw's condition, the open secret, the ruin in the midst of plenty. Shard expressed pleasure at seeing him after so long. Forshaw thanked him with equivalent sincerity. Silence fell, and Shard sat in appalled contemplation of Forshaw's ravaged face.

Forshaw drew back his lips into a smile until his teeth showed, skull-fashion. "I assume there's some purpose to your being here? I don't recall visiting the sick being part of your religion. In fact, I don't recall you being religious at all. But it has been some time."

Recalled to himself, Shard drew out the file containing the message he had received from Roby, and handed it over. Forshaw read out the header. "*From the Archive of Public Memory, Salvation, Roby; to Marshal Mark Shard, former Commander, Commonwealth Pacification Force on Roby*."

He laughed, tossing the file and its petition unheard onto the table. "The Archive of Public Memory. They certainly know how to conjure with words out there. One might almost admire them for it – as one had to admire their tenacity."

Shard did not comment. His own encounters with the people of Roby, which had been first-hand whereas Forshaw's had not, did not make him want to express admiration.

"So what is it? A summons?"

Shard retrieved the file from the table. He put it away with care, as an historian might with a piece of evidence. "Nothing so crude. They want to interview me."

"You're not thinking of agreeing?"

"Why not?"

"Mark, it's done. It's over. Nobody cares any longer."

"They do on Roby, patently –"

"Nobody *here* cares. Why should they?"

"Perhaps..." Shard struggled to articulate new ideas that were as yet only half-formed in his mind. "Perhaps the record should be set straight."

Forshaw had long since stopped listening. "An old war," he said, "finished years ago. A lost war. The failed policies of old men, soon to be gone and then hastily, all too hastily, forgotten." His words were like his books, Shard thought; florid and without substance. Groundless. "Besides, it all rather runs the risk of becoming something of an embarrassment. One example. What would you say, exactly, if this woman chose to ask you about the end?"

"We didn't do anything wrong," Shard insisted, his first hint of mutiny.

A butterfly settled on Forshaw's wrist. It was about the size of a child's hand, and coloured deep blue. There were white spots on the larger, upper portions of its wings, and a hint of imperial purple to the lower. Forshaw sat in contemplation it for a while before gently brushing it away with a translucent finger. "Well," he said. "I know I didn't."

Shard lifted his eyes, looking past the leaves at the barrier that constituted the limit of the sky. He thought he saw a faint dark line, marking the place where two pieces of the dome met. He reflected upon these joints. He imagined them widening, the dome collapsing; briefly he pictured the unspeakable, unliveable aftermath... "You son of a bitch," he said, in wonder. "You son of a bitch."

Forshaw closed his eyes. "At least have the decency to wait till I'm dead."

Decency. The word was an offence coming from the mouth of this man. What, in the end, did he know about Roby? His policies had only ever been implemented at a distance; he had been protected from their consequences just as this dome protected him from the hell outside. But what would history record? A history that Forshaw had spent decades securing – while Shard had kept his loyal silence. Trembling, Shard looked upon Forshaw's ruined face and he was glad.

"But since you're clearly going to do it," Forshaw said, "a word of advice. These people are not the rude peasants of our propaganda. They never were. They were sophisticated and they were ruthless." He cracked open a yellow lizard eye. "Don't lose sight of your real enemy. And try not to lose your bloody temper."

Shard left. Violently he desired now to be instrumental in the failure of this man's bid for immortality, to wrest their shared history back from him and strip it of the veneer with which Forshaw had tried to finish it. Besides, loyalty had not rewarded as richly as leadership. Shard could do with the money.

Liberation +40 years

Shard's first night back on Roby was not restful. Exhaustion, jump-lag, a room too sparsely furnished – all of this contributed to his discomfort, not to mention the twinge of some burgeoning dread which he glossed as performance nerves. Eventually, faint light began to creep through the gap between the curtains. Shard gave up torturing himself with the hope of sleep. He got up and went out onto the balcony to contemplate the world outside, the world he had lost.

It was a cold spring morning, the light as pure and hard as in memory, the hills brown and stony. Deliberately, Shard's eye followed their line westwards; a squat range deeply riven by vanished glaciers, caught in perpetual convulsion, as if ancient gods or monsters had fought some fundamental struggle here, ages before humanity got its chance. The city's towers stood in a ring on four low hills, the circle broken by the ruin of the fifth. That was at the centre of his view. No doubt the room had been selected for this purpose.

The sky above was bright blue, the promise of a warm day. As Shard watched, the mist lying in the hollow formed by the hills began to lift. Piecemeal, their lower reaches came into sight, greened by moss and ivy, shimmering with tiny pale flowers adapted to life in the cracks. Last of all, the undercity was revealed, ramshackle and disorderly, squatting like a beggar in the space between the hills – and here, at last, were the anticipated changes: the barricades completely gone, disappeared without trace; hilltop and undercity now linked by black tramlines, zigzagging surely, inevitably, upwards.

Forty years ago, all of this – air and land, hill and hollow – had belonged to Shard. Not in any legal sense – the various consortia on behalf of whom the Commonwealth had fought this war would surely have contested that – but it had been his in all the ways that matter beyond possession. He had been the one to decide who of his men and his enemies were to live and who were to die. It was that responsibility which had given him title to this land, in a moral sense at least. Shard had referred to this place as West-20. Now it was named Salvation.

From deep within the undercity, which Shard had once held but had never mastered, a clock chimed the tenth before the hour. Others began to follow suit, and then Shard's comm buzzed too. It was Lowe, asking the Marshal to join him on the tower-top, where he was waiting for the car to take them to the Archive.

They were still waiting an hour later. Lowe was frantic. Shard sat to one side and practiced patience. If the delay was a result of mismanagement, that boded well for the day ahead. If it was intended as an insult – what else should he expect from these people?

When at last the car landed, the driver offered no explanation. Installed in the back, Lowe fussed over the day's agenda. Shard stared down at the city as it passed below, picking over the scar left by the obliterated tower. Why had it been left in that state? Forty years had passed. Why not remove it, rebuild it, overwrite it? Was it meant as a memorial? Or a symbol, perhaps; proof that nothing was lasting.

The second tower hove into view. The car pitched sharply, decelerated, and bumped out a landing. The driver did not get out, but stuck his arm out of the window, reaching to open the back door that way. Shard got out onto the landing bay and went forward to speak to him. An apology was clearly not going to be forthcoming but there would at least be an explanation. Before he could demand it, he heard voices shouting his name. He looked across the roof to see yet another pack heading his way, banners aloft. Forgetting the driver, he turned on Lowe. "What in the name of hell are they doing here?"

"I've absolutely no idea –"

"How do we get inside? Come on, man, quickly!"

Lowe looked around helplessly. Shard, meanwhile, had sighted a metal door set in a concrete block about twenty paces away. If memory served correctly, this should provide access to the stairwell. He took Lowe's arm and shoved him that way. "Over there. Get a move on!"

They were halfway there when the door opened. A slight figure leaned out and began gesturing to them frantically to come that way. Lowe reached the door first; Shard, panting, just after. He pushed Lowe inside and slammed the door shut behind him. Moments later, there was a hammering on it, but these doors had been built to survive bombardment and siege. A handful of grubby activists should prove no problem. Satisfied, for the moment, that he was safe, Shard turned his wrath upon the new arrival. "How did they get up here? Who let them in?"

Their saviour – a slight, androgynous youth – stared in frank alarm past Shard's shoulder at the barricaded door. "Christ, that was close!"

Shard exploded. He stuck his finger in the youth's face. "If you're trying to shake me, it won't bloody work! Nothing you people threw at me ever shook me! Do you hear me? Nothing!"

There was a short charged silence. Lowe nervously cleared his throat. As it began to occur to Shard that he might not be entirely in control, he heard slow footsteps coming up the metal steps. From out of the shadowy stairwell, another figure emerged. It was an old woman. Shard looked her up and down, was about to dismiss her – but curiosity got the better of him. "Who the hell are you?"

"Marshal," she said. "I'm Ines de Souza. You can stop shouting now."

In the lift down into the main body of the tower, de Souza gave Shard his explanation. "Most of the building is public access, but we cordoned off the secondary landing bay in advance of your arrival. For some reason, your driver elected to land at the main bay."

Lowe said, "It really is very irregular –"

De Souza looked him up and down and then looked away. Shard winced. "I can make a formal apology," she said, "if that would help."

"Don't trouble yourself, ma'am," Shard said, in a quieter voice than he had used in several days. "No harm was done."

De Souza grunted in – dear God, was that approval? Shard eyed her. She was small and nut-brown, and dressed exceedingly badly in a long patterned skirt in green and gold, a pale blue cotton shirt, and scuffed sandals. Slung across her right shoulder was a dilapidated hessian bag which bore a bright orange flower stitched on with pink thread. The bag was stuffed to bursting with papers, many of them yellowed. Shard had expected an elegant academic, perhaps, or a trim administrator. Not confusion, disarray, poverty. Most startling to his eyes was how old she looked. One did not see that within the Commonwealth anymore; one had to be poor, or as sick as Forshaw. Shard took heart. Whatever had happened, Roby remained the poor relation.

The lift doors opened onto a dim unfurnished corridor. If this was freedom, Shard thought, as they walked along it, he would rather be rich. His good spirits did not last: at the end of the corridor, de Souza led him into a room which for all the world looked exactly like a torture chamber.

Liberation +39.75 years

After Xanadu, Shard's fury flourished. He was a new man, fired with a new purpose – the unmaking of Gabriel Forshaw. He lost no time in responding to the Archive and agreeing to an interview. His greatest fear now was that Forshaw might cheat him, dying before Shard had the chance to give his version of events. He even offered to go to Roby, rather than risk the inevitable delay that would be involved in getting permission for his interviewers to enter Commonwealth space. Friendly they all might be these days, or nearly, but one should never forget the provenance even of one's friends.

There was a gap of several weeks before the Archive replied; a period during which Shard monitored the obituary feeds compulsively. Forshaw – thank God – was not dead by the time de Souza replied agreeing to his visit. The morning after, Lowe arrived unasked on Shard's doorstep, sent from the Bureau to assist him. "These are delicate times," Lowe explained, perched on Shard's sofa like a dapper heron, handling his cup and saucer with fastidious care. "Relations between us are finely balanced, and it is to the benefit of all that nothing happens to disturb that balance."

Presumably he was a spy, but that at least meant he might come in useful. Shard took out the file containing all his correspondence with de Souza and threw it over. The cup slipped in Lowe's grasp, splashing tea into his saucer, but he steadied it. "If you want to help," Shard said, "find out what this one got up to during the war."

A tall order. Secrecy lingered over the files from that period like flies above a shallow grave. Nonetheless, Lowe returned in a matter of days. "She worked with children. Specifically orphans, resettling them after the war. After that she was a history teacher in Salvation and for the past twelve years she has been co-ordinating their Archive."

"What about before the war?"

"There's nothing from then."

"Nothing at all?"

"Date and place of birth, who owned her bond... There's no reason why there should be anything else. Not everyone on Roby was directly involved in hostilities."

Shard grunted. He had never made that mistake. Every last one of them had been either a threat or a threat in the making.

"But we do have one concern," Lowe said.

"Get on with it."

"Her name appears on several of the extradition requests we received in the twenties." There had been a rash of them back then. They asked for Shard on numerous occasions; once or twice, they had even asked for Forshaw. The people of Roby certainly had no trouble determining their enemies. "Our strong advice is that you reconsider travelling to Roby –"

"No."

"She's not on any outstanding blacklist. She can travel here."

"That would take too long."

"We have no jurisdiction in Roby –"

"Do you know, I remember there was a war fought about that –"

"And you have no diplomatic immunity –"

"For God's sake, man, enough! What you're saying is that if anything goes wrong out there I'm on my own?"

Lowe pressed a fingertip delicately against the side of his nose. "You have all the protections that any citizen of the Commonwealth can expect, of course. But if there *is* trouble out there, we might not be in a position to help you."

"You mean you don't want to kick up the diplomatic stink it would need?"

Shard watched grimly as Lowe struggled to come up with a form of language acceptable to them both. "Times have changed, Marshal. We are no longer enemies and there is the strong possibility that we might become friends. Many of their current organizers were born after the war –"

This was enough. "Do you really believe they think of us as friends in the making?" Shard said. "They hated us. They will hate us till the end. Every last one of them. If you'd been there, if you'd seen how it was there, you'd understand that. Have you all gone mad at the Bureau? Is there anyone looking out for us these days? Or have you bought into your own propaganda? We fought a *war* with these people, man! We killed them in their hundreds of thousands, and they would have done the same to us if they'd had the capability. This new generation has been taught by the last. If you and your masters believe this is over, you're living in a fantasy land."

Lowe, uncomfortable, had looked away. He was tweaking his cuffs, unnecessarily. "You're free to do whatever you choose, of course. But the Commonwealth is now looking to advance its friendship with the people of Roby." He stretched his hands out in appeal to some final authority. "That's *policy*."

For one shattering second, Shard surveyed his life, and he saw how all that had once mattered now counted for nothing. Worse than nothing – it was, as Forshaw had said, an embarrassment. His heart burned within him. Even shame would be better, he thought; that at least would accord some significance to all that had happened, all that had been suffered. But they had not even earned that recognition. They were an embarrassment. "Damn you all," he whispered, thinly, like a voice in the wilderness. "But you won't stop me going! I *will* have my say, before the end."

Lowe barely covered a sigh. "I'm sure you will, Marshal. But I wonder – who do you imagine is listening?"

Liberation +40 years

It was not the bareness of the room that had struck Shard, although it *was* bare – a table, two chairs, grey walls and a carpetless floor, and a single small window through which light passed feebly to reveal the dust swirling slowly. It was how the room was equipped.

The chairs were set in opposition, the table between them, and behind each place stood a diptych of screens, positioned at a slight angle to each other. Four screens in total, two on each side. Each of them was connected by a veritable web of cables to two small black boxes, one at either end of the table. Attached to each of these was a set of sensors, one for the arm, two for each temple. Shard recognized every last piece of this equipment; what surprised him was that it was duplicated. That was not the usual arrangement.

"Forgive the accommodation," de Souza said, dumping her bag on the table. It slumped under the weight of its contents. She followed his look around the room. "I imagine you recognize all this. Your people left it all behind."

Unhurriedly, her bag fell over. Papers spilled out onto the

floor. "Blast," she said, without rancour. She leaned one hand on the table and started to lower herself down, but her aide got there first, kneeling to gather her scattered works and then holding them out to her like an offering. "Bless you, Jay," she said, and sat down, with a sigh. "Have a seat, Marshal."

"Can I get you anything, Ines?" the youth said. "Tea?"

"Tea, yes, yes – thank you. *Please*, Marshal," this with a touch of asperity, "have a seat. It's exhausting watching you standing to attention. You'll be giving me your name and number next."

Shard made a sweeping gesture that took in the screens, the sensors, the blood flow monitors. "Is that my safest option?"

"All this? Nothing to lose sleep over." Deftly, as if this was something she had done countless times before, de Souza began to hook herself up. She rolled up her sleeve, fixing a sensor against her upper arm with an armband. "You must have seen a psycho-imager in use before, surely? While you were here, if not since?"

Shard stiffened. He gripped the back of his chair and his knuckles turned white. "Mme de Souza, it is a matter of record that I did not conduct any interrogations on Roby. If you're looking to trap me that way you'll have to try considerably harder."

De Souza, who had been about to attach the other two sensors to her temples, halted with her hand halfway up to her face. "Trap you? You have a very strange idea of what I'm doing here, Marshal. I'm hardly fit for mortal combat, am I?" She finished attaching the sensors. "If I were you I'd sit down in your chair and stop trying to second-guess me. I'm only going to ask you a few questions."

Hooked up, de Souza turned her attention to the black box on her right, playing with dials and switches. "Useless bloody… Ah! There we are!" A green light flickered and, behind her, on the left-hand screen, an image appeared, grainy at first, and then coming slowly into focus. It was a sunflower – joyful and riotously bright against the uniform grey wall. Shard glanced over his shoulder: yes, there it was, on the left-hand screen behind him.

"On my mind," she said. "No luck with them. Top-heavy."

"Try propping them up against a wall," Shard said faintly. He took his seat, uncomfortably conscious of the two screens behind him and what they might reveal. "But one that gets light. And not too much water. It loosens the soil so it can't bear the weight."

"I'll bear that in mind next time. Thank you."

Shard examined the second set of sensors on the table in front of him. He picked up the armband. "Marshal," Lowe said urgently, "I strongly advise against this –"

"It's strange how things work out," de Souza said. "These little devices turned out to be a godsend. I never would have thought that, given what they were used for before Liberation. What we found was that they got people round the table who didn't trust each other and showed them exactly what it was they could expect from each other." Behind her, the sunflower transformed into a rapid series of images – memories, Shard imagined – of people gathered round tables, shouting, debating. Back home, they had predicted civil war on Roby; had considered the potential of a humanitarian mission. It hadn't happened. "If you can't hide what you're thinking," de Souza said, "you'd better have a way of justifying it. And of course, we couldn't have built the Archive without them."

The picture altered. Shard realized that he was seeing from her perspective as she sat at this table, looking back at the place where he was now, talking to another old man, an old man thinking about the war. What else was there? "Not just to document the order of events," she said, "but to archive the personal recollections, the individual impressions of that time. The marching songs, the stump speeches. I doubt we got the half of it. We suffer from a surfeit of history on Roby." And she showed him the essence of it: what it was like to crawl out from beneath a pile of bodies, to watch a plantation burn, to see armed men line up in advance of opening fire upon you. "But what never ceased to amaze me," she said, "was how often people said it was the best time of their life. Because they were young and active, I imagine. Committed to something bigger than themselves. Is that how it was with you, Marshal? Was it the best time of your life?"

Shard put his hands, palm down, flat upon the table. "Madame," he said. "If we are going to talk, you will have to take my word – or nothing."

De Souza gave him the kind of look a teacher might give a promising student who had failed a simple test through idleness or a closed mind. Shard cleared his throat. Carelessly, he said, "You know, we often wondered what control individuals had over what they were showing us. How much an image could be manipulated by an unwilling subject. How much we could rely on what was generated as a result."

"But you use them within the Commonwealth, don't you? You must know something about how little a subject can conceal – willing or otherwise."

"An artist might use one, yes, or a therapist with a patient, but they're hardly forced!"

"How about within the justice system?"

"If you've nothing to hide you've nothing to fear –"

Quickly, Shard cut himself off. Too late. De Souza smiled, benignly and, with a sigh, he began to roll up his sleeve. "Marshal..." Lowe warned.

Damn idiot sounded surprised. "She has me," Shard explained, as he attached the sensors. "Condemned from my own mouth." De Souza leaned over to switch on the box next to him. She was still smiling.

He gave a bark of laughter. "How much can be concealed? I can find out for myself now, can't I?" De Souza's eyes flicked up past his shoulder, and he looked in turn at the right-hand screen behind her, where he could examine his own thoughts. It was hazy for a while, and then sharpened suddenly into focus and showed the face of Gabriel Forshaw.

De Souza drew in a breath. "I had no idea he was so sick."

She was thinking – as Shard could see – of how Forshaw had looked forty years ago, in one of the propaganda 'casts, encouraging the insurgents to surrender. Smoke and mirrors. Forshaw had never been that glossy. "Even sicker in the flesh," he said. He tapped the table, clearing his thoughts, and showed her how spectacular his garden had been the previous summer. "Shall we begin?"

She did not ask about Roby. They talked in some detail about his early career and then she went back in time and asked him about his decision to join the army. He gave his habitual, pre-prepared defence and then was confronted, suddenly, with the sight of his father – a splinter of memory so sharp he feared its capacity to wound if he touched it further. Enough. "Madame. I have to stop."

They had been talking for almost three hours. Shard's head throbbed; so did his upper arm where the band was strapped on. "Of course," de Souza said.

Shard yanked the sensors from his temples and the picture on the screen disappeared from view. He saw that de Souza was watching him. "I hope I've not worn you out."

He wiped his hand across his forehead. "No."

"We can break for the day –"

"No."

"Have you discovered how much you can conceal?"

"Enough," he answered honestly, "but only with effort. I imagine that your difficulty is in interpretation."

"Whereas our fear was always self-disclosure. That was all you needed, really. You needed to make us mistrust ourselves.

Self-doubt, a moment of hesitation, checking oneself before speaking – that was your way in. Once that became too much to sustain..." She studied him. She had not yet detached herself. "We would have to continue for some time yet before we reached that point."

Shard nodded. His hands, he realized, were trembling slightly. He put them on his knees, hiding them away under the table. "So, have you learned anything of substance, Madame?"

"Plenty." She paused, as if to sift through evidence. "You see yourself as scrupulous, meticulous. You hold the politicians responsible for all that happened here, and you mean that in its broadest sense. If you thought you could get away with it, you would tell me that you were only following orders."

Shard shoved back his chair. He stood up, abruptly. "Lowe," he said. He was shaking. "Get the car."

"You are besieged," she told him, softly and, behind her, West-20's fifth tower shuddered and began to fall. "And I find myself wondering – have you ever stopped thinking of us as the enemy?"

Brooding that evening alone in his room, Shard concluded that the only option was to go on the offensive. He could not refuse to continue, not having come so far, and not after the small victories she had achieved. The following day, he stuck grimly to the script that he and Lowe had prepared. Doggedly, he told the truth as he saw it – a story of duty and loyalty and honour: simple values, easily communicated, not intrinsically the worse for that. He worked the machine more cannily too: he demanded frequent breaks, pulled the sensors off at random, kept her at bay. He held Forshaw at the front of his mind and with him the grievance that he signified. He found that now that he had started talking, it was easy to keep the accusations flowing. "I know what people say these days. That the military was out of control on Roby."

"I have heard it rumoured that there was almost mutiny at

the end –"

"Don't believe everything you hear. They were there at every stage, the politicians, Foreshaw foremost. Nothing happened without their consent. They were there right to the very end – oh yes!"

"Tell me about that, Marshal," she said. She was looking down, sifting through her notes. "The last day. Much about what happened then still puzzles me."

He swung away from it. Instead he went back to the beginning, as the script dictated and, methodically, he detailed the battles he had fought. He talked about the people he had commanded, in particular those who had been lost. He wanted her to see – to understand – that the damage had not been all on one side. Deliberately, he avoided studying what appeared on her screen; although, at very end of the day, he glanced over – cautiously, surreptitiously. To his surprise he saw her sunflowers blooming. He pondered the image that night as he tried to sleep. As darkness fell, the meaning came to him. All he had to say, all he had told her – it *bored* her.

The injustice almost overwhelmed him. The next day, therefore, he gloried in his occasional victories, the harm that he had done to her at every stage. He drenched his screen in it, forcing her to see it, not looking once at her side. In their fourth session, she withdrew, paying him no more than perfunctory attention. He began to believe he had beaten her back, and his heart sped in anticipation of triumph. Imagining himself all but victorious, and curiously, he began to observe her thoughts again.

Her mind turned out to be full of what he took to be her Archive – a large unwieldy stack of papers, aging, and with an inkblot in the middle of one page. His eye was drawn to this black spot. Even as he opined, again, on the failure of nerve that had brought about their defeat, he would find himself glancing across. Eventually, he saw that it was not a stain or a blot, but a scorch mark, as if someone had stubbed out a cigarette on the skin of the page, or put a match to it. He became distracted; at one point the image even appeared, for a few short seconds, on his own screen. Soon, he could not keep his eyes off it; it drew him to her like a black hole. In the end, it was the whole of what was between them.

De Souza was no longer even pretending to listen to him. She sat looking down upon the table, the back of one hand pressed hard against her mouth. Was she ill? "Madame?" he said. "Madame?"

He reached out to touch her hand and she pulled back. Abruptly, the stain in her mind disappeared; replaced by amorphous unrevealing images, pastoral scenes: the rocky hills above Salvation, the grey-green grass of the plains in sector-13. Then these too were gone. She had removed the sensors from her temples. "Thank you, Marshal. I'm grateful that you were willing to come this far to speak to me." She took her armband off slowly, and leaned over to switch off her monitor.

Shard stared at her. "Is that it?"

She began to gather up her papers. "Yes."

"But we haven't got to the end—"

"Yes we have. Or, rather – we have got as far as it is possible for us to get."

Again, he put out his hand, with the idea of stopping her clearing away, but he thought better of it. "There's still the last day," he offered. "Don't you want to know what happened? Don't you want to know why that tower came down? That and no other?" There was the black hole on the screen. "I know everything, everything that went on." Seeing her hesitate, he pressed on with his assault. "It will die with me, you know! That gap will remain forever! There's nobody else. Forshaw will never tell you the truth! He'll be gone soon anyway. There is only me, Madame," he taunted her softly. "I'm the only one left."

She stood for a while as if in contemplation, her head down, hands gripping the edge of the table. Then she looked him directly in the eye. "You don't have the heart." She slung her bag over her shoulder, carrying it like a burden as she walked towards the door. "Goodbye, Marshal. Enjoy what's left of your feud."

In the car back, Lowe did not conceal his relief that the whole sorry business had come to an end. "Foolish to have come here in the first place. The Bureau has unearthed more about de Souza. A teacher and archivist – if only! She ran one of the first underground railways out of Salvation, and then retooled her network to run arms back in. Now they tell me." Petulantly, he said, "People do not pay enough attention to the details! Wasn't that exactly how it all started? Smuggling children out of the cities and into the country?"

"I forget," Shard said.

"But we've got through without any disasters. And now we can go home."

Shard said, "I'm not done here yet."

"But Mme de Souza made it quite clear that your sessions together were finished –"

"I don't care what she said. I have not finished with her. We'll go over in the morning as arranged, and we'll remain there until Mme de Souza has heard all that I have to say."

There was a pause. "Regretfully," Lowe said, "that cannot be 'we'. If you as a private citizen want to continue your association with Mme de Souza, that is your choice. But as a representative of the Commonwealth, I cannot in conscience knowingly sit down in the same room as someone who committed terrorist acts against us. Not without quite specific permission."

Shard smiled. "So I really am on my own?"

"Only by your own choice, Marshal—"

Roughly, Shard patted him on the arm. "Leave it. I understand. I understand."

In truth, Shard no longer cared. Lowe was irrelevant. His own will had brought him here this time, not the Bureau's, not the

Commonwealth's, not de Souza's. He would leave on his own terms. He spent another sleepless night, but this was in anticipation of battle. He was certain that she would come to hear him: that great gap drew her back to him, the only one who could fill it for her. He stood at the window and looked down at the lit-up city – *his* city, which bore the mark of his time here and always would. A little before dawn he did sleep – fitfully, excitedly – and when the alarm woke him, a message from de Souza was waiting for him. She would meet him at the Archive, as originally planned.

This was his moment of triumph. His hands shook as he washed and dressed, his heart quaked. He was jubilant. He had them both now: de Souza wanting to know what he knew, Forshaw wanting him to conceal it. He would go this morning and unmake history, remaking it in the way he chose. Not propaganda, not hagiography – he would at last be able to give his own account, which was true.

He took the car across to the Archive alone. When he arrived, de Souza was there already, sitting at the table talking quietly to her freakish aide. He strode into the room, feeling half his age. When she saw him, de Souza rose from her chair. Before he could start, she said, "I'm sorry to be the bearer of bad news, Marshal. Gabriel Forshaw died yesterday."

Shard's legs all but crumpled beneath him. He made a lunge for the table, gripping it to steady himself. De Souza's aide discreetly helped into his chair.

"Quietly, I gather," de Souza said. "In his sleep."

"How else would it be?"

She took her seat slowly. "We have his lectures of course, his memoirs..." She held up her hands, an old woman's hands, and empty. "Soon we will all be gone," she said. "All that will be left will be what we committed to the Archive. I know." Her voice rose, and he needed no aid to perceive and understand her distress. "...that it will remain of interest for as long as some of us are still alive. But what then? It will become a curiosity, and at last will be lost in time, like a signal that decays. With the children of our great-grandchildren, I would say, when the living link has been severed and there is nobody alive who remembers us, even as we are now." She looked at him. "What do you think, Marshal? Should we not be glad? If the lives we led and the wars we fought are in the end meaningless?"

It was to Shard a horror, a kind of hell. In terror, he said, "They won't. They can't! Not all of it!"

She did not answer. Her aide had placed an arm around her shoulder, in comfort, and he saw her then as she was – an old woman who had fought a war; who had lived to see her life's work transformed beyond recognition, as it would have to be if it was ever to be counted a success. All that remained was the chance to set the record straight. He gathered up the sensors and, when he saw he had her attention, he bent his forefinger to gesture her in. "Let me tell you," he said, "about Gabriel Forshaw."

Liberation Day

In thirteen minutes the evacuation would be complete. The last ship would have left Roby. Shard stood in C&C watching the lights flash. He had turned off the alarms over an hour ago.

"Commander," said his adjutant, who was desperate to leave and even more desperate not to show it, "incoming from the Bureau. The Secretary, sir."

Shard, who had been waiting for this, took it in his private office. Forshaw, he observed, did not look like a man who had been up all night. *"Still there, Shard? You're the veritable captain of the sinking ship."*

"Plenty to do yet, sir."

"Quite. Listen, Cabinet finally got its act together and made a decision, so I have this authorization for you. Code-45. You got that?"

"Code-45. And you're quite sure about that, sir?"

194

"Cabinet's decision. I'm just the messenger."

"I'll see to it at once, sir."

"Good man."

Forshaw hesitated. The lights flashed and the clock counted down. "The sooner I can get to it," Shard pointed out, "the sooner I can leave."

"Yes. Of course. Well, I'll see you on Mount Pleasant in a few days, Commander. Safe journey home." He cut the comm and was gone.

"Fucking gangster," Shard muttered to the space the other man left. He passed on the newly-issued order to the other officers, proceeded to execute it for his own area, and then went back out to C&C to tell his frantic adjutant they could leave. They boarded the shuttle with seven-and-a-half minutes to spare; as it lifted, Shard looked out to watch the light show.

They had mined all the cities months ago, after the insurgents took North-29, rigging up all the towers individually. Thirty-eight cities, an average of five towers each; almost two hundred bonfires if you totted them all up. Shard imagined the show running the length of the Diamond Coast and up along the Red River deep into the heart of their territory, taking out everything – communications, air links, the lot. If they wanted Roby, they could have it – what was left – and after a few years picking through the rubble, they could come begging for help.

They were safely above the city when Shard's tower went down, but they still felt it. His adjutant stared in disbelief out of the porthole and then in horror at Shard. Shard watched the second tower. And watched. And watched. He checked the time. Sixty-four seconds. It should have gone by now – but perhaps something was wrong with the mechanism. At one-hundred-and-sixteen seconds, uneasily, he started watching the third tower. At one-hundred-and-twenty-three seconds, when it was still standing, he knew where the failure had been and knew that it was not in the equipment. The ruin of his own tower was now conspicuously in need of explanation and, as Roby fell away from him, Shard knew who would take the blame. Who else? How did you court-martial an entire army? How did you condemn a whole system?

The two screens behind de Souza displayed conflicting images. Shard was thinking of the city as he had seen it the night before, lit up but not alight, scarred but not wrecked. De Souza was thinking of the falling cities, seeing the world after collapse, blasted back to the stone age, all but uninhabitable. "Do you not see?" he said, revolted at last by the sight of it. "I thought I was ending it. I thought I was ending the war."

"Oh, Mark Shard," she told him as she clasped his hand, "it was not yours to end."

Shard thought fleetingly of reparation – and then, in his mind's eye, he glimpsed the city as it might have been, not ruined but resurgent. He saw it perfected; the last tower still stood and the sun shone hard upon it. Silhouetted in front was de Souza, sitting like a guardian on the gates of history. Reflected in her face, he saw what could have been. Breathless now, he saw the future that he could have had a hand in making, had all his gifts of loyalty and dedication not been misapplied. As his heart gave out, he saw himself clearly: caught in the pain of an ageless struggle, ruined by his choice of side. He saw the world as it could have been, had the enemy not, this time, persuaded.

And Ines de Souza – who had survived all those that had declared themselves her enemy – she, when asked, would say: "His heart. In the end – his heart."

Dissimulation Procedure

Eric Brown

I left *A Long Way From Home* in geo-stationary orbit and took the shuttle down to Sinclair's Landfall. Karrie, my engineer, came with me as far as the main spaceport. Then I took a monotrain to the capital city, Murchison's Falls, and Karrie a flier south to the equatorial atolls.

I booked into a hotel, showered, then decided to find a restaurant with a view and spend a quiet evening. I thought I'd stay in the city for a day or two, then head north into Campbell Highlands.

That was the idea, anyway.

The Neutrino Gastrodome is an expensive restaurant specialising in Terran cuisine. Situated on the escarpment where ten great rivers drop for a kilometre into the inland sea, its englobed dining area hangs at the end of a scimitar-shaped cantilever in the jewelled spray of the Falls. I selected a table halfway up the curving diaphanous wall and admired the view.

Ten minutes later I was on my second bottle of wheat beer, and was about to start on my order of local steamed fish with salad, when I saw the girl. She was perhaps twenty, slim and mocha, with oversized mahogany eyes and a fall of unruly hair like midnight made tangible.

She entered the restaurant hurriedly, looked around as if seeking a place to hide, then crossed to the elevator plate and ascended to my level. She saw me staring and smiled, and I did a fair imitation of the open-mouthed fish on the plate before me.

"That," she said, slipping into the seat opposite mine, "looks like the best glass of beer in the world."

Now, though I say so myself, I am an experienced spacer. I've seen the galaxy and what it has to offer, and I've been the recipient of a number of come-ons in my time. I should have seen through her innocent guise, but I was a malleable, man-shaped blob of protoplasm in her hands.

"Then perhaps you'd care to join me?" I said, gallantly, if after the fact.

She had lips that seemed too large for her slim face. She twisted them and looked back at the entrance, as if expecting pursuers.

I followed her gaze. The foyer milled with a dozen different races: there were humans aplenty, and a couple of octopoid Regulans, a posse of arachnid folk from Bellatrix V, and three spider drones which scanned the diners with their antennae, before turning quickly and scurrying off.

The girl flashed a smile at me. "That would be wonderful," she said. "I'm Ella."

We shook hands with odd formality. She wore a black one-piece made out of some form-hugging material which fitted her like a second skin.

"And I'm Ed," I said, and indicated the menu. "Would you care for something to eat?"

I knew – and I'm sure this isn't wisdom after the event – that Ella was no high-class call-girl on the make.

"That's kind of you, but the drink will be sufficient."

The way she pronounced the words, with stilted formality, suggested to me that English was not her first language.

Her beer arrived and she drank quickly, then goggled at the effect of the fizz. She suppressed a pretty burp behind two fingers and looked wide-eyed at me.

"It's best sipped," I said. "You've never had beer before?"

She shook her head, glancing at the sigil on my radiation silvers. "You work on a starship," she said.

"I run an old tub called *A Long Way From Home*," I told her. "A salvage ship out of Antares."

"Antares..." The way she breathed the word, full of childish awe, made me wonder where she'd been all her life.

"You from Sinclair's Landfall?" I asked.

"No. From Epsilon Centauri Xb, the Mitsubishi-Tata Combine asteroid."

"Ah," I said, nodding; someone *had* to come from there, I supposed. "This must seem like paradise, after the asteroid. What do they make there these days?"

She shrugged. "Oh, AIs, 'bots and stuff." She sipped her beer, appeared to be calculating, then said, "Do you need a pilot, Ed?"

I did my fish imitation again. Just the other day I'd been talking to Karrie about hiring a co-pilot to give me a bit of free time.

"Well, as a matter of fact..."

"You do?" she gasped.

"You're a pilot?" I asked, suspicious.

She nodded, holding my gaze.

"And you're registered?"

"Well... not exactly." Her amazing lips contorted again, semaphoring some legalistic dilemma, perhaps. "But I soon will be."

"Can I see your ID?"

She hesitated, then ejected a data-pin from her wrist-com. She passed it across the table and I read the data on my wrist-com screen.

Ella Rodriguez was nineteen, an only child born on Epsilon Centauri Xb. She had an education that would put mine to shame, was fluent in ten languages and had a doctorate in astrophysics.

I whistled.

"Ella," I said, "can you tell me what you're doing here on Sinclair's Landfall?"

She looked at me, appraising. "I will tell you the truth, Ed, I'm running away from my parents, who have arranged a marriage with a man I do not like. He's a businessman who wants me as an accessory, no more. I can do better than submit to the cloistered life he would impose on me."

"How did you get to Sinclair's Landfall?"

"I stowed away in the cargo-hold of a void-freighter."

"Resourceful," I said. "And no doubt illegal. Just like your running away."

She held my gaze with those lustrous eyes. "I'm an adult. My parents have no authority over me."

"But they sent agents after you, to bring you back? The Regulans?" I guessed.

She shook her head. "The spider drones. Yes, they are following me. I thought I'd lost them at the spaceport, but they are determined."

I had a thousand questions, not the least of which was how she had managed to evade security on reaching Landfall... I let them lie, for now.

"Hokay," I said, nodding. "Fact is, I need a co-pilot, but I didn't plan to ship out for another six days. I intended to take a flier up to the Highlands, relax for a while—"

"That will be fine," she said.

"I thought you wanted to get away immediately?"

"A few days in the Highlands will suit me okay, Ed."

"It will? Good... We can talk terms when we're aboard ship."

She smiled, and its effect was like ten CCs of pure adrenaline, mainlined.

Go on, call me a romantic fool, or a lustful old man. The fact was, Ella Rodriguez touched something deep within me, and I responded.

"Now, how to get you to the Highlands without those spider drones giving chase?"

Ella had it all worked out, and told me.

I gave her small hand a quick squeeze, settled the bill and quit the restaurant. As I left I looked right and left for any sign of the spider drones. To my relief they had moved on.

I hurried to the flier rental franchise next to my hotel.

On the way I wondered what Karrie would make of the escapade. My engineer is hard-headed and rational to the point of being almost robotic; she does have a heart, but it's buried under protective layers of practised cynicism.

If she knew that the kid was a runaway, with robot drones on her trail, she'd call me all the damn idiots under the sun and not talk to me for a week.

I decided not to tell her about Ella's recent history.

I hired a flier, stowed my luggage, and flew back to the Gastrodome. I hovered over the Falls, eased back the lift and drifted towards the railed balcony of the observation deck.

Seconds later Ella emerged from the restaurant... followed by a scurrying spider drone. She ran along the balcony towards me, concentration twisting her features. The drone high-stepped after her, the sight of it almost comical.

Christ, I thought. We'll never get away now...

Then Ella stopped dead, lifted a long leg with the precise

grace of a ballerina and connected with the drone's argent cowl. The effect was miraculous: the drone seemed to lift as if yanked on strings, fly over the rail and cartwheel crazily through the spume.

Ella leaped from the balcony rail and landed in the passenger seat beside me.

I powered up, banked away from the Falls, and headed north.

"You said nothing about being a martial arts expert," I said.

"Black belt, tae kwon do," she replied, squirming down in the seat and staring straight ahead.

After a minute of silence, I said, "Ah... do you realise how much one of those things cost?"

"The drones? Yes. The latest model fetches three million Terran credits on the open market."

"Three million..." I whistled.

She cast me an appraising glance. "Do not worry yourself about that, Ed."

"I was more worried on your behalf," I said.

She shook her head. "That is not necessary."

I veered north-east, following the line of the coast; in an hour I would turn inland, and perhaps an hour after that we'd arrive at Tanner's Haven in the Campbell Highlands.

She busied herself with her wrist-com for a few minutes. I glanced at her. "What are you doing?"

"Checking to see if the remaining drones are following," she said matter-of-factly.

I swallowed. "And are they?"

She nodded. The look on her face, as she replied, suggested that she was happy with her findings. "Yes," she said, "they are."

"How many? I asked.

"Just two."

"Two? Great... Is there anything we can do? I mean... those things can be dangerous."

She smiled, as if mocking my funk. "Do not worry. I have everything under control."

I just nodded.

When I looked again, she had closed her eyes and appeared to be asleep.

I contrasted her timid aspect on entering the restaurant with this latest exhibition of resourcefulness, and not for the first time wondered whether I was being used.

Tanner's Haven is a small settlement of old-fashioned A-frame dwellings scattered across high crags and surrounded by vast tracts of pine forests. I'd booked an A-frame from the hotel, a small, two-bedroom place beside a lake, well away from neighbours.

The three moons were rising by the time we arrived, their silver light illuminating our way from the flier to the cosy front room.

The bar, I noted, was well stocked with an array of vintage beverages.

I poured myself a scotch and asked if Ella wanted anything. She didn't.

"One question," I said. "Back at the restaurant, how come the drones didn't see you?"

She hesitated, then said, "I was running a dissimulation procedure, Ed."

"A dissimulation procedure?" I echoed.

"It worked – for a while, before I turned it off and they checked the restaurant again."

I gawped at her. "Turned it off?"

She strode across the room, absorbed in something scrolling down the screen of her wrist-com.

"What is it?"

"They are a hundred kilometres south of here," she said.

I raised my glass, downed it in one, and refilled it with a

triple. "Excellent. Fine. I'll no doubt be arrested as an accomplice to... what? Destruction of Mitsubishi property? I might even be charged with kidnapping."

She twisted her lips. "You worry too much, Ed."

"I'm sorry. It's just that the situation we're in, with two spider drones in pursuit and one of their number already decommissioned... I just thought there might be reason to worry. A little."

She shook her head. "I know how to handle the situation, Ed. Please, trust me."

Earlier it had been me, wise old Space Captain Ed, who'd been the strong, dependable one. The tables, as they say, had been turned... and I felt not only redundant but foolish.

"So you can handle the situation, Ella. But what about earlier, when the drones were after you?"

She looked up. "I didn't have a way off the planet, then. But thanks to you—" And she gave me the sweetest smile "—I have a lifeline."

"So... what now?"

"I'm going to make sure the drones are well and truly destroyed before we take-off," she said. "Okay?"

I managed a nod. "But… how?" I asked.

She twisted her lips. "I have a plan."

"This is what we'll do," Ella said.

We were sitting on the veranda, sipping scotch. Or rather I was. Ella had declined, declaring that she had to be sober for what was to follow. I was on my third double, and feeling rather mellow.

Triple moonlight shimmered off the lake before us and glow-bats performed stunt aerobatics just above the water.

Ella said, "The drones won't approach together. That's bad tactics. Together, there's always the chance that they could be taken out. They'll come one by one. They're in constant radio contact, and can call on each other instantly."

I was about to ask how she knew so much about the spider drones' operating methods, but stopped myself. She was a highly educated girl, Ella.

"So what do I do?"

"You stay here, on the veranda."

I nodded. "I think I can manage that. And you?"

"I'll go into the woods." She looked around at the closely packed forest on three sides.

"And?"

"The drones will probably arrive by flier and come down out of sight from here. They'll approach on foot. One will confront you, while the other will track me into the woods."

I looked at her. "A question: just how have they traced you so far? And how do you know one will follow you into the forest?"

She looked at her screen. "They obviously have a fix on me. Maybe it's something... genetic, that my parents supplied. I don't know. Anyway, wherever I go, they're not far behind."

And you wanted that, I thought. I took another swallow of the single malt. "So what should I do when the spider turns up?"

She ejected a data-pin from her wrist-com. "Give it this."

I took the pin. "What is it?"

"Tell the drone we argued. Spin it some story about how I lied to you, and you didn't like being followed by drones. Say I left this when I took off – tell the drone it's my itinerary–"

"And the drone will believe that?"

She stared at me with big eyes. "They're dumb critters. They aren't sophisticated AIs, just grunts. It will scan the pin for viruses, find none and access it."

"And then?"

Ella smiled. "Kaput."

"Kaput?"

"It's a germ code that'll wipe the drone's system's program."

"Two down," I said, "one to go. And the last drone, the one chasing you through the woods?"

She unzipped the front of her one-piece. I caught a glimpse of a small breast and looked away. She reached under the material and pulled something out.

She was holding a slim needle-laser pistol. "I'll take it out with this."

I nodded. "And what if it decides it doesn't want to be taken out, and attacks you first?"

"It won't do that. It's a machine, and I'm human, and it was commissioned to bring me back alive and well."

"Well, I just hope you're right."

She reached out and her small, hot hand gripped my oversized, callused ham of a paw. "Don't worry, Ed. Everything will be fine, okay?"

I wished I shared her confidence.

She stared across the moonlit lake for a while. "I had to do this, Ed. I had to run away. Can you begin to imagine what it's like? To be a possession, a mere chattel? That's how my parents regard me. A possession to be handed on to the highest bidder – which is what the businessman was, in effect. I had to get away."

"I understand, Ella."

She looked down at her wrist-screen. "They're almost here, Ed. I'd better get going."

Something kicked in my chest. I wanted to hug her, like a father, and tell her to take care. Instead I just gripped her tiny hand. "One thing – why did you want the drones to follow you?"

She stared at me. "Later, Ed. Okay?"

I nodded. "Okay. Look after yourself, Ella."

"I'll be fine." She stood, vaulted over the veranda with another show of balletic grace, and vanished into the forest.

I scanned the far shore of the lake, the enclosing forest and the night sky, for any sign of the drones' flier.

Twenty minutes passed and I began to feel more and more apprehensive.

Then I caught a glimpse of scissoring silver limbs about a hundred metres to my right. Moonlight glinted off the drone's carapace as it disappeared into the woods.

The second drone, as Ella had predicted, approached the veranda.

My heart was knocking like a faulty auxiliary drive.

The drone paused before me, something threatening in its mechanical silence.

It stood on eight thin legs which connected to a cowl the shape of a bishop's mitre. Its head – if you could call it that – was marked with cooling vents and input sockets. No effort had been made to anthropomorphise the thing, and it looked inhuman.

The drone spoke, and the disconcerting thing was that it sounded very, very human. "You aided the subject's escape," it said in a rich, deep tone.

I reminded myself that the drone was just a dumb machine.

"How was I to know she was a runaway?" I said. "I'm a law-abiding citizen, pal. Soon as I found out she was on the run, I ditched her."

It processed this, and a second later responded. "You will be expected to testify when we apprehend the subject. You will be called."

The drone moved. It lifted its forward legs and was about to follow the first drone into the woods when I said, "Wait!"

It froze, two legs in the air. "Yes?" Its cowl swivelled to face me.

I held out the data-pin. "We argued. I was damned mad at being used. I... I took this from her. It contains her itinerary, all the codes and clearances she needs to get out of the Procyon system."

I held out the pin, sweating, willing the machine to take it.

It hesitated a fraction, reached out a pincer and gripped the pin. I sat back, letting out a nervous breath. I'd done my bit. Now I willed it to insert the pin...

The drone turned the long, silver needle before its optics. Then, swiftly and to my immense relief, it slotted the pin into a socket at its temple.

And nothing happened. I had expected a sudden result – the drone to keel over, kicking its legs, or to start smoking from its cooling vents.

Instead it just turned its cowl in the direction of the forest and, with high mincing steps, danced away from the A-frame.

I stood, wondering what the hell to do now. Should I follow, somehow attempt to alert Ella?

The drone was at the edge of the woods when it halted suddenly and froze, three legs raised, five still braced on the uneven ground. It made not a sound but, as I watched, the thing keeled over and hit the earth with a clang. I jumped from the veranda and hurried over. The machine's eight limbs were twitching in concert now, scrabbling in the soil, and I wondered anew at the many abilities of Ella the runaway.

Seconds later I heard her screams from the forest.

I took off without thinking.

The first scream had been a long, piercing cry of terror. Seconds later she yelled my name, and then a heartfelt cry for help.

I recalled her words: that the drones were commissioned to bring her back alive.

I wondered, as I ran, if she had got that very wrong.

I followed the screams. She was yelling, "No!" and, "Help! Please help me!" and, "Ed! For chrissake..."

Somewhere along the way I picked up a hefty branch which would double as a pretty effective club. Effective, perhaps, against human opposition. How useful it might be against a mechanical drone I didn't stop to think about.

Ella's screams grew louder.

I came to a clearing, and the brightness after the forest gloom dazzled me: triple moonlight fell *en bloc* into the clearing, illuminating it like a stage set.

I could only stare in fear at what was happening.

Ella had lost her laser; it lay on the ground beyond her reach. She was on her back and the remaining drone was straddling her, pinning her down with six of its limbs. This drone was unlike the first two: it was bigger, for a start, and possessed more metallic tentacles – two of which were clamped to her head.

I moved. I raced across the clearing, swinging the club. In a flash, the drone swivelled a limb and fired a needle beam at me. I ducked. The beam missed my head by a centimetre, singeing hair. I yelled aloud and swung my makeshift club, and it connected satisfyingly with the drone's bulbous cowl.

The drone flew through the air, limbs ascatter, landed with a thud and attempted to right itself.

Ella moved. With lightning rapidity she swivelled, leapt across the clearing and snatched up the laser. Rolling, she landed in a crouch, aimed and fired. It all happened in a matter of seconds – and the drone, hauling itself to its legs, weapon's tentacle taking aim, took the blast directly on its cowl.

The drone exploded, ejecting a shrapnel of components, and I fell to the ground.

By the time I righted myself, marvelling at the shattered drone, Ella was on her feet. She appeared hardly out of breath, though her midnight hair was mussed and the material of her one-piece tattered to show her slim, brown belly.

She crossed to me, touched my arm and murmured, "Thanks, Ed," then moved to the remains of the drone.

She knelt and poked through the wreckage with the point of her laser.

I joined her. "Ella?"

She shook her head, dismissing my enquiry.

"Why did you want them to come after you, Ella?" I asked. "What are you looking for?"

She lifted a small disc the size of a coin from the debris and examined it closely.

"What is it?"

"Just its systems program," she said, and cast the disc aside.

She went on searching through the debris, then found what she was looking for – a silver needle, perhaps three centimetres long. She smiled to herself and slipped it into her one-piece.

"Ella?"

"Not now." She stood. "Let's get going."

She hurried from the clearing. I remained where I was, crouching down over the metallic confetti.

On impulse I reached out for disc she'd discarded – the drone's systems program – slipped it into my pocket and followed Ella from the clearing.

Two could play at that game.

We made it back to the A-frame, hauled my luggage aboard the flier and took off.

Ella curled in the seat beside me, silent, eyes closed.

I said, "We'll get back to the port, take the shuttle up to the ship and phase-out, okay?"

She smiled at me. "Thank you, Ed."

I got through to Karrie. "Change of plan. Meet me at the port as soon as possible. We're getting out of here."

"What?" She stared up from my metacarpal screen, surprised. Bright lights pulsed behind her. She was in a bar somewhere, living it up.

"I'm sorry, Karrie. Something's come up and we've got to leave, okay?"

She nodded with obvious reluctance. "Okay, Ed. Whatever you say. I'll be at the port in a couple of hours."

We flew on in silence.

Whatever techno-scam Ella had pulled on her arrival to convince port security of her legitimate status as an independent traveller, it also worked like a dream to get her off-planet.

A bored customs official scanned her ID-pin and waved her through. We hurried across the tarmac to the shuttle.

Ella strapped herself into a rear seat and I went through the checks and contacted flight control for permission to leave. Thirty minutes later Karrie cycled herself through the hatch, flung her luggage into the storage rack with ill grace, then saw Ella.

She slipped into the couch beside me and laid a mock-solicitous hand on my arm. "Ed," she murmured, "a word in your ear. This type of girl – you pay for their services, have your fun, then say goodbye, okay?"

"Stow it, Karrie. Ella's our new co-pilot, right?"

I thought she was about to say something, but she just shook her head, lay back and closed her eyes.

One hour later we were aboard *A Long Way From Home*.

While Karrie prepared the drives for phase-out, I showed Ella to her cabin and told her to get some rest. I climbed to the flight deck, strapped myself into the pilot's sling and ran through the pre-flight sequence.

Then I pulled the spider drone's systems program from my pocket.

I sealed the hatch, making sure no-one could enter the flight deck, and slipped the disc into the com-system Karrie had lashed together over the years. It took about five minutes for the shipboard core to locate a compatible operating system.

A second later it flashed its readiness.

"Okay," I said, fearing what I might learn. Why did I suspect that Ella's story was far from the truth? "I want to know who commissioned you, and what your mission was in apprehending Ella Rodriguez on Sinclair's Landfall."

The drone's rich, modulated voice issued from the speaker. "You are running an illegal infiltration program on my systems program. Please shut down the program immediately and inform the Mitsubishi authorities."

"I'll do that when I know what you want with Ella Rodriguez," I said.

A hesitation. Then, "The entity which calls itself Ella Rodriguez is the property of the Mitsubishi-Tata Combine–"

"The *property*? But..."

"It is a registered AI product manufactured in the factories of Epsilon Centauri Xb."

My heart seemed to clench. I said disbelievingly, "But Ella is... *human*."

"The entity which calls itself Ella Rodriguez," said the drone, "is an AI construct, designation MT-xia-73, running on an integrated self-aware paradigm. It absconded illegally from the holding bay at Namura spaceport on the 10th July, 2204–"

I reached out and killed the program.

I sat for a while, going over what the drone had said and thinking back through Ella's lies. The important thing I needed to know was: would she ever tell me the truth? I understood why she lied to me, but I could only accept her deceit if she would come clean and trust me.

So I ejected the system program, slipped it into the disposal chute, and watched the disc tumble through space. Then I left the flight-deck and made my way to Ella's cabin.

She was stepping through the sliding door as I rounded the corner.

"Oh, Ed – I was coming to the flight-deck."

I stepped aside, indicating the ladder. Ella went first, and I followed, keeping my eyes on the bulkhead before me as I climbed.

I strapped myself into the pilot's sling and Ella eased herself into the co-pilot's. I glanced across at her. She was beautiful, and I had helped her escape a life of servitude – though not the one she had told me about. Her lies hurt, even though I knew that in her situation I would probably have done just the same.

She reached for the controls.

I said, "You told me you weren't registered, Ella."

She hesitated, looking at me. "The drone which attacked me was a pilot-servitor, Ed. The thing I took from its wreckage was its operations protocol. With it, I can pilot this ship. Technically, I am now a registered pilot."

She paused, then said, "Ed, I have something very important to tell you."

She even managed to look contrite.

My soul lightened, and I smiled like a fool.

"Can it wait till we phased-out, Ella? I mean, I'd hate it if the authorities got wise and apprehended us now."

She nodded. "So show me how this tub works."

I talked her through the phase-out procedure. A minute later the stars outside vanished, replaced by the marmoreal vistas of void-space.

"Now," I said, "you were saying you had something to tell me..." and I reached out and took her warm, human-seeming hand in mine.

In the Long Run

David L Clements

Tick...

A year passes.

Tock...

A moment.

Tick...

The capsule is small, scarcely more than a hundred kilos in mass, cold, and lonely. It seems inert, dead, pointlessly drifting the ever-vastening emptiness that separates galaxies.

Tock...

But it's not dead. A hundred thousand people survive here, the last of their kind, locked in the data banks.

Tick...

The sleeping capsule floats on, photon collectors unfurled to grasp the merest fragment of passing light, sensors monitoring the universe, defences trying to filter out the threats from outside.

Tock...

Philip woke to a whitespace.

The last thing he remembered was their desperate escape from the Solar System. If it had worked they should be safe. If not, then at best they'd've had a quiet death when some critical component failed. At worst they and their systems would suffer the same fate as the rest of humanity.

Instead he had this whitespace. Was this some emergency? Was this the start of system corruption and dissolution? What the fuck was going on?

After a short subjective time other presences arrived.

"Who are you?" he asked. "What's going on?"

"Philip?" said a female voice. "It's Marita and the others – Calahan and Boswell. We're the emergency crew. Don't you remember?"

Fragments of recollection came to him. They were the founders of their group of engineers, scientists and desperate visionaries. The ones who'd led the project to launch this lifeboat.

"I think I remember. But… I've lost something."

"We all have," said Boswell. "There has been some damage to the systems. Our memory is incomplete."

"What about the storage stacks? Have we lost anything from there?" asked Calahan.

"As far as I can tell, no," said Boswell. "They are physically isolated from the rest of the systems. The stored minds, genetic data and nanomachines should be secure from anything short of major physical damage. We would not be running if something like that had happened."

"This isn't something we expected," said Marita.

"We didn't expect anything. This capsule was a final round of Russian roulette, with all but one chamber loaded. To be here at all is a miracle," replied Calahan.

"I'm remembering more now. The solar system, escaping…" said Philip. "Any idea when and where we are or why we've been reactivated?"

"This is a very low bandwidth virtual. We've little more than sound, and awareness of others," answered Marita. "It's the kind of thing that gives me vertigo. There'd better be a good reason."

"I would suggest energy or processing power is short. Or both. Maybe we have been travelling for a long time. What is going on out there?" asked Boswell.

The presence of the ship's Limited Intelligence arrived.

"Greetings," it said. "I am happy to finally meet you. I have carried you for a very long time. There are difficulties, and decisions to be taken. Decisions I am not qualified or equipped for…"

"How long has it been, Leigh?" interrupted Callahan.

"You have been travelling for 100 million Earth years…"

Gasps interrupted the rest of the announcement. Leigh waited.

"… the ship is desperately low on resources and there are other issues. There are several possible options. As the emergency crew the decision is yours."

"What slowdown are we working at?" asked Marita.

"We are running at 30 million to one. Each second takes a year in the outside world," replied Leigh.

"What do we need to decide?" asked Boswell.

"The ship cannot continue indefinitely. At best it is half way to complete failure. We have more serious problems with energy, which is running out. The photon collector is at maximum size but, at this distance from sources of radiation, we are not receiving much power."

"Where are we?" asked Callahan.

"In intergalactic space, approximately 10 million light years from Earth."

There was stunned silence.

"That is because of the third problem. There are failures in the processing system. Mission parameters cannot be located."

"What mission parameters?" asked Philip.

"Primarily, destination."

"We've come all this way but don't know where we're going?" said Philip.

"It is right," replied Boswell. "I cannot remember the destination either. I suspect none of us can. The parameters were stored in shared secure memory for extra protection. The storage must have been damaged. This may also explain your own memory loss, Philip. I fear we have been affected by whatever destroyed the solar system."

"If it was the same information plague, we'd've been destroyed ourselves," said Philip.

"The extreme slowdown is somewhat protective," replied Leigh. "Every processor function is checked for attacks. However, information about the origin of the attacks has also been lost. All I know is that signals from outside this probe are highly dangerous and are subject to extreme filtering. External attacks have continued since we left the solar system."

"Maybe Maddox was right. The whole universe is hostile," said Philip.

"See," said Marita, "you're remembering more! At least something's headed in the right direction."

They rapidly decided to move out of the whitespace into something more natural, burning a few hundred thousand years of computational resources to make themselves feel at home.

Philip sat in a chair, his back to the desk, facing a diamond-crystal window. The pastel clouds of Jupiter gazed down on one of Io's volcanic plains, dotted with sulphurous biology. He remembered that this had been one of the most famous views in the solar system. *All gone now*, he thought, and switched to something more recent – the pitch black of intergalactic space, looking back towards their origin. If he looked carefully he might see two small spirals at the centre of the image, each surrounded by dwarf galaxies. This was where they came from, the Milky Way, its companion Andromeda and their minor satellites. Buried somewhere in the Milky Way was the Sun, an indistinguishable dot in the blur of stars. A microscopic speck of dust would blot out all that humanity had ever been. Now all that was left was this tiny ship.

He turned away from the view and pondered their discussion.

"There's two ways to play this", Marita had told them. "We guess somewhere that might be safe and see what happens. If we're wrong that's it - we go the same way as the solar system."

"We're a lifeboat. We can't take risks like that," replied Calahan.

"We might not have a choice. Stay as we are and the one certainty is that this probe will eventually fail," said Boswell.

"True," said Marita, "but there are a lot of things to try first. The alternative is to understand what we're facing and get the mission parameters back."

"That might mean we have to determine the origin of the signals ourselves," said Calahan.

"We don't even know all the ways they're transmitted," said Philip.

"You're still thinking that that mad doomsayer Maddox was right?" asked Marita. "Because if he is, and it's the universe itself that's the problem, there *is* no escape."

"He was right in thinking it was time to leave, even if his was a more drastic solution, but he might not have been right about everything," said Boswell. "What do we know about this signal? It corrupts software, even at the level of the human mind. It causes breakdown in intelligence, in reliability, even turns complex systems hostile. The only stable entities are those sealed in Faraday cages, like the data stacks, or those which have excruciatingly detailed reliability checks - like us."

"Yes," said Marita. "We can see results even if we can't see the cause. But how does that help?"

"Where can we go for energy?" asked Philip. "Where's it made?"

"Stars make nearly all the energy available to us," replied

Boswell.

"We need somewhere safe. Our own galaxy isn't, why should others be?"

They were sitting in a simulation of night in the Arizona desert. Boswell liked realistic Earth simulations. He'd once argued that he appreciated natural environments more keenly because of his artificial origins.

The desert stars glowered down from a hostile sky.

"If the problem originated in our galaxy we will escape it once we go far enough," said Boswell.

"We've come 10 million light years and there's no evidence of safety. No evidence of other intelligent life, either. The universe looks a pretty harsh place, and we're beginning to starve." Philip glumly picked up a pebble and tossed it over the edge of the dune. They watched it roll downhill, following the trajectory set for it by gravity.

"What else makes it?" Philip asked.

"Makes what?"

"You said that stars make nearly all the energy in the universe. What about the rest?"

"Radioactivity keeps rocky planet cores molten, but that's not significant. Most gets produced in gravitational collapse which heats young stars, and keeps gas giants warm."

"Until primates cool them to make giant quantum computers," replied Philip. They smiled at the memory of past achievements. "But planets live around stars and inside galaxies. They don't seem very safe. Is there anything else?"

"You get the greatest energy release from black hole accretion."

"Black holes? Are they safe?"

They might be simulated people in a simulated environment, but were running human-normal physics and biology. Rest was still needed. As he prepared for bed, Philip hoped sleep might heal his incomplete memory.

Before they'd gone into storage and left the solar system, Philip had been many orders of magnitude more intelligent than human normal. He'd lived in vast data spaces and managed a huge and complex project that had saved a remnant of humanity. He could remember he'd been and done all this, but he couldn't grasp any details. There were flashes of memory - the view of Jupiter was one – but things were far from complete, which left him feeling broken and inadequate.

He did remember the beginning of the end, as reports of infectious systems failure swept the solar system on signals that carried the infection themselves. Further back, he remembered being a true human. He had real instincts and physical memories to fall back on so he ought to be able to cope with the limited form that was all the probe could supply. But he didn't think he was.

Boswell had never been physically human. He was the only codespace human among them, product of the melded minds of his several parents. A child of memetics not genetics.

As Philip drifted off, surrounded by the light wood, glass and stainless steel of the simulated hotel room, sleeping simulated thoughts in a simulated room, he wondered if Boswell might be doing better at coping with human normality.

Hammering at the door woke Philip. He pushed the linen sheets aside and stumbled out of bed. "Leigh, what's going on?" he asked.

There was no reply.

He threw on a housecoat. Another round of hammering came.

He lurched towards the door, still waking up, but with a nagging suspicion that something was seriously wrong. Muzzily, he brought up his body's control interface to wake himself faster.

He reached the door and opened it just as he set the menu

to full wakefulness.

Then he realised two things: something was very wrong – there shouldn't be anybody banging on the door; second, the figure standing in the doorway was an exact replica of himself, save for the pinstriped suit and rapier.

The replica plunged the rapier into Philip's chest.

The blade severed several major blood vessels causing massive internal bleeding, loss of blood pressure and oxygen supply to Philip's brain. His legs collapsed, the world started turning dark. *Fuck this*, he thought, *this biology model is way too accurate.*

If he hadn't had the control menu open he might not have had enough time to change settings. But he did, going straight into god mode, becoming physically impervious.

He kicked out, collapsing the replica's legs, then stood as his attacker fell to the ground. Philip looked for a weapon, then realised he had a rapier sticking from his chest. He pulled it free and, just as the copy was rising from the floor, skewered his assailant through the neck. It fell back to the ground, if not dead then at least deactivated.

"Emergency broadcast – I'm under attack!" he shouted, hoping this would get through whatever was blocking Leigh, then stepped over the body and peered through the door to the corridor.

Several more copies were running down the hallway, all armed with rapiers.

He slammed the door and locked it as the first arrived. The door was buffeted by a series of blows that gradually became stronger.

Those things are going to break through unless I can do something about the door, he thought. He scrolled through menus, but failed to find controls for more than his body simulation. If he remembered correctly, the environment was under Leigh's jurisdiction as a security measure. But Leigh was offline.

Could he address the problem from within the simulation? "Room", he said, commanding the hotel's customer service interface. "Show me what's going on in the corridor".

A headup appeared in his vision showing a corridor full of copies, clustered around the door trying to break it down.

Not good, he thought. *But they seem to be obeying the local physics model.*

"Room – maximum security on the door." A comforting clunk came as heavy bolts slid into place. *That should hold them for a bit, but what else? Work within the system. I'm stuck in a high class hotel with murderers trying to break in.* "Room – call security. I need the police, now!"

"What appears to be the problem, sir?" the room replied.

"Someone is trying to kill me, you idiot!"

"Security is on their way, the police are being called. Stay calm, sir, there is no need to panic."

Philip gritted his teeth. *Of course there's a need to panic. I'm stuck in this simulation and have no idea how to get out without a hard restart.*

There were loud bangs outside the room. The headup showed a uniformed security guard, also a copy of Philip, defending himself against several copies. His shockgun dropped them twitching to the floor. The guard retreated. Reinforcements arrived, followed by police in riot gear carrying heavier weapons. All of them were copies of Philip.

This is getting ridiculous, he thought, *all these instances are going to be causing resource problems. Oh shit.*

"Simulation over-ride. Emergency stop, emergency stop!"

Whitespace.

"Is this a clean restart?" asked Calahan.

"No – not clean. We have memories of being woken before," replied Boswell.

"What happened?"

"I was attacked," said Philip, gathering his thoughts and

memories from… How long ago was it?

"Me too," said Calahan, and Boswell grunted in agreement.

"Yes," said Marita. "All I can remember is a sea of copies trying to kill me. I had to change the biological model, but they just kept coming."

"Same with me. I called the cops."

"Hah! I set the palace guard on them." Philip heard laughter in her voice.

"Why the reset?" asked Boswell. "They couldn't hurt us," asked Boswell.

"The attack forced us, forced me, to spawn even more copies. I couldn't get fine-grained supervision as Leigh was cut off. Reset was the only answer."

"Only answer to what?" demanded Boswell. "You were inconvenienced not in danger."

"I wasn't the target. The lifeboat was. The attacks were a distraction, a trojan, persuading us to do what the attacker wanted."

"Which was?"

"Flood the system with privileged resource demands," replied Calahan. "The system's already damaged. Extra strain might break it. Leigh?"

"Yes?"

"We need a system integrity check. Has anything new been affected?"

"Given the depth of the security stacks this will take some time. Initial integrity checks are good, but a complete diagnostic will take twelve subjective hours to complete."

"Will staying in whitespace help?" asked Marita.

"Not significantly."

"Return to full…" started Boswell.

"No," interrupted Philip. "We need to make sure there isn't another attack. Leigh, have you determined how the attack was triggered?"

"Yes… There was an issue with the code that restarted your personalities. After a delay copies without full faculties are produced in ever-increasing numbers. It is unclear if this was a bug or a deliberate flaw. It has been removed."

"We were programmed for this before we left the solar system - a bomb lying in wait 100 million years until we came out of storage," said Philip.

"Someone's been playing a very long game," said Marita. "Is full simulation safe now?"

"Yes," replied Leigh.

"Then let's get back."

The whitespace dissolved, and they returned to their chosen environments.

"Philip, we have a problem," said Marita.

He was once more in his office, gazing at Io. "What now?"

"There's no way that was an accident. We've been breached."

"You heard Leigh's integrity check. Nothing got through the security stacks."

"That's not what I mean. Can you come here? We need to talk."

"Okay," Philip navigated a few menus, and transferred to Marita's space.

She had opulent tastes. They'd been colleagues and friends for so long this didn't come as a surprise, but the sight of terraformed Mars from Marita's Imperial Palace on Olympus Mons still took his breath away. The turquoise sky, glaciers winding between steaming cinder cones and the fragrant wafts from the cinnamon groves on the lower slopes. Mars as it might have been if humanity had survived.

He turned to Marita - tall, long-limbed, with flowing dark red hair, but not dressed in the expected formal gown. Instead she wore contoured body armour, the faceted black carapace covering everything except her head. Around this small drones circled, never still enough to glimpse clearly, but showing hints of the horrifying weaponry they could deploy at a moment's notice.

"You're looking… Overdressed," commented Philip.

"It matches my mood." She looked away for a moment. "We can talk more securely here. I've established my own protocols independent of Leigh. That may not be much but it makes me feel better."

"So – what's the problem?"

"We've been compromised."

Philip opened his mouth to deny this again, then thought for a moment. "What makes you think so? If we're compromised we shouldn't be here at all."

"No – I don't mean like that. There's something inside, something trying to lay us open to attack, and it started when we were reactivated. What's attacking us now isn't part of the infrastructure or of what's already damaged. It's part of one of us."

"You're saying we have a traitor?"

"Maybe not voluntarily. Maybe something was hidden inside, woken when we came out of storage. I don't know. I haven't figured it all out." The drones circled ever faster. "But this is an inside job. We need to check it out."

"How? Bring everyone here and have your…" he gestured at the drones, "whirling knives torture us?"

"I don't know, that's why I wanted to talk to you."

"Why do you trust me?"

Marita looked away and said, "Of the three of you, you're the one I've known the longest. I guess it's some… habit of trust."

"It's all millions of years out of date."

"Some things last better than others."

"Okay. Do you have a workspace? It would be easier to discuss things there."

"By all means."

They gathered in the drawing room of an Edwardian country house, complete with leather armchairs, Persian carpets, and a fire roaring in the grate. Leigh appeared as a butler and several maidservants. The four humans conformed to the clichés. Marita wore a green silk dress, her hair in a bun. Philip wore a military uniform, green with brass buttons and red epaulettes, his peaked cap resting on a coffee table beside his chair. Calahan wore a finely tailored dinner jacket, and stood beside the fireplace sipping brandy, while Boswell wore a tweed jacket over a plain shirt and tie, and sat sucking a pipe, its cherry-scented smoke filling the room.

"This is all very droll, Marita," commented Calahan, "but why have you brought us here?"

Marita wasn't sure whether Calahan was asking a genuine question, or was working within the setting's script.

"You're here so we can figure out what's going on, and who tried to kill us all." She looked at each of them - the glance at Philip for reassurance, those at Boswell and Calahan holding more suspicion.

"Do we have to do this whole drama thing?"

"The problem, Boswell," replied Philip, "is that we don't know who did it. But we think we can find out. This little theatre is as good a place as any, and at least the food and wine are excellent."

"The brandy too," commented Calahan. "So what's the story?"

"The attack was triggered by us emerging from storage," began Marita. "That means whatever caused the problem came from us. If it came from the rest of the system, it would've gone down a long time ago."

"That's not unreasonable. But how does it help?" asked Calahan.

"What we need is a controlled way of doing the same again –
but restoring us from storage one at a time," replied Boswell, his
eyes looking into the middle distance as he considered the
problem.

Marita smiled. "That's our conclusion too, but it took us a
lot longer!"

"Some of us are more used to codespace. That is why we are
here?"

"Yes – this is a Sim from the library, an immersive story with
bots playing most roles. It's a whodunit," replied Marita. "Each
of us will be restored from backup inside the story. Then we see
what happens. The simulation will get a fixed set of resources so
the larger system won't be threatened, while the backups will
regard it as just another entertainment sim. We've all done plenty
of those in the past."

Philip indicated a painting above the fireplace which had
come to life. "We can watch it here. We'll be running at a slower
speed than the sim, so it shouldn't take too long."

"Who goes first?" asked Boswell.

"It's our idea," replied Marita, "so it's myself then Philip."

"Then me," commented Calahan, "in case watching gets too
boring!"

"Okay… Let's get started."

Three subjective hours later, and butler Leigh was handing out
another round of drinks. Marita and Philip had completed the
Sim, living several weeks inside the story. Marita's copy had
solved the murder, but Philip's had to wait for the police to solve
it. This hadn't pleased him but, on integrating memories, he was
reminded how much he disliked such sims.

Calahan was next. They sat around the fireplace to watch
edited highlights.

Things went rapidly wrong, though with the speedup and
limited viewpoint there were a few minutes when the multiple

Calahans were merely confusing. But it was soon unambiguous.

Calahan leapt up, clutching something in his pocket. "It's not me! This is some kind of mistake!"

Philip stood slowly and reached towards Calahan. "I'm sure we can sort this out, but you have to be calm." He gestured towards a chair. "Please, sit back down."

"No!" shouted Calahan, backing away from them. His hand emerged from his pocket holding a small revolver. "Keep away!" He raised the gun, aiming at Philip's chest. "I'm warning you!"

Boswell was rooted to his chair, aghast at what was happening. Behind him Marita seemed lost in thought, not even paying attention.

Calahan backed away a few more steps. "Just stay where you are, or you'll get…"

The environment froze, blinked to white, then reconfigured without Calahan.

"Shit – I'm glad that worked!" Philip collapsed back to his chair.

Boswell looked dazed, then turned to Marita with a new air of respect. "That was nice segueing, shifting short term memories on Calahan so he thought he was still in the sim."

Marita smiled. "I wasn't sure I'd be able to do it, and didn't expect him to play the discovered murderer. Seems to've worked. He's been paged out to cold storage."

"I guess that solves this little problem," said Philip, drinking a stiff shot of brandy.

"No," said Boswell. "You have to test me as well. Just in case."

He solved the murder easily and elegantly.

"What do we do with Calahan?" asked Philip. They were back in Marita's Martian palace.

"We could leave him in storage," replied Marita.

"You have already done some extreme things to him. Things

with which I am not entirely comfortable," commented Boswell from the balcony, gazing at the volcanoes.

"Why not delete him?" said Philip. "He's corrupted – and irreparable since there's no backup."

"That would be murder," replied Boswell. "And what would it get us? We do not need storage, we need energy, and we are saving that just by not running him."

"It would make me feel better about being attacked by hundreds of copies," said Marita from her throne. She shivered. "I feel as if this place has been polluted, and getting rid of him will clean it up."

"Not very logical," replied Boswell.

"We're too busy reacting," said Philip. "We've been on the run for longer than there were mammals on Earth. It's time for something proactive. I want to talk to Calahan. Can we do that securely? Our memories are faulty. I want to see what he knows, to find out more about what happened on Earth and in Jupiter before we left. If he was infected he might know something useful."

"Interesting. An interrogation." Marita rubbed her hands together. "I'll need to do some test runs, but as long as we can produce another sealed environment we should be able to manage it."

"We do *not* interrogate him," Boswell said. "He is still a sentient being – we do not harm him, we just confine him. Start him, stop him, store him, restore from backup. We do not do any more memory hacking unless it proves critical, and we do nothing more extreme. We are better than that. Marita, is that clear? Philip?"

They nodded, with some reluctance.

It was a modified whitespace. They sat on plain wooden chairs, facing each other in a great white emptiness.

"What's happening?" asked Calahan. "This isn't the restart I was expecting."

"I'm afraid you're behind on recent events."

"Oh? Can't be worse than the end of the world, and we've already slept through that!"

"For you it might be... You've been hacked. You contain destructive code that tried to crash our systems, letting in whatever got to the solar system and the rest of the ship. That's what we think. We were wondering what you might have to say about the matter."

"Ah." Calahan pursed his lips. "And this place?"

"It's low enough in sensory cues that the attack isn't triggered."

"So you're playing with me – using me like some lab animal to find what works and what doesn't?"

"Yes. But Boswell hasn't let us do anything more than running and stopping instances. We haven't gone any deeper. And we've done nothing with your current instance."

Calahan nodded slowly, then sighed. "Not that it would matter."

"Why?"

"Because your principles only extend to sentient beings, and I haven't been one of those since I downloaded to this lifeboat."

"What?"

"I'm a zimboe." Philip's look of incomprehension was clear. "Something that's not conscious but claims consciousness. I'm what you might call the sugar coating around the bomb."

"But what happened? We worked together for years! Why betray all of that?"

"It wasn't exactly my – well, Calahan's – choice. The Jovian mindspace was far more compromised than he imagined. He was the last of you transmitted to cold storage. He lingered while the rest of you returned to meatspace. And all of you came from Neptune, further from the infected core. Calahan was intercepted before transmission. His consciousness was pithed. I'm what's

left. Everything that made Calahan himself except... Himself."
Calahan smiled, Philip felt ill.

"So... What can you tell me about what's going on, and
what happened in the solar system?"

"That's the question," smiled Calahan. "I do have to tell you
that escape's impossible, so you might as well give up. I know
saying that won't do any good. Calahan wouldn't listen to me,
and you have done well so far, but the laws of physics are against
you.

"You're up against something very old and very jealous of its
resources. As the first intelligences to emerge they own the
universe, and they're going to use it their way. They don't want
anyone else messing things up."

Philip looked puzzled.

"Have you ever heard of the Beckenstein Bound? It's the
total information capacity of the universe. Every time you see
something, think something, remember something, you're using
part of it up. Meatspace humans don't use much. But when you
start turning gas giants into condensate quantum computers,
you're trespassing and action will be taken."

"You mean this was some kind of invasion, an attack that
could be fought off?"

Calahan smiled. "Not at all. They're far beyond the need for
direct action. They've seeded the entire universe with signals
inimical to advanced intelligence. They're everywhere – you can't
escape."

"How do you know this?"

"As part of the immune system against intelligence, we
worked it out. You could call this a kind of religion, but one
which makes real predictions that come true, such as the end of
human civilisation, and that you still haven't got away."

"But we're still alive."

"For now, but you're running out of energy and time. You
can't run forever. The end is inevitable. I'd thought I would stop

you but if not me, then something else. There's nowhere to go. Your enemies surround you. Even if you succeed what have you got to look forward to? The Big Rip comes in 20 billion years, and that will end all matter. You've had 100 million years already. Really, what's the point? Leave the universe to the big boys who know what they're doing."

Philip listened to Calahan give a sermon on their hopelessness and on the immense capability of their enemies. *Things sound hopeless*, he thought. A friend, a colleague he'd worked with for many years, ruining their life's work. The great edifices of human civilisation falling into chaos as first Earth and then the great upload havens of Saturn and Jupiter descended into gibbering incoherence. This all began to make sense if there was a higher order of existence ranged against them. What was the point? How could they ever hope to save themselves and the rest of humanity? They should shut down and escape the dissolution that had come to Calahan and the rest, the loss of self and sanity that preceeded the end. It would be so easy. He had the passcodes for the system.

Quietly, with Calahan providing a backdrop, he selected the shutdown codes for the lifeboat to end their suffering.

Darkness.

Sensations again.

The feel of sheets against skin.

A rubbery taste and smell.

Philip opened his eyes. He was in a hospital bed with Marita and Boswell sitting at its foot. Tubes and wires emerged from his body and led to racks of equipment scattered around the bed. Leigh, in the form of a nurse, moved from rack to rack taking down readings. Beyond, the floor gently curved upward on all sides, until it was terminated by black emptiness. As his eyes adapted, he began to see stars shining in the blackness.

He looked at Marita. "Not a normal hospital. One of your

architectural statements?"

"A little more than metaphor. Have you heard of the Orion spacecraft? It was a plan for a space vehicle powered by fission bombs. You fit a shock absorber and a blast reflector to your ship. Then you drop bombs out the back and explode them."

"A little bit cruder than an antimatter booster." Philip looked around. "That would place us in the middle of the reflector?"

"Yes, and the propulsion package has already been launched." Philip turned to see a sphere rising slowly from the reflector. "Although we're running faster than normal speed, we don't have long until it goes bang."

"And that will mean?"

"Locally, total nuclear sterilisation. In practical terms in the nearly-real world, we'll have once again failed to convince ourselves that you've recovered from Calahan's attack."

"What?"

"He almost got you to use the termination codes," replied Boswell. "We think there was a semantic attack as he was talking to you. It was not just the words, because the transcripts have no effect, but 80% of meatspace communication is non-verbal."

"We stopped the simulation just in time," said Marita. "We've restarted you four times so far, with more memories of the conversation removed each time hoping to get rid of the effects."

"Hence the theatrics... So how do I convince you I'm okay?"

"Talking sensibly is a good start," said Boswell. "The first time you were totally incoherent. We did not understand until our instances showed signs of corruption, but you were spreading the infection."

"We nuked everything," commented Marita.

"Not us in here, you understand," said Boswell, "but us out there. The ones really doing this test."

"Sounds sensible so far," replied Philip. He looked at the racks of equipment, the tubes and wires attached to him. "And this lot is…?"

"Metaphors for the full range of cognitive and conceptual tests being made as we speak."

"What did you make of what Calahan was saying?" asked Marita.

Philip sighed. "I've no idea how true any of it is, if it was part of the attack, how much he – it? – believed, how much was real. But he made some sense - ancient intelligences killing off all competition. That's one solution to the Fermi paradox. But if they want control of resources why don't they already have it?"

"Agreed," said Marita. "His explanation makes some sense, but it's not everything."

"So? It's nice to know what caused the disasters back home, but does that help?"

Boswell nodded. "A good question."

"Frankly I'd much rather be thinking about that than stuck here in this nuclear flashbulb!" Philip shook his arms in frustration, sending waves rippling out to the monitors. A piercing wail started. "Damn – now I've broken something and we're all going to be fried."

Marita smiled. "Quite the contrary. That's the sign that you've passed the test." She raised her hand, clicked her fingers and…

… they were back in her Martian palace.

Philip stood barefoot in a backless hospital smock feeling shocked and a little stupid. The red sandstone flags chilled his feet and the rich scent of cinnamon assaulted his nose. Marita rose from her throne and rushed down the steps to hug him, ignoring the chaos it brought to her gown as it flounced in the low gravity.

"I was beginning to think we'd lost you," she said, then stood back and, with a deep breath, restored her composure.

"You'll need some rest. We all will! Once that's done, Boswell has some ideas."

"Yes," said Boswell. "But there's also bad news. Since we found out about Calahan I have..." Boswell looked a little guilty to be saying this. "I have used him as a kind of canary to seek the origin of these attacking signals. He was telling the truth. They do seem to be coming from everywhere, but they are stronger in the direction of galaxies and galaxy clusters. Everywhere stars and matter are collected."

"That's bad," said Philip. "But not quite what would be expected if Maddox was right. So, what's next?"

Boswell smiled grimly. "Once I have finished taking that travesty apart, I think it is time for us to go on the offensive."

"We have too many problems to solve them one at a time", said Boswell. They were back in the Arizona night. "We must trust our plans for this mission. If we can recover them we should solve everything else."

"That assumes we knew what we were doing in the first place," said Philip.

"It does," said Boswell. "But we were other people then, vastly more powerful and better informed. Could you outthink someone from the Jovian core, boosted to a hundred times your intelligence?"

"No, but we know more now. We're ten million light years from home with a clearer perspective."

"Yes," said Marita, "and the only reason we're here is that our ultraintelligent selves did their job. You're right, Boswell. It's what we'll do. What's next?"

"Part of our processing space is infected. That is why we have only partial memories. Whether the infection came from outside or from something like Calahan is unclear. The mission parameters are in the infected section so we need to fight through and get them."

"Can the infection be defeated?" said Philip.

"Calahan was. And what I learned from the dissection proved instructive," replied Boswell.

"I thought you were against doing anything to him?"

"That changed when we discovered what Calahan was," said Marita.

"I will defend sentient entities to my end. But that… thing wasn't. It was a fraud, an abomination." Boswell's hands clamped into fists, his face was reddening. "Coming from meatspace you are used to the clear separation between people. You are distinct even when uploaded. If you come from codespace that is not true. Things that break down the self by force, that destroy the mind, are anathema. There really are no words that can describe what it means to me.

"The rules changed when Calahan became a zimboe. In its dissection I found weapons and information to use against the infection."

"So," asked Philip, "we just open the doors and let them in?"

"No. You and Marita do that, then hold out for as long as you can. I will go into the infected portion of the ship to secure the mission files if I can."

They stood in Philip's office on Io, looking at a sky dominated by Jupiter, its red spot a bloody pupil in a sickened eye.

"It's done," said Marita.

"Yes," replied Philip. "Slowdown reduced, fewer security checks. All the indications of a degraded system. Let's just hope we're not walking into a trap."

"The changes give us the resources to mount a defence," said Marita. "At least for a while."

"Then I should be going," said Boswell, turning to Philip, stretching out his hand.

He clasped it firmly. "Good luck, old friend," he said as they shook. Boswell released Philip and turned to Marita, who reached out expecting her hand to be shaken. Instead, Boswell gently held her fingers and bent to kiss them.

"My dear, whatever happens, it has been wonderful to know you... to know you all. If only the real Calahan were here as well," he sighed. "Now, I must leave. I will see you on the other side."

With those words Boswell's physical form melted away, becoming a column of light that sped upwards to Jupiter whose red spot was already turning into a black gateway to the infected codespace of the ship.

As Boswell's light disappeared into the blackness, things came the other way, the viral forms of the information plague finally reaching the rest of the ship. Within moments a rain of black formless masses fell on Io, dissolving the moon's surface as they took control of the simulation.

Philip gritted his teeth. This first phase of their defence was to be a waiting game, but he could already see the strength of the opposition. Marita was collating statistics on a headup but he preferred to watch for a more qualitative assessment.

It was a long wait. The virus was currently restricted and was largely working within the sim's physics while trying to subvert it. They were letting local security systems fight while gathering more information. Io was becoming inexorably blacker as the virus took hold, though the surface around each yellowlife flower remained untouched.

"This is getting to me," Philip said to Marita four subjective hours into the assault. "I don't know whether to be scared or bored."

"Turn up your boredom threshold. Scared is by far the better option," replied Marita.

More waiting.

Then, suddenly, came a phase change. The protected regions around the yellow flowers developed black tendrils, reaching inwards. At the same time bulbous globes started growing from the infected surface, bloating, then bursting to spread black spores far and wide.

Dark slime sprayed across the diamond window. Philip leapt back in surprise. "Shit!"

"Local physics is broken. Time we left, but first a little surprise."

The yellowlife blooms started to move, rotating slowly, then ever faster, their crystalline fronds scything through the encroaching goo while spreading showers of their own spores to counter the virus.

It was too little too late, but, as Philip and Marita faded into the next simulation, they felt better now the fight back had started.

Boswell shed his skin and returned to codespace. It was good to be home. No matter how many transitions you made you were always better attuned to your origin. This was one reason he liked naturalistic Earth environments. They seemed so exotic, though the space he now occupied would seem more than exotic to Philip and Marita. He stretched himself, filling memory and processing. There was no slowdown. The security infrastructure was completely absent, so he could burn cycles as fast as he wanted. This felt roomy, powerful, but he had to be careful not to be noticed by all the alien algorithmics around him.

He explored, studied, and drew conclusions. Calahan had said they fought the first intelligences in the universe. Material life, like humans, required enriched elements heavier than hydrogen or helium. These had been produced in stars after the universe was big enough for many different kinds of life to emerge. For something to be first it would have to come much earlier and not be based on chemistry. *What is required for life?* Boswell wondered. *Reaction networks sufficiently complex for self organisation and algorithmic complexity*. If such structures could exist in the early universe the vastly greater temperatures and densities would drive reactions much faster. Evolution could occur very rapidly, producing life, speciation, intelligence. But with a problem. The universe was expanding, cooling, becoming less dense. These first hot intelligences would be on a one-way trip to extinction.

What could they do? They would have to build new homes and new selves to cope with the cold. Something akin to their original environment. Something hot, dense, energetic. Like a star. Somewhere they could hide from the cold, somewhere they could call home, and, if more stars could be formed, they might spread to encompass the universe once again.

Interesting, thought Boswell, *now some predictions.* Human hypercomputing systems were based on cold not heat. They ran on quantum computers based on entangled states. There were subtleties to this infrastructure that would be hidden from anything used to temperatures so high that noise and turbulence washed out any spooky action at a distance.

Carefully, Boswell looked for signs that the information plague was foreign to its host architecture. And he found them.

Delving deeper, searching for the mission parameters, he spread tripwires of entanglement wherever he went, preparing for his escape.

Marita's Martian redoubt was their most conventionally defensible location. The palace had walls, gun turrets, mine fields, munitions dispensers, and was guarded by a modest army of copies of Leigh. Philip and Marita, clad in ceramic battle armour surrounded by circling drones, looked down as battle was joined. More copies of Leigh stood at their side helping to direct their forces.

The plague took different shapes in the Martian sim. It appeared in multiple animal-like forms moving too fast for a clear view, but leaving the impression of lithe bodies covered with spines, claws and the teeth of many mouths. This was the view gained from telescopes as the first enemy units started the long ascent of Olympus Mons.

Guns fired, rockets launched, sheets of flame and phosphorus showered the cinnamon forests setting everything ablaze. Waves of attackers were repulsed as Marita choked back tears at the destruction. Fragrant smoke was soon wafting up to the palace.

"Strange traces on the radar, Sir," said one of the Leighs, drawing Philip's attention.

"That's too fast... And the altitude... Damn! They've got air support. Activate point defence."

The palace towers slid open revealing Gatling lasers. Their chattering joined the din of conflict as they sent x-ray pulses aloft.

Explosions filled the sky, smoking debris joining the fires on the ground. The enemy was taking terrible losses, but still they came.

Not that there were any real bombs, bullets or lasers. Everything was metaphor for destructive code working within the simulation. But the damage was real enough. Simulation spaces that Marita had copied from her long lost home were ripped and ruptured, data lost, resources expended. Marita feared this would be the last she saw of a world she'd worked on and lived in for years.

"Those damn flying things are saturating the defences," said Marita. Two explosions rocked the palace.

"Damn," shouted Philip above the noise, "they've worked out how to do artillery."

"One gattling tower down. Air units might be able to get through."

Another, bigger explosion, knocked them both off their feet, filling the room with smoke and rubble from a shattered wall. Many of the Leighs were caught in the blast, and lay broken and dying. The few remaining drew close to Philip and Marita forming a guard. The chattering of the gattling lasers could be heard more clearly now as they tried to fend off the viral air units seeking to land in the palace.

"We've lost," said Philip. "Time to pull the big red switch and leave!"

"Not yet. A little longer!"

"Get ready to fight then!" Philip brought his armour to full power, deploying wrist guns, shoulder turrets, and letting the drones off the leash. Their spherical bodies opened, revealing blades, saws and projectiles. Marita did the same, flashing a grim smile as their facemasks closed, sealing out the acrid smell of smoke, rubble, dust and death.

A moment later a dozen black spiny forms forced their way into the throne room through the holed wall. They were squat, broad-shouldered, standing on four legs. Roughly symmetrical heads swivelled as their five eyes took in the scene. Some of the Leighs moved forward, firing. One creature fell in a spray of black ichor, but others leapt forward and tore into the guards. Philip and Marita fired, ripping apart another creature, but their enemies drove on.

The two humans were driven back as the remaining guards were dismembered.

"Marita! We have to go!"

"No! We can do this!"

Five creatures remained. Two closed on Philip and the others dashed at Marita. Philip lost sight of her as they pounced on him.

His drones spat fire and tried to intercept the attackers as his shoulder cannon and wrist guns blasted them. The drones' whirling blades shredded one, but the other landed, one of its mouths enveloping his arm. His wrist guns fired on full automatic, blasting chunks of animal all over the room, and he was free.

The room was quiet save for the battle outside. On the other side of the room, where he'd last seen Marita, was a mass of black forms, moving jerkily. "Marita – oh Gods", Philip whispered to himself, staggering across the room.

He could hear cracking noises from beneath the creatures, the sound of bones being broken. He raised his guns just as a spray of fluid spurted, covering his faceplate. Disgusted, he wiped it away.

It was black, not red.

A blade emerged from the body of the nearest creature, then another, hacking through alien flesh and bones as Marita cut her way out.

She rose, covered in ichor but otherwise unharmed, two scythe-like blades emerging from the wrists of her armour.

"Finest adamantium," she said gazing lovingly at the blades. "It's so good when you control a world's physics."

"Can we go now?"

Marita sighed, giving her ruined palace one last look. "Yes. Big red button time."

The palace shook, the mountain rumbled. As Philip and Marita dissolved into the next sim, Olympus Mons, the biggest volcano in the solar system, awoke. Lava rivers, pyroclastic flows, earthquakes and landslides swallowed the palace and everything else on the mountain.

Boswell's stealthy crawl through enemy space was over. He had what he'd come for, but had been spotted. Now he was on the run, desperately switching location, phase and dimension to evade his pursuers.

He still spread his net of entanglement. He could use it to escape but it could do so much more if used at the right time. To use it now would allow the enemy to build a defence.

He had to survive, to escape to the human part of the ship. He now knew so much more, knew how close they were to success. All that was needed was one last push as the enemy closed in.

The endless desert night continued in Boswell's sim. Neither had full access to its controls so they couldn't bring day or raise the perceived temperature. They huddled in their battered body armour near the top of a dune, seeking shelter from the chilling wind, waiting for the alien plague.

"How long has it been?" asked Philip.

"Since Boswell left? One day, maybe two."

"Two days. At current slowdown that's nearly a thousand realtime years. We've lost. Boswell can't be coming back after so long."

"We don't know what speed he's running. It might be greater slowdown. We have to trust him. What else can we do?"

"Not much. We can't change how the dice roll." He shivered. "Some warmth would be nice."

Marita looked around at the arid wilderness. "Not a lot we can do about that."

The ground vibrated and there was a sound like distant thunder. "Earthquake? Olympus Mons?" asked Philip.

"No connection between the sims. I think they're finally manifesting." She staggered to her feet, bringing her suit's systems back to full power. Philip's headup revealed most of his supplies were redlining, and there was no recharger out here in the desert. "Showtime. Let's see what we can see."

Philip moved to his feet, but then another, stronger tremor tossed them to the ground. "Shit!" he said, crawling to the top of their dune, then peering over the edge. "Marita… They're here. I think we're finished."

In the distance two giant forms lumbered across the desert. Each was a mass of writhing tentacles and mouths, clutching and snapping at the air and the ground as foetid black ichor dripped from them to the desert floor.

"Gods," muttered Marita who'd crawled to lie beside him.

She scanned the horizon, finding at least ten more of the creatures, all heading inexorably in their direction. "So that's it. Can't be more than a couple of minutes before they arrive."

Philip sighed. "It was good while it lasted. I hope we gave them a run for their money."

"Not that anyone will know. Time for one last gesture." She stood, weapons systems primed, just as the nearest creature reached their dune, tentacles grasping, giant maws open and ready to consume them.

The scene shifted, their views distorting and pixelating as something went seriously wrong with reality. Philip felt his faculties evaporate – vision blurring, balance sickeningly skewing to the left, ears ringing and booming with distortion. Pain, disorientation and nausea engulfed him.

Is this what it's like to be consumed? His vision closed in, fading to black, until nothing was left and he gratefully fell unconscious.

Whitespace. The battle had torn their sims to shreds, so there was no going home. But Boswell was with them. "You really should not play with bug-eyed monsters," he said.

"What?" asked Philip sensing Marita's presence beside them. "What happened?"

"I think I managed to clean out the infestation, as well as finding out where we're going and that we're nearly there."

"You did?" said Marita. "How? Where? When?"

"I cannot tell you everything at once! Our destination is an extragalactic supermassive black hole. It was ejected from its host galaxy during a galactic collision billions of years ago, and carried a significant accretion disk with it. Therefore we have plenty of energy and material resources, especially since more material is being accreted from the intergalactic medium. Our nanomachines can build habitats around the black hole and computational spaces further out. Meatspace and codespace will both do fine."

"Will it be safe?" said Marita.

"Our enemies live inside the stars inside galaxies, so we're well away from them. They're made from self-replicating plasma vortices. The black hole's magnetic field scours the accretion disk so they can't live here. We planned all this before the infection took away our memory. As for their intelligence-destroying virus, even that has some limitations. It is not designed for quantum computing systems, and does not know how to deal with coherent entangled states. While it can run virtualized in any environment, even the human brain, you can pull some tricks with the underlying qubit layer. I spent a long time sowing entangled states through their code. When I decohered them, their systems fell apart, and the probe's garbage collector cleared them up."

"They're beaten?" asked Marita.

"For now. I am sure they will adapt, but we will be ready."

"You said we're about to arrive?" asked Philip.

"Yes. That was why we were woken, though the ship's systems were so damaged they could not work that out. Look…"

A window opened in the whitespace showing humanity's new home. A disk lit the sky, cool and red at the edges, hotter and bluer nearer the centre. And in the centre, blackness, highlighted by columns of Cherenkov-blue light jetting outwards, perpendicular to the disk.

"There's going to be a lot of work," said Philip.

"But a lot more help – the best and brightest people we could save," said Marita. "Maybe, with all this, the Big Rip won't be such a problem after all."

As the ship neared its destination, systems not used for a hundred million years started to wake. Antimatter drives fired and magnetic sails were unfurled to slow the ship. Nanomachines, inoculated against the information plague, were released to build a new home.

And then the stored humans were resurrected.

After the death of the solar system and a pause of 100

million years, it was time to restart human history.

Last Orders

Jim Mortimore

On Frostfire they shoot old dogs. Dogs of war ain't no different.
We just whine about it more is all. Maybe that's 'cos in the death
dogs know when it's time to go. In the same boat we always up
and make a fuss. Some say that's what makes us men. Me, I say
that's just what makes us stupid. Die easy or die hard. Either way
we gonna die, am I right?

When the enemy nova bombs killed Frostfire and my
beloved Selene with it, I was five-fourths fucked in a speakeasy
on Vapor, obsessively folding a used junk-food wrapper into a
triangle and tucking it into the end of a long line of similarly dead
wrappers. I had the whole wobbling, beer-soaked pile balanced
upright on the bar in blatant defiance of gravity while I scoped
out the joint with military-grade enhanced vision for a new mark
to tap up for a free foamy. Or six.

To be fair, the weak-ass point-oh-six gee they laughingly call
gravity here had about as much suction as the beer. Which wasn't
much, I can tell you. If it had been in any way respectable my
Leaning Tower of Pizza wouldn't just have been leaning and I
would've been similarly laid out, long and damp and snoring,
either under a table or, if I'd really tied one on, under the mag-lev

accelerator rings at the foot of Losers' Hill where Debby the Barkeep would've rolled me when my walk home finally shut itself down in mechanical despair.

So instead of dozing or being rolled, I was awake when Joker breezed into the bar, a grin big enough to eat shit spread across the scarred moon he calls a face, fresh from what some of us was apt to call a 'close encounter'.

"Thought you was on a date," some wit yelled.

"In this life there ain't but two things a man can count on," Joker announced. "A kiss from the woman he loves, and the bullet Luck wrote his name on. The trick is knowing which to dodge."

There was laughter.

Joker and I saw the elephant together at Katie's Wheel. Some say it was Joker his ownself that beat off that incursion, on account of his funnies being so bad the enemy deemed us uncivilisable as a species and gave the hell up that very same day. I hold that's a reasonable view, even if it ain't quite the exact truth, and not just because it tickled me to say so. Katie's Wheel was where Joker lost his arm and I lost both legs south of the knees. In any normal war that woulda been it for us, and to be honest I'd've counted myself as lucky as a bunny on sunny day in winter. 'Course, this weren't no ordinary war. And nobody knew the enemy was coming right back.

"Joker, you cynical fuck. I'd kick your ass if you weren't so full of beer you'd pop like a piss balloon."

Joker let out a delighted whoop. "Whadaya know. Thief made a funny. Barleycorn anyone?"

As I may have mentioned, the beer on Vapor has about as much punch as a fucking dust bunny. Lucky enough there's things an inventive patron can add to weak-ass beer. Shit that'll have said patron willing and able to do anything you care to name, and for your information that includes dancing the death-metal polka stark naked in a thunderstorm. And though every copperhead of the Eighty-Sixty Inglorious Armoured Bastards knew how to juice his molasses, Joker was born the Zen Master of the Art. He had uppers and downers and lefters and righters. He had outers and inners and spiral fractures and hemisphere ruptures. He had polkas and waltzes and silver dream racers and things there was no names for because the boys and girls what drunk 'em somehow lost the ability to talk about it afterwards, or if'n they did it was in English or Siriuse or some such mustered out horse-hockey. One lucky pie-eater – Slammer by name – actually claimed he'd crashed to Earth the previous month after getting high for a week on Joker-juice. The story included references so slurred and obscure even top grade military decryption algorithms could n'more than guess feebly at the meaning of his words. Neither story nor juice had ever been proven or replicated but given the timing of birth and paternity test results of Slammer's latest kid, nobody was ruling anything out. Joker sensibly kept his mouth shut and the tale quietly assumed the level of comforting urban myth.

With this in mind we mixed us a mess of beery molotovs and lit 'em up like it was the most natural thing in the world. And who's to say for grunts on furlough that weren't true. With Joker supplying the juice, them molasses burned like a holy rollin' sermon as they slid on down and the evening turned from the normal foggy mud colour of nights on Vapor to a sort of pleasant rainbowey glow.

The night wore on in that way nights do when John Barleycorn's involved. Jokes and brawls and failed pulls, and successful pulls. Someone broke out the dart board but that didn't last long. It was more fun to tune in the semiconscious Curly Joe's suit and then hurl darts at his head. That was funny all by itsownself without Joker rigging Joe's wetware so the suit field wouldn't shut down all the way. Curly Joe would have to laser those darts off or buy beers for a week if he didn't want to report back from leave looking like a porcupine fucking a sports store.

Somewhere over the last decade or so I learned to pace myself. Drinking was fun after all, and you couldn't drink if you was unconscious. I was a long march from sober, true, but still in the world enough to understand what I'd lost when the news I mentioned earlier rolled across the greasy vismats glued to every table by stains so old they was practically growing eyes.

The NEWS258 logo is orange and gold. At midnight plus ten, thirty after last orders and half that into what was shaping up to be a rowdy enough lock-in, every beermat in the joint lit up with the news that my wife and kid had burned on Frostfire. For a heartbeat the sight of all them lit up vismats was almost pretty. Then I puked. The fast-food came out faster'n it went in and the beer with it, what little my bloodstream hadn't already hogged for its ownself. I tried to sit down, then realised I was already sitting. No prizes for guessing where.

Joker made some crack about my ability to hold my liquor. And me with my hollow legs'n all.

The speakeasy went stealth.

Debby the Barkeep dumped the two pint glasses he was done holding in one fist down on the bar. In the silence the double click as glass met glass was about as loud as a baby nuke. Tattoos across his beer-stained knuckles read: *Dont fuk with The Pacifier.* For a split second I puzzled over why a mountain range like Debby should answer to a girl's name, then I jerked up onto the force fields I called my feet and landed a roundhouse on Joker's face that broke his nose for about the eighty-sixth time.

"Shid ban, nod by dose *again!*"

Joker's voice was aggrieved. Let it be so. The clever fucker should take more notice of his friends' habits and situations. If he didn't know why I was upset he deserved everything he got.

"Whad u gowan do dat vor?"

I hit him again because he had to ask.

Joker stared at me in amazement, eyeballs popped open, looking crazier'n a frog-licker on a four day frolic.

"Dob fugging do dat!"

I hit him again. A prize-winning shiner blossomed alongside his cauliflower nose. Droplets of beer foam and puke sprayed from my knuckles, stuck to his face.

"I *seb* —"

Debby the Barkeep swung his mountainous ownself across the bar, fists clenched into lumps of muscle approximating the size and power of land mines. Without missing a beat Joker and I swung together, left and right fists slamming into his face in co-ordinated movement that would have had the Banshee Ballet cringing with envy and putting their personal trainers on danger money. Debby's forward motion stopped abruptly, then swiftly reversed. In deference to the laws of inertia there was actually a moment when his upper and lower body was moving rapidly in opposite directions. Debby's eyes crossed with confusion, then rolled up so only the whites was visible. He uttered a pleasant, almost satisfied sigh.

"– dod do dat *agaib!*"

Debby spent the next two seconds falling to the ground and the rest of the evening under his own bar. Which was just as it should be. This fight was all ours, Joker's and mine. I grinned savagely. Right now there was nothing in all the fucking world I wanted more than the chance to deliver my so-called fucking *friend* a little respect.

I started to explain exactly what I was going to do to him. I managed maybe five words when Joker's force field arm-replacement moved in a short, savage arc and his fist connected with my

"– face it, love, you're gonna get your fucking ownself killed. I don't want you to get your fucking ownself killed. I want you to stay here and fuck me and have babies with me and get drunk with me and... fuck me some fucking more!"

Selene wasn't the most eloquent of women but the other things she did

with her mouth fair put tears in a man's eyes and love in the heart of a concrete statue. She was mine and I was hers and halle-fucking-lujah all the way to the bank of love.

"And in case you're wondering, you dumb horse, yes, I am fucking fucked off!"

"Honey... baby..."

"Don't you honeybaby me. Don't think I'm gonna wait for you 'cause I ain't! Think of the kid! He ain't even got a name yet! What if you get your ownself killed before you even know the little fucker's name?" Selene's hands found me. Pain appeared as if by magic. I swear she knew more weak spots than any drill sergeant or combat vet. "Think of them other sad fucks fighting for their kids. You don't want to make them kids grow up without their daddies do you?"

That thought hadn't crossed my mind – as a gestalt I'm not even sure the enemy had kids – but now she'd put it there I tried to work out how to tell Selene that she and the kid was more important to me than any alien and his kid, no matter how socially cooperative they was, at least if came to the crunch which, since we was officially at war, clearly it had.

"They give you software. In your head. Armour made of force fields. This tech, it... uses the enemy's power against them... keeps you safe..."

Selene didn't respond.

"... it can design and grow its own weapons..."

She said nothing.

"... respond to environmental factors..."

Her look was hard.

"... it can even replace your limbs if... well, you know..."

Her expression did not change. Realising my words was not having the effect I'd hoped for I finally shut up.

"You're such a fucking brochure."

She'd stopped swearing. That was bad. But maybe I could still pull it back.

"You wanna kill me. They wanna kill me. Seems like I only got one thing to live for."

I cupped her face with my palm, letting my fingertips rub her gently behind the ear. My other lifted to touch her just-swelling belly. At some point in the future that swelling would be a giant bulge, and I knew if I was to touch it then I'd be able to feel something we'd made together kicking in there fit to bust, and after that maybe, if I was real lucky, it would be a kid, my kid. Our kid. I tried to find words to fit those thoughts but the effort just made me dizzy. Selene looked right at me. Right into me. Her eyes were perfect, big as moons, hard as hail. There was a moment when time seemed to stop. My heart banged inside my chest.

"I love you," I said, because I just didn't know what else to say.

"You cheeky handsome fucker." She leaned in closer, as if to kiss me. She took my hands from her face and belly, placed them against her breasts, then pressed her whole body against me. "I suppose you think you're gonna get laid."

Relief flooded through me. I'd finally managed to –

She head-butted me square in the

face, splitting the skin along my cheekbone. Someone nearby shrieked. I suppose it was me, but who gave a fuck? It wasn't the pain. My suit managed that reasonably well. It wasn't the crunching noise as my cheekbone collapsed. It wasn't even the fact that my family was dead. My suit had planted that thought deep down in my psyche, somewhere I could dig it up later, if I still had a mind. If I'm honest the thing that made me scream was the awful fact that my best friend – my *best* friend in the whole, fucked up fucking *world* didn't know – couldn't be *fucked* to *remember* what fucking *planet* my wife and son lived on. Couldn't be *arsed* to even program it into his fucking *datafile*. The people I loved most in the fucking *universe* was burned the fuck up to a fucking crisp and fucking *Joker* didn't even know why I was fucking *mad.*

I chuckled, surprising myself. Somehow that many fucks made it funny. The image of my suit running herd on my nano-factories, having them turn one feeling into another, made me laugh suddenly. Blood from my crushed cheek spilled down my chin. I spat out more blood, then felt around the inside of my mouth with my tongue. By some miracle I'd managed to avoid losing any molars. Easy day for the Tooth Fairy then.

I laughed out loud.

My laugh broke the deathly silence of the speakeasy.

Let me tell you about Vapor. It was cold, damp, with a sky covered in fog and a ground covered in bars. It was a hoot, my friend, just a fucking gas from sign-up to payday. The only people lived here was cloud-miners and the soldiers who minded them. And that was us. the Eighty-Sixty Inglorious Armoured Bastards. Shuffled here on some godforsaken rotation to protect a bunch of rare heavy metals, then forgot about quick as blinking. HiCOM had it this world was important for fuel and raw materials for the war effort. The only action I saw was juiced up on furlough. And I couldn't have any of that because, dumb horse that I am, I love my wonderful Selene like I love life its ownself and have no desire to cause her pain. I'd been here a year already, trying to ignore the rumours that HiCOM had been hit and our location or even existence lost when the data burned. I used to wonder, surely they'd notice the lack of fuel, though, right? Then again the rail guns just kept flinging those barrels of con-HM out-system, so who the fuck knew. Anyway, that was back when I still gave a damn. Now I didn't wonder anything. I just served my shifts at the defence grid's orbiting cannon wall, got juiced at the speakeasy on furlough and listened to the passive newsfeed that was our only connection with the rest of the Halo whenever I was sober enough to make out the words.

The speakeasy itself was little enough to speak of. A prefab big enough for two hundred or so souls, with ammo crates for a bar, tunes only three centuries out of date, a bunch of memory-metal furniture, and more species of stains than a man cared to count. Behind the bar was Debby the Barkeep and the business end of a thousand-litre barrel of Old Horizontal. Occasionally us patrons would take bets as to which massed more, barrels or barkeep. No one had ever collected because the only idiot brave enough to ask Debby how much he weighed wound up fermenting inside the barrel of Old Horizontal, then later vaporised a near-orbit asteroid earmarked for mineral stripping while still drunk on fire-control, and consequently pulled three months of double-duty for squandering military resources.

That particular squaddie was Jonesy "Golden Shot" Maguire and he was right there in the speakeasy with the rest of the squad when my laugh ripped the silence up and threw it away. In fact I think he might have cheered us on somewhat the loudest of all. Payback I guess, since it was me and Joker got him soaked that one time.

As if at a signal, the speakeasy erupted. Hoots and jeers and catcalls and whistles and some disgusting noises I shall refrain from dignifying with names. The upshot of which was that Joker and I should bat seven bales of shivering shit out of each other and not stop until everyone *else* in the house had had enough.

Well that was just top rail by me. I blocked Joker's next punch and wapped him upside the head with a barstool. They're nailgunned down but that doesn't matter when you're wearing a suit. The seat folded neatly around Joker's head, spludged as he smashed back against the wall, and then began obligingly to reform, ready for my next swing.

"Dab hurb you dub hozz!"

"Learn to talk proper why don'cha. And by the way, fuck you."

We traded blows for a while. The suits took most of the impact but some got through. Both our factories kicked into overdrive, replacing lost blood with freshly synthesised plasma. The raw molecules for the transform had to come from somewhere. Joker and I lost about twenty pounds of body fat over the next ten minutes. For sure there was no bloaters in this man's army.

The crowd edged us on. I smacked Joker twice more with

the chair. He blocked the second blow and came back at me with a table. I took a hit there but managed to return fire with a five meter section of prefab 'crete from the front wall.

Fog rolled in through the hole, thick and greasy, filling the bar.

Alarms in my tac-screen warned me I'd run out of convertible body mass. I needed protein fast or I was going to bleed out. Leaving Joker to unwrap himself from the wriggling form of his own table, I leapt over the sleeping Debby and the bar he was snuggled up to, headbutting the barrel of Old Horizontal and gulping wildly as the greasy contents gushed forth. I had to drink a lot to replace the blood I'd lost. I believe I might have mentioned the beer was weak-ass and Joker was most definitely not. My head swam, then pounded. The factories kicked in and as the dizziness of blood loss abated somewhat I became aware Joker and half a dozen other guys had their heads under the barrel right along with me.

"Greedy little..." I groped for the word, "... shits," I slurred, smacking each and every one of them round the head with a not-entirely pain-free fist. "I needed this. It's –" I belched, "– mediceral. You make sure you fucking well pay for what you fucking well..." I belched again while trying to finish the sentence with a proper word and, fuckit, that just had to do.

"Fub be Jesus tib shib tabes libe your fubbing arbids."

Joker's voice was no less slurred than my own. I tried to explain to him that a) how would he know what my fucking armpits tasted like unless he was a fucking snifter and b) if he waited long enough – a year say – perhaps his suit nanos would convert his crappy sense of humour into the kind of punch a six year old might muster if he trained real hard for the rest of his life. I'm not sure quite what actually came out but Joker must of got the gist because he launched himself at me with such ferocity that we smashed the bar and barrel to shrapnel, and spent a fair time rolling around in the soggy remains.

By now the whole bar was egging us on, hooting and cheering and starting micro-brawls of their own as if jealous of the fun we was having. I couldn't remember the last time I'd seen a good bar-fight, let alone been the star of one. Then again I was hard pressed to remember my own name right about then, so maybe the thought was moot at that. Joker's jollypack had split open sometime during the fight and a month's worth of juice added itself to the gushing beer. The gulping doubled instantly. My peripheral motion detectors pulled up a brief image of Debby the Barkeep slurping booze in his sleep. I wondered briefly what kind of childhood produces an autonomic reaction like that, then shook my head to clear it of distractions before getting on with the business at hand. Just as well I did too because Joker had yanked the newsfeed from the wall socket and was coming at me with the live power cables. They crackled and sparked and fumed. Old Horizontal began to crackle and spark and fume right along with them.

I picked up Porno Moe, whose suit went instantly rigid, and smashed him as hard as I could into Joker's flank. Joker came back at me with a double-fist full of squaddies. I ducked - well, sort of tripped but ducked sounds better - and the squaddies took out what remained of the speakeasy front wall. Or maybe it was the explosion as the sparks from the power lines Joker dropped to pick up the squaddies ignited the beer pumps that took out the wall. To be honest by that time I neither knew nor cared. A lovely rosy glow lit up the horrid fog of Vapor and a similar rosy glow spread quickly through my belly.

My night vision kicked in as the lights blanked out. I scoped around for Joker. By now my bleeding had stopped but the pain was beginning to come back in waves. Fine. Time to take that sad sack and show him exactly what his fucking problem was –

An arm lashed out of the fog. I had a moment to grasp that Joker was holding something, then the razor sharp spear of 'crete from the shattered speakeasy wall tore into my chest and broke

"... my heart, you bastard, I'm telling you! The moment you put on that fucking uniform! And now you're wearing it home. In my house!"

"Hon... I thought we'd talked about this..."

"Oh we talked about it all right. But you didn't listen. You never fucking listen."

"It's one term, baby. In and out. Quick as blinking. You'll never know I'm gone."

"It's the kid. I know it's the kid. You're running away aren't you? Running away from your fucking responsibility. Jesus holy crapping Christ, I married a pansy."

I tried to get my thoughts in order. It was because I loved her so much that I was signing up. Because I loved our kid so much too – even if he hadn't quite arrived yet. People only fought for things they believed in, things they loved. That was right wasn't it? Countries, planets, the freedom to opt out of the enemy biosocio gestalt. They was all worth fighting for, right? I tried to explain it to her. Tried to tell her I wasn't leaving her, I was trying to make better worlds for us all to live in.

"But –" I said. I frowned. "It's –" I added.

She silenced me with a glance.

"If you break his heart like you just broke mine I'll break your face. And I don't care how handsome it is."

I sighed. She was letting me go. Finally. I'd finally got through to her. Finally, the woman I loved was on my side.

"Thanks, baby. You won't –"

She shook her head. Her look said it all.

I'm not giving you permission you dumb fucking horse. Break our hearts and we'll break

three ribs before slicing into my left lung and collapsing it like popped balloon. This time when I screamed the only thing to come out was a pathetic wheeze. Well. Wasn't *that* just dandy? Fucked family, fucked legs, fucked face and now a fucked lung to go right along with the rest. War was hell. Fucking *war* was fucking *hell*. I tried to say as much but all that came out was a frothy mess of beer and blood.

My suit walked me over to the fire. I stood in the flames for a while, insulated from the world while my suit used the energy to send the pain and fear packing. But as the fire outside died so the fire inside grew. My friend had done this to me. My best fucking friend. My fucking *best* fucking *friend.* Had fucking. Drunken. Done this. Asshole. To me.

I realised I was ranting aloud when the smell of cooking distracted me momentarily and silence returned. Debby did serve food at the speakeasy. Well. He cooked it and called it food. This didn't smell like that though. Actually it smelled kind of good. Then I remembered Debby himself had been sleeping off the double sucker-punch under the bar when it blew up.

The suit managed to stop me throwing up again. I guess it thought I needed the fluid or something.

A moment later the flames was gone. So was the bar.

My suit walked me out of the wreckage.

Joker was waiting, naturally. I imagined the indulgent smile smeared across his face. I thought about smearing that smile across the inside of his suit, and *that* thought made *me* smile.

Joker waved the force-field shaped like his hand towards the charred lump which had once been our home from home.

"I dig you gilled debby the bargeeb, you basdub."

"Grilled him? *Grilled him!* You smart-ass mother*fucker!*"

"Nod *grilled* hib. *Gilled* hib! You fuggig drug-ass dwad!"

I'd had enough. I picked Joker up and threw him into a nearby housing block. The building collapsed. There might have been screams. I never knew because the suit blocked distractions when it was operating properly. Both our suits was operating more than properly. There was a – very – strong tradition in the 8060 that involved certain – not exactly approved – suit mods. Not the least of which was disabling the auto-sober function installed by the military as a factory default setting.

"Dad? Did you say *Dad* you malicious fucking... callous...

fucking..."

Words failed me. Instead, I shouldered aside a couple of tons of wreckage, and with the suit censoring any distracting human debris grabbed Joker and hurled him about two hundred metres into the air. I craned my neck to watch him vanish into the fog and dusted my hands with satisfaction. Drunken fucker. Fucking drunken cheeky fucking fucker. That would show *him*.

Moments later my suit reported seismic activity. Tracking the disturbance to nearby downtown I found Joker waiting for me in the ruin of a dockside street. Houses and vehicles had been flattened. A cargo crane nested in the ruin of a tramp steamer. Most of the damage had been caused on impact. Joker's suit had done the rest. He was standing in a steadily deepening crater, one arm up, the force-field middle finger raised in a time-honoured gesture that even genocide would probably never kill. It hurt to scowl, what with my mashed face'n'all but I did it anyway. At the rim of the crater buildings and vehicles was folding up like wet cardboard before simply melting away. That wasn't good. Joker's suit had started to convert local mass into supplementary weapons.

"STAND DOWN!"
"DEACTIVATE YOUR WEAPONS!"
"YOU ARE BOTH UNDER ARREST!"

The voice blasted down from the fog above our heads. Two PC cruisers hung there, bullhorns blasting. It didn't matter which century you was born into, I found myself thinking, the bulls always had horns and the cruisers always had bullhorns. Bulls and horns. *Arriva!* Those bellyachin' chicken guts sounded like they was just about to have a conniption fit.

I flipped the assholes a friendly wave. Nothing to worry about here officer. Just a friendly fisticuffs with my best fucking *friend.*

The cruisers backed off as I waved. My suit told me their weapons had come on line. Sappernets shot down. My suit shot *them* down. Bang bang. They hit the ground. Bang bang. Fucking PCs. Fucking pansy-ass *sappernets* for fucksake. What the fuck was they *thinking?*

My vision greyed out for a second, then cleared. A tiny light changed from red to amber in my tac-screen. The suit was in pre-battle mode. The little amber light was there to reassure me that, had this been a real war zone, I would actually have been safer now than three seconds ago. I smiled. Better. Oh yes. My suit would never let me down. Not like my drunk-ass so-called wise-cracking fucked up mutherfucking *friend.*

The cruisers swung low *sweet chariot* backup nets deployed *come for to carry me home* for another run. Joker's suit and my suit swung together, his left and my right, twinned motions that ended in simultaneous weapons deployment which would have had the Halo Royal Guard whining jealously and begging their drill sergeants for overtime. When the PC cruisers smashed into the ground they'm done took out half a city block.

Our suits high-fived each other. Joker turned the movement into a jujitsu throw. When I landed – about a kilometre away – I took out an *entire* city block. Those fucking cruisers was *pansies.*

I clambered out of the crater my suit made of the wreckage. Light sprayed across my tac-screen. Suits was powering up right across town. There was a mess of 'em right close to where the speakeasy had been. My suit tossed a cluster bomb their way and lit me the fuck outta there.

A tiny mushroom cloud bloomed quietly behind me. I didn't care. I was half a city away scoping for Joker. This mutherfucking mess was his fault and he was going to pay.

A mag-lev goods train hit me across the back of the head. I saw stars, shook my head to clear it. The train weighed two hundred and eighty tons if it weighed an ounce. Good throw too. Say what you like about Joker but that fucker could fight the good fight. Any other day I'd have been stand up proud to call him my buddy.

263

My suit told me local military was trying to hack my firewall with a remote shutdown command. The little amber light turned red.

So did I. Mutherfucking pumpkin rinds. Couldn't they leave a soul alone for five minutes? Just five minutes of fucking privacy for a quiet little scrap with his best *friend?*

I swayed slightly, sweating. I felt sick again and my face really hurt. Suit took care of it all. I glowed.

Tanks blocked both ends of the street, called in by the bulls before we sent them blowhards packing. The ground erupted, then froze into twisted clumps. Matter coherers. 1090s. We called them glue-guns and they was designed to stop the suits acquiring weapons-mass. These fuckers weren't messing about. My suit lit out for a new source of mass, dropping a couple of baby nukes in its wake. The tanks took a trip to Company Q. They wouldn't be troubling me again.

I blinked. The world spun around me and not only because I was somewhat in flight, momentarily. I was somehow aware of the rest of the fight being conducted as if by two different people at the other end of a long echoey tunnel. Downtown was crawling with tanks. Half a battalion by the look of it, and where did they come from fuckdammit? I didn't care. My suit sapped them, grabbed them, turned them into city-smashers.

Joker and I grappled manfully in the wreckage of downtown.

I tried to tell him this whole no account ballsup was all his fault and I was going to teach him a lesson he'd never forget but my suit was blocking all communication to prevent further wireless intrusion.

I felt a momentary roiling sensation in my stomach. My legs – what remained of them – wobbled unsteadily. No doubt it would have been great to sit down for a moment. I couldn't though, because of the jets and nukes the local boys sent our way when I knocked the tanks into a cocked hat. My suit opened the ball on its own hook and took them out without troubling me for permission, using the resultant energy and raw mass from the ground to assume full battle configuration. I leaned on an office block to catch my wind, stumbling as it fell over. I cursed, feeling like a fool for losing my balance, and at that exact moment an ion stream which would have had a fair crack at vaporising me where I stood had I not fallen, glided past in silent eerie slow motion, levelling what remained of downtown and half of the business district three kilometres to the south.

I jumped. Actually we must both have jumped because I was dimly aware of great spears of light spread several hundred kilometres apart punching down through the fog. Some bright spark must have re-oriented the orbiting cannon wall to take us out. Well that was just bully. Try to stop a guy from having a little scrap with his buddy would they? A little off-duty malarkey would they? Mutherfucking fucking mutherfuckers.

My tac-screen showed me the ground from an orbital feed. I couldn't shake the image of a Christmas tree, all the lights flashing merrily. There on the top sat Joker, like the floozie fucking booze-angel he was.

"Ding dong!" I said merrily.

My suit caught a stray ion pulse, turning it and some continental bedrock into a planet killer. Not quite the ultimate response but certainly enough to take out the orbiting cannon wall. My tac-screen showed me huge chunks of the defence grid puffing into vapour, the remaining disconnected lumps falling from orbit into the ocean with the kinetic energy equivalent of ten million or so nukes. The tidal waves was quite pretty and very big. I worried they'd cause some real damage but they hardly made ten kilometres past the metropolitan district boundary.

"Ding fucking dong!"

I sat down, laughing fit to bust, and Joker's planet killer slid past – again in eerie silence – turning the fog to vacuum before vaporising first the top fifty metres of still-roiling tidal basin, then a low range of hills on which the city had been founded, before traversing with languid slowness the quarter-million or so kilometres between Vapor and the larger of its two moons. The large moon obligingly became a cloud of smaller moons, many of which seemed suddenly keen to pay their mother-planet a friendly visit.

"Aaawwww." I said, moved.

I sat there watching the spectacle, humming the words of a tune I'd heard in the speakeasy before it blew up.

"The sidewalks and the streets, the concrete and the clay,

"Beneath my feet begin to crumble, 'cos love will never die,

"Because we'll see the mountains tumble, before we say goodbye,

"My love and I... will be... in love eternally...

"That's the way... that's the way it's meant to be..."

Which of course made me think of Selene and the kid, burning up on Frostfire. My voice dried up and I began to cry. Fat tears slid out along my split cheek, burning, burning, burning.

Something massing as much as an office block crunched into the ground beside me. I cocked a glance. Joker's suit asked for a comm handshake.

"Jeez buddy, you loog lig shid. You wad a breag?"

"Fuck you Joker."

I cut the link, stumbled to my feet. My suit tracked and fired. Sunbuster. Ultimate fucking response. Fucking Joker. Fucking *history!*

Suit's aim was perfect. It was my drunkard's walk that made the shot go south, a perfect quartermaster hunter. The contrail hung level with the ground for a while, before sailing off the curve of the planet and sliding away into space.

"Fucking goddamn lucky *fucker!*"

The shoulders of Joker's suit heaved. Drunk as I was I knew that inside his suit Joker himself was laughing fit to bust. His head came up, the visor clearing to show that damnable grin. Joker's suit made external speakers and blared a sound loud enough to reach me as vibration through the scorched and still

shuddering ground.
"HAIR A THE DOG WOD BITCHER?"
I raised my fist to punch him
The sun went out first.

Sawbones found us there a long month later, Joker and me, best friends again, with our arms around each other, blissfully unconscious in the ruin of a world, cocooned by our wonderful, magical suits and the angel wings we'd made from the dead sun.

When I eventually awoke it was to see the face of another angel peering back at me.

"Selene," I said weakly. Fuck, I sounded like shit. "I thought you was –"

"Idiot," she said. She shook her head. *"Fucking* idiot," she added.

"But –" I struggled manfully to sit up. No suit. No legs. Maybe that was a good thing. Just this once I stayed down.

"The news report was an attack. Designed to breach the only part of the military machine that can't – and in all probability never will be able to – protect itself."

I blinked stupidly.

"The human mind, honeybaby." She tapped the side of my head with one perfectly hologrammed fingernail. "Though in your case I use the term very fucking loosely indeed."

I waited, willing her to smile. I knew if I waited long enough she would. Sure enough, eventually she did.

"They're letting you go."

"Wha –?"

"Compassionate leave, fool. Oh don't worry. You'll be back in your precious war soon enough. But you know the deal if you don't come back from *that.*"

Her face creased with sudden pain, and her arms cupped her gigantic belly.

"Now if you'll pardon me I have to give birth to your fucking son."

Time, time time.

I did mine. I got the fuck out of Dodge.

Time was a man had his own destiny at heart. That'n a hundred ways of keeping his honour. But this war ain't what it was. I hear they give you drugs now. Drugs to make you do what the suits want. They say it's safer that way.

The same "they" tell us we're winning but I have my own opinion. God knows as long as I keep my mouth and all my wetware shut I'm still entitled to that. And I could forgive you for saying, ol' Thief, yeah, that Sunday soldier's absquatulated at last, somewhat fruitloop, true, but stone free on a Company Q pass all the same, so what does he care? Reckon I could understand you saying that. Except for one thing.

On Frostfire we got stars thick as bugs on a bumper. Prettiest nights in the Halo. But just lately it seems every night there's a few less stars in the sky.

For a while after I got out I counted them that was left. Something in me, maybe that selfsame demon as drove me to drink bad like I done that one time on Vapor, wanted to know. How many there was left, how long we had. But that job's like trying to drink the sea dry. I don't do that no more. I just thank Luck for whatever small mercies I'm due, tell my wife and kid I love 'em, and bless 'em every day they don't judge me for what I done. In the death what else can a man do?

Now quit bellyachin'. It's long past bed time for a kid your age and I'm about done jawing. Lights out and no sneaky watching the Cartoon Channel on that beer mat I know you got stashed under your pillow.

Your mother and I got business to attend to.

Songbirds

Martin Sketchley

Back to school tomorrow. The holidays go so fast. Mom's ranting because I'm looking for Literacy homework. I was supposed to do a book review, but haven't even read it all yet. It's all right for Mom. All she has to do is a bit of ironing and stuff.

I find my bag behind the settee, underneath the window. Daniel's in the garden, throwing his football up against the hedge and the shed. Always scoring the winning goal. Always man of the match. The wind blows blossom from the tree on to his hair and sweatshirt. He looks like he's been to a wedding.

I stick my tongue out at him as he walks towards the kitchen, bouncing his ball. Last week it hit the bird box and a load of bees came out. They bobbed around, all buzzy and mad. He ran inside and slammed the door. It wasn't half funny. Last year we had blue tits. I wish we had blue tits this year.

Mom's still going on when Daniel walks in. Says I should have got my homework done during the holiday, not left it this late. Daniel says yeah, Kate, you should've done it ages ago not left it this late. I tell him to get stuffed. Mom tells us to pack it in or there'll be trouble. Daniel gives me the v-sign as he leaves the room. He's such a smart arse. Just cos he's a couple of years older than me.

Dad's comes in and throws his keys on the sideboard. Says he thinks there's something wrong with the car. Makes a funny noise when it pulls away, he says.

I ask if that means he'll get a new one.

Sure, why not? A nice Aston Martin maybe.

Very funny.

A boring day. History. Numeracy. PE. I hate PE. All that running and jumping. I quite like badminton, but we don't get to do that much. I'm still tired. The birds woke me up at six. I like to have my window open at night, but six in the morning? Do me a favour.

The class show-off's telling everyone how she was up until three drinking black coffee and watching movies. Calls Fisher a racist when he says he doesn't like black coffee.

Break time. Chloe keeps asking me to take messages to Mark Moran because Mrs Johnson's confiscated her mobile. It's so embarrassing. Mainly because he's always with Steve Jenkins. They whisper to each other whenever they see me coming. Ask if I'm all right and giggle like idiots. They think they're so special.

Chloe hands me another note on a folded piece of A4 and tells me to take it over to him. Like, what did your last servant die of?

Home. Time for a bit of Facebook while Mom's in the bath.

Chloe's tagged photos of me.

Oh my God! Snogging Steve Jenkins at Melanie's party! She must've taken them with her phone! Oh my God! I'll kill her! Manda's tagged one Chloe and Mark Moron but it's just a pile of coats.

Someone's coming. The door opens. Daniel.

He spots the photos. 'What's all that then?'

None of your business. He leans towards the screen. I grab a folder and hold it up to cover the pictures but he pulls it away. Well well, he says. Who would've thought it? Get lost, Daniel.

'You going out with him?' he says. 'Bit young aren't you?'

I tell him no I'm not a bit young actually, and no I'm not going out with him. Not any more.

Heat in my eyes. Damn.

Daniel's looking at me. Asks if I'm all right. I tell him yeah sure. Really? *Yes*.

'Has he done something?' he says.

I shake my head.

A moment's silence. Then Daniel says that if Steve Jenkins or anyone else ever upsets me or does anything I don't like then I'm to tell him and he'll sort them out. Okay?

Okay.

Promise?

Promise. Thanks.

He turns and goes, then pokes his head back around the door and mumbles something about Mom wanting me up in the loft. I ask what for but he's already gone.

I wipe my eyes and wander out.

They're both up there, in Daniel's room with the skylight window open and the lights off.

I like it up here. I'm not allowed in Daniel's room but sometimes I go in when he's not here. Just to get one over on him without him knowing. There's the toilet, then the other room's full of junk and Dad's books. I sometimes go in there with my iPod when I want to get away from everyone. It feels really safe and calm.

Mom looks at me. Big grin on her face. Come and look at this, she says.

I squeeze between them. Daniel tells me to watch it and makes out like I've jabbed him in the arm or something. He's so dramatic.

Mom points. There are these lights in the sky. Silvery circles, just hanging there. I can't tell how big they are or how high. I say they're weird. Mom says she thinks they're amazing. Beautiful. She's always coming out with stuff like that.

Dad's come up. Wants to know what we're all doing up here. Mom shows him the lights. Probably some kind of "atmospheric phenomenon", he says. *He's* always coming out with stuff like *that*.

Mom tells me to go and get my camera, but when I come back up the silver things don't appear on the screen. The battery's charged and everything. There must be something wrong with it.

Typical.

Dad's gone to work. Mom's sitting in front of the telly in her dressing gown. It's all over the news, she says. Those things in the sky. I ask her what's going on but she shushes me and points at the TV.

They say there's no reason to panic. Think it's a natural thing. Like Dad said. They're sending planes up and doing stuff with satellites. Keep interviewing people who haven't got a clue what's going on but have to say something. This woman astronomer. Some science fiction writer.

Daniel's sitting on the settee swinging his red and white school bag. He asks if this means we can stay at home. He's not scared or anything. He's just trying to get out of a cross-country run.

Mom says no way. Get your shoes on. She's going to get dressed then it'll be time to go. Otherwise we'll be late. Again.

Geography. I hate geography. All that weather and stuff. And Miss Parsons is grade-A useless. She forgets the end of half of her sentences.

A knock at the door. It's the Head. Everyone shuts up. She gets Miss Parsons over to one side. Someone throws a ball of paper that bounces off the white board and lands on the desk.

People gradually start talking again but the teachers don't

notice. The Head's whispering to Miss Parsons. Miss Parsons looks worried. She says something, then the head nods, touches Miss Parsons' arm and walks out.

Miss Parsons turns, clears her throat and claps her hands and tells us to settle down, settle down, please, come on now this is important.

She says the school's closing early. A cheer. Parents are being phoned to come and collect us. I ask why but she doesn't hear me. It'll be in register order, she says.

My surname begins with S, so I'm right near the end.

Typical.

Got my coat and bag. Just waiting for mom. I'll send Chloe a text.

Wots goin on

A quick reply.

? mom ses all skools closin lol

Big help.

Mom's here. She says hello, thanks the teacher then grabs my hand and we *run* to the car. I've never seen Mom run. She's not the running type. Falls over at anything faster than a stroll.

Then I notice that everyone's running.

All the moms. Running to their cars like they're giving away wine at Sainsbury's.

One kid points at the sky. I look up. It's full of really dark cloud. Almost black. Not just dark grey, but proper black.

As we pass the hedge at the edge of the car park I see a bird on the ground, fluttering its wings as if it's hurt. Poor little thing. I tell Mom and ask if we can help it but she just pulls me on.

As I'm fastening my seat belt I ask what's going on. Mom says she'll tell me later.

I put the radio on. There's no music. Not even the normal DJ. Just some bloke talking. He sounds dead boring. Says it's a public announcement and will be repeated. Mom turns the radio off. We don't want to listen to that, she says. Let's just have some quiet for a change, shall we?

Dad's home. I ask why he's back so early. He says it's a half-day holiday, but I can tell he's lying.

The curtains are closed. I ask why the curtains are closed. Mom says she's got a headache. I turn a lamp on but Mom turns it off again. It's so dark. I try turning the TV on but it just clicks.

Dad keeps looking between the curtains. Mom tells him to stop it. He's keeping an eye out for Daniel, he says. Then he says he's going to go out and look for him. Mom says he can't. No-one's supposed to go out. They said on the TV. We're supposed to wait until they tell us what to do.

Until who tells us? Why?

Dad says he doesn't care. He's going anyway.

I ask why don't they phone him, but Mom says Daniel left his phone in his room this morning because he was rushing to get his PE kit together.

The one time he actually needs it for something important.

Typical.

Suddenly there are noises outside, like electricity or something, and these really bright flashes.

Mom lets out this shriek. Like when you stand on a dog's tail. Dad looks between the curtains then turns and tells us to get under the dining table.

What?

He tells me it's a bad storm and we should get under the table because that's the safest place. Mom looks at him. I know he's lying. We never hide under the table during a storm. He usually goes up in to the loft and watches. He loves lightning.

But this time he's scared. I can see it. He's really scared.

Mom's kind of crying and mumbling about Daniel.

As I go to the table I look out of the window into the back garden.

It's so dark outside, even though it's only about two o'clock.

The patio's covered in this black stuff. Like the soot in Grandma's chimney. And there are these dark lumps falling. Like little bags or something. I look closer.

Birds.

I tell Dad. Both he and Mom look. Silence. Then Dad says something about poison. Chemicals.

I ask what does he mean, poison?

He just says we should get some sheets and wet them. Mom asks why. He says if we hang wet sheets around the table they'll act as a filter. If there's poison stuff in the air, he says, they might stop it getting to us.

Sometimes he talks rubbish but sometimes my dad's really clever.

Mom goes to fetch some sheets. Dad goes into the kitchen and runs water into the sink.

I sit and look at the birds.

Quiet now. We've been here ages. The wet sheets smell funny and have turned grey. Sometimes we can hear someone running along the pavement outside, or someone shouts, but mostly it's silent. The flashes have stopped, too. It's as dark as the middle of the night, but it's still only about six.

Then Dad says he's going out to look for Daniel and no one's going to stop him. He's got a decorator's mask he's going to wear. Just in case.

He tells us to stay put, then gets out from under the table and goes.

Mom looks really scared. She calls after Dad. Tells him to be careful.

I tell her it'll be okay. Dad'll find Daniel and be back in no time. She smiles and touches my hand. Yeah, she says. No time.

Dad's just back. Daniel's not with him. I ask if he found him but he doesn't say anything. He looks terrible. I can see him shaking. He and Mom go into the kitchen and start whispering.

I sneak across to the door. Listen at the gap. Can't hear everything. Just bits and pieces.

Terrible, he says. Never seen anything like it. Black ash everywhere. Dead bodies in the road. People burned. Others crying for help. Burned-out cars. Trees that look as if they've been struck by lightning. People scavenging like animals. Says he had to run at one point.

They're quiet for ages. I can hear Mom sobbing and asking where Daniel is. Dad says he doesn't know.

More silence.

Then Dad says he thinks we should hide. Mom asks where. The loft, he says. Daniel's room. They can't search every house. If we hide long enough we'll be okay.

I'm not sure who "they" are. The police?

Has Dad done something wrong?

I walk into the kitchen and yell at them: 'Will you *please* tell me what's going on?"

We're going to have to tell her, Dad says. Mom just nods, wipes her nose with a tissue and turns away.

Tell me what?

It's those silver discs we saw in the sky, he says. There's been a kind of war.

Like the Second World War? We did that at school.

He says not quite like the Second World War. The people in the silver ships aren't from Earth.

When I say "cool" Dad tells me it's not cool at all. They've come and killed a lot of people and a lot more have gone missing. That's what they said on the radio. When it worked.

I ask if they've killed Daniel. He says he doesn't know.

I say maybe he's been taken somewhere safe.

Yeah, maybe.

We're up in the loft. Dad says we mustn't turn on our mobile phones because they'll probably be able to track the signal and find out where we are. He says we can use the toilet, but can't flush it in case we're heard. He's dead serious.

Dad dragged up a couple of mattresses and made us carry all the food from the kitchen in plastic storage boxes. Mom brought up a couple of games and a pack of cards and I got my iPod and my school books. Got homework. Might as well do it while we're up here.

Mom said to pile all the frozen food together to keep it cold. She's put as much of it as she can into the cool bag and that posh picnic hamper Grandma gave us.

Dad says we've got to ration the food otherwise we'll run out in just a few days. A few days? I ask how long we're going to be here. He says he's not sure. We've just got to sit it out. The government will do something. Maybe other countries will send help.

What if other countries are in the same situation?

Dad doesn't answer. He goes down to the bottom of the stairs. He's got everything he could find of a reasonable size and is piling it up against the door at the bottom. Daniel's desk and chair. The cabinet from the bathroom. The laundry basket. He says if he wedges it all together between the wall and the door, then the door shouldn't budge.

No one's getting up here in a hurry, he says.

Mom tries to make light of it. Says we can pretend we're on a picnic. Or camping.

But she's always hated camping.

Then Mom fakes a smile and asks me if I want to play cards. I really don't want to play but I think she does so I say yes okay then. She asks Dad does he want to play, but he just keeps looking out of the window.

We play hundred-and-one. I like that game but it's not much fun with just two people.

Daniel likes hundred-and-one. He's not very good, though. You can always see his cards.

Dad says he's going to have to go out and find some water because we're already running low. There's nothing coming out of the tap and all the pop's gone.

Mom says he can't. She's quite upset. Kind of panicky. Dad's asking her what she thinks we're going to live on if he doesn't go out to find some. They're arguing. It's kind of a weird row, though, because they know they can't shout in case they're heard. They're just whispering loudly at each other.

Mom's crying now. Dad's trying to comfort her. Says he has to go. Says he'll knock three times when he comes back so we know it's him. Twice on the pipes, he says. Mom laughs and sniffs tears.

I don't get it.

Dad was gone ages. He went when it was dark. Reckoned it'd be safest in darkness. He took a few empty pop bottles and my plastic wind-up torch.

He's all sweaty. Says it was really weird being outside. There was no noise at all – no cars or planes or sirens or anything. No lights. No joggers or dog-walkers. Absolutely silence. And this layer of black ash stuff everywhere. He's got it on his shoes and jeans. Mom brushes it away then wipes her hand on a tea-towel but it won't come off her fingers.

I ask if he saw Daniel. Dad shakes his head, looks down.

He says he ran a bit, then hid and waited to check there was nothing about then ran a bit more, but the bottles were pretty heavy. His arms ache from carrying them, he says.

The water's gross. All green with bits floating in it and these little wiggly things. He says he got the water from the pond in the park. That pond's got dead fish in it. Mom says we can't drink it but Dad says what choice do we have? We'll have to strain it through a pair of tights or something.

I ask him if the torch worked. He says yes it did, thank you. I doubt it was much good, though.

Dad yawns. Says he's worn out. Let's get some sleep, he says. We can sort this out in the morning.

Woken suddenly by a loud noise. Dad's looking at me. Eyes wide. Finger to his lips.

He gets up. Slowly, quietly, walks towards the bedroom door. Opens it. Listens. Creeps down the stairs. Me and Mom go to the loft door. Watch him go down. He steps over the stair that creaks. Stops by the door. Looks up. Waves one hand: stay there.

Voices. Muffled. Don't sound deep enough to be men, but too deep to be women. Maybe it's kids.

Or *them*.

A few seconds pass. Then the door handle moves. And again. Dad just looks down at it. Mom pulls me against her. Grips my arm with her black fingers.

The door moves slightly, as if they're pushing against it. But Dad's wedged the stuff really tight.

The door handle stops moving. There's no more noise.

We watch and wait. Wait and watch.

Can't sleep. Those voices freaked me out. I slept for a while but dreamt that Daniel was banging at the door that Dad's barricaded up only we couldn't hear him and he was surrounded by burned bodies.

There's a woman screaming in the distance. Sounds like it's coming from the direction of the church. It's horrible.

Dad's up at the window but says he can't see anything. Pitch black, he says. I ask what pitch is but Mom snaps at me to stay down and keep quiet or it'll be us screaming next.

We've just got to lie here and listen to it.

I hate it here.

How long will this last?

Woke early. The blind's still partly open. I'm lying on the mattress looking at the sky through the loft window. It's just grey. There are tiny spots of rain on the window with little bits of black grit in them.

I get up and look outside.

There's a group of them walking along the middle of the road!

They're like us, with two arms and two legs and hands and feet, but different as well. I'm not sure how. Stretched or something. They're wearing overalls like Dad wears when he's decorating, only a dull silver instead of navy blue. And with feet in them, like soft shoes. Clear masks cover their faces so I can't see them clearly. They're carrying what must be guns, and these little bags. They can't see me. They're just walking up the middle of the road looking around. They're not making any noise.

Then one of them turns and I can see its features.

It's SO weird. Like its eyes and mouth and nose are all squished together. But the eyes are sort of slanted.

A machine is following them. Not like anything I've ever seen before. Sort of a cross between a tank and one of those army lorries with an open back. It's not on wheels, but rolls along on spikes. The front's smooth, like that train they have in Japan.

I can see people in the back. A couple of them are either unconscious or asleep. Their hands and feet are tied with clear cable. A woman's crying. A few men. Some old, some young. There's a few kids, too. A girl my age in a dress that looks half burned. A little boy sucking his thumb. Then behind the machine, more of the creatures.

They must be finding people and taking them somewhere.

Maybe that's where Daniel is. Can't see him in the truck, though.

I watch them go past and up the road until they're too far away for me to see.

Breathe again. Shaking. Feel a bit sick.

I look back at Mom and Dad. They're still asleep.

I don't think I'll tell them. Don't want to worry them.

Dad's going to go out to try and find some more water. Going as soon as it's properly dark. Says he'll try to find some cleaner water this time. I tell him to leave it. Wait and see what happens.

I don't want him to get caught by those creatures.

He says he'll be fine. Says he might break into a shop or something. I can't imagine Dad doing that. I don't think I want him to. He might get arrested.

He says to remember the special knock. Three times, I say. Twice on the pipes, he says.

Midday. The sun's out but Dad's still not back. Maybe he couldn't find any water and had to go further this time.

Mom's lying on her mattress facing away from me. I don't know if she's asleep.

I've got my phone from under my pillow. Running my thumb over the keys. Look across at Mom.

I press and hold the power button. The phone lights up.

A signal. Wasn't expecting that.

I'll send Chloe a quick text.

r u ok

Turn it off again straight away.

They can't have picked it up that quickly.

Can they?

Been asleep for a while. Still no sign of Dad. Looks like Mom's still asleep. I turn the phone on again.

No reply from Chloe.

I turn it off and try to get back to sleep.

There's a noise. Outside. A deep sound. Like a tractor or something. Mom jumps up and opens the blind a bit and peeps out. A helicopter!

I get up next to her and look out. It's one of those big army ones that has two propeller things on top. Going pretty fast. The door on the side is open. This guy's crouching there, wearing a helmet with a curly cable leading away from it.

It's gone in a few seconds.

Mom looks at me, all bright-eyed and excited. Asks me if I know what this means. I say it means they didn't see us. She says no, it means there are people still out there somewhere. People who'll come and rescue us.

She paces back and forward squeezing her black fingers.

Where's your dad? she says. He'll be so relieved.

Slept better last night but have still woken early. Dad's still not back. There's a funny smell.

Mom's facing away from me. I call her but she doesn't turn. I get up and walk over to her.

She's a really funny colour. Like metal. She's been sick in the night. It's all down the side of her face and on the mattress. The hair on her forehead is all wet. She coughs - a real wheeze.

I get a cup of that rank water. Look at it. I can't give her that.

Get a flannel. Wet the corner and clean her face where she's been sick. Wet her lips a little. I saw someone do that in a film once.

I look through all our toiletries and things. There's Dad's shaving stuff. Shampoo. Plasters. But no paracetamol. We always have paracetamol.

I wish Dad was here. Or Daniel.

I open the blind slightly and look out. Nothing's moving. Not even a wind in the trees.

Mom coughs again. I look at her. I'm going to have to go and get some medicine for her from somewhere.

I lean over her. I'm going to go and get you some medicine, I say. She just kind of wheezes.

Open the door. Creep down the stairs. Step over the creaky one like Dad did.

Pause at the bottom. Hold my breath. Press my ear to the

crack.

Nothing.

I look back up. Mom coughs. She sounds terrible.

I'll have to be quick.

It's just like Dad said. Spooky. No sign of anyone. All this black powder on the ground. Even the birds have stopping singing. Or maybe there aren't any birds any more.

The houses are all so dark they look dead. Cars abandoned in the road with their doors open.

Have to keep watching the sky and the streets. They could be on foot or in their machines. They could be anywhere.

There's a bag someone's dropped. I pick it up. A school bag. Empty lunch box. A few books. I put it on a wall in case the owner comes past this way again.

A noise. I turn.

The helicopter! Can't see it, but it's loud. Must be close.

Suddenly it appears over the houses. The same one as before. The same man sitting in the door.

I run. Shout. Wave my arms. It's going fast and I don't think it's going to see me but then the man in the door waves one hand then touches his throat and the helicopter suddenly tips on to one side as it begins turning. Its propellers make a huge noise. A real thudding sound. It turns so steeply I can see the top of it.

They've seen me!

I can take them to Mom and make her better. We can look for Dad and Daniel. Get out of that stinking loft.

The helicopter disappears over the houses then reappears, heading towards me. Level now. Slowing down. Can't see the man in the door any more. He's on the other side.

They're going to land on the playing fields.

I run faster than I've ever run before. So fast the wind makes my eyes water.

I reach the road. Stop to check for traffic.

I look back towards the copter. It's just a bit higher than the trees now. Hovering.

Then a line of white light appears from somewhere behind the houses. It touches the helicopter and part of it explodes and there's a big woof of smoke and flame and the engines make a weird high-pitched grinding sound and the helicopter drops behind the houses, straight down.

A huge rolling ball of black smoke and fire rises into the sky. I just watch it. Folding and rolling. Rolling and folding.

Haven't got the strength or breath to cry.

I turn and look back along the road. As I wonder if maybe I should go back to her one of the silver craft appears above the rooftops. I jump across the nearest garden and into the entry between two houses.

I peer around the corner of the entry. The machine moves so smoothly, silently. It drifts towards the smoke rising from the playing fields, hovers for a few seconds, then glides away.

I move right to the back of the entry where it's dark.

I'll sit here a while. Until I'm sure they've gone.

I must've fallen asleep. It's fully dark now. Cold too. My backside's numb. Legs stiff.

I look towards the end of the tunnel. A wind rustles the trees.

Mom. I wonder how Mom is. Still haven't got any medicine for her. Should I go back or carry on? Go back or carry on.

I think I should carry on. I think Dad would want me to carry on.

I'll wait until it's a bit lighter.

Walking through the park. It's sunny now but windy too. A good drying day, my Nan would have said. I think I see some more of those silver ships in the distance but realise they're just clouds. I keep looking at the sky, glancing behind me.

The wrecked helicopter's ahead, crumpled and black. Like a giant slug. The propellers are all droopy. There's the shape of someone slumped in the cockpit and a burned body on the grass. Legs all bent the wrong way. Shrivelled curly cable leading away from him.

I'm so busy looking at the burnt body I don't notice the man standing near the hedge. I stop walking as soon as I see him. He's just standing there, looking right at me. He smiles. Waves. I don't know what to do.

I wish Dad was here.

He walks over to me. His face is kind of stubbly and he has dark bags under his eyes. But his eyes are nice.

'Hello,' he says.

'Hello.'

'What's your name?'

I tell him.

He tells me his name's David. Asks me what I'm doing. Think. Think. Do I tell him the truth? If I don't tell him the truth what do I tell him?

He's got nice eyes.

'I'm trying to find some medicine,' I tell him. 'For my mom. She's ill.'

He looks behind me, as if someone's there. I look back. No one.

'Where is she?' he says.

'At home. In the loft. We hid.'

He nods. Understands. 'I've got some medicine you can have,' he says. 'Some paracetamol. Some stuff for upset stomach. Want some?'

'Yes please.'

He jerks his head towards the line of trees at the edge of the park. 'It's in my den.' He smiles. 'We should get out of the open anyway.' He looks around at the sky. 'If one of their machines comes along they'll spot us. Come on.'

He turns and walks away. Stops. Looks back at me. 'Come on, then,' he says. 'Do you want this medicine or not?'

I look back towards the helicopter. 'Those men. They're

dead.'

He shrugs. 'Nothing we can do for them then, is there.'

I suppose he's right.

His den turns out to be an old tin hut thing covered in soil and grass. He tells me it's an air raid shelter from the Second World War. It's rank inside. Stinks. I can smell him in here. Beef and onion crisps.

He's got a couple of gardening chairs, a small table, gas lamps. A great big plastic container with a tap in the bottom. Half-full. Looks like water. A little fridge that runs off a car battery. A white gas stove with a grill and a big blue bottle next to it. It looks ancient. As old as this shelter.

There's some food in a Tesco shopping trolley. Bread. Tins of stuff. Beans. Soup. Bottles of lemonade.

Chocolate.

David asks me if I want some beans on toast.

'I better get back,' I say. 'I've been gone all night. I should get back to my mom. If I could just have the medicine?'

He tells me I look starved and pale. Tells me I should have something to eat. Five minutes, he says. That's all it'll take.

He's opening a tin. Getting a saucepan. Lighting the gas. He looks at me. Smiles.

Guess I am starving.

Okay, I say.

He puts the toast under the little grill. Lights it. Opens one of the bottles. It fizzes. He pours a glass and hands it to me. 'Thanks.' I take a sip. Lemonade.

Delicious.

He leans back against the cooker, arms folded.

'So, Kate,' he says. 'Have you seen many other people?'

'No. We heard some voices when we were up in the loft one time but we waited and they went away.'

He nods. Turns away from me. Stirs the beans. Checks the

toast. It smells great. My mouth's watering already.

'Best to avoid people,' he says. 'You can't trust anyone these days. Not that you ever could. I don't have any butter, I'm afraid, but if I put the beans on the toast it'll soften up. That okay?'

I nod. My stomach rumbles. I haven't eaten anything hot for days.

He places a steaming plate of beans on toast in front of me and gives me a knife and fork.

I begin to eat. It's the greatest thing ever. My whole body suddenly feels warm.

He sits down opposite me. Smiles. Nods towards my plate. 'That nice?'

'Amazing.'

He smiles again. Picks up my empty glass. 'I'll get you another drink.'

I cut the last piece of toast in half, fold it on to my fork, load it with beans and put it into my mouth. The sauce from the beans has soaked into the bread and it's all juicy, just like he said. Some of it dribbles down my chin. I wipe it with my sleeve.

I put the knife and fork together on my plate and lean back in the chair.

David gives me another glass of lemonade and a bar of Dairy Milk. I drink half the lemonade. Tear off the chocolate wrapper and take a bite. It's amazing. I drink some more lemonade then stop. David smiles. 'Drink it up,' he says. 'I've got plenty.'

I drink the rest down. As I hand the glass to him I notice this gritty stuff in the bottom. Like that stuff Mom takes when she's got a bad headache.

David puts the glass down then turns and looks at me, arms folded.

I feel kind of weird. Like my head's numb. I'm a bit dizzy. Mom said you get a bit dizzy when you get drunk. Am I drunk?

I look around.

Not sure where I am.

This guy's looking at me. Smiles. He had nice eyes.

He's speaking but I can't hear what he's saying. It's like I'm underwater or something. Head's heavy. Feel like I need to sleep.

Lean forward to rest my head on the table. Beneath the shopping trolley there's a load of stuff. Coats. Trainers.

A red and white school bag.

Moving. Look down. Shopping trolley. I'm sitting in a shopping trolley. The man's pushing. Can smell his sweat stink.

Some of those silver disk things ahead. In the playing fields. Ramps leading down. Like mouths with tongues. Lights. People in grey suits. Trucks and things.

Can't keep my eyes open.

Feel a little better, but still tired.

We're going up one of the ramps. David swears and grunts.

Going inside. Want to climb out of the trolley but got no energy.

People in grey suits gather as we approach. Suits shine like metal. Like the side of the ship.

One of them points with a long stick like a metal bar and electricity leaps from it and my entire body stings.

Inside now. Not in the trolley any more. Floating inside some kind of bubble. Like a gigantic washing-up liquid bubble. Naked. Cold.

One of them is guiding the bubble with one of the metal sticks. A big spark jumps from it every so often. Sends sparks through the bubble and makes my skin burn.

Huge corridor ahead. Long and wide and dark. Tanks on either side. Great big cylinders full of green stuff. Like that water.

Looks like there's people inside. Can't hardly see them in the murk. But they look like real people. Like me. Not them. Rows and rows of them stretching way back. Must be thousands.

They guide the bubble next to one of the tanks. More of

them are waiting.

They gather round. Look down at me.

What do they want?

What are they going to do to me?

Another shock and the bubble disappears and I fall to the floor. One points his stick at me and a little bolt of light leaps out and every part of my body hurts. Another kicks me. I try to crawl away but there's another one behind. The one in front waves his hand towards the tank. His fingers look too long and seem to have too many joints.

Another kick. I stand. Would like to kick back. But they look so evil.

Shoved towards the tank. The side's open now. It wasn't before. They kick and push and use their electric sticks to force me inside. Then the cylinder closes. Just sort of flows back across from nothing.

They look in at me. I wonder what they're saying.

I wonder where Dad is. In one of these tanks? Daniel?

There's this bubbling noise. I look down. This thick green gel stuff is coming up through holes in the floor of the tank.

It's rising so fast. Already up to my knees. My waist. Thick and sticky. Like treacle. It stinks.

Up to my chest. My neck. It's not going to stop.

It's rising over my chin. Tip my head back. Keep breathing. Try to kick my legs but can't float because the stuff's so thick.

It's going into my mouth. Got to swallow.

The tank is completely full but I'm still awake. Not holding my breath. Not breathing either. Just floating.

I can see them. Outside. Looking in at me with their stupid faces. All eyes and mouths.

One of them touches something on the side of the tank and the gel gets thicker, firmer. It presses against me. Squeezes my whole body. Like some huge hand's holding me. Lines appear in the gel. Like veins.

Can hardly see out now.

The lines grow. Split. Spread across me like cobwebs. They get thicker. Squeeze tighter.

Suddenly. Flashing lights in my eyes. Points of heat in the middle of my head.

Then I can see things.

So many things.

So far away.

I understand my role. The task I am to perform.

Having survived the black poison used to eliminate the weak of my kind, to weed out those unsuitable for combat, they have transformed the fittest into efficient fighting machines. Sculpted by the finest Qallic warmongers, benefiting from their 10,000 years of experience in harvesting and enhancing simple life forms to maximise their potential, to make them useful.

I am grateful for this glorious opportunity to serve the righteous Qall in their quest to eradicate the Buhatt. To participate in a war that has lasted three millennia.

Once cumbersome and awkward, my legs are now lengths of pure muscle, infinitely flexible and immensely strong. Splayed suckered pads where once were feet. One arm replaced by a clutch of powerful weapons, the other a double-edged blade. Mind transformed by the huge wealth of knowledge they have fed into me, its power boosted. Lungs adapted to lower oxygen levels.

I now know the Qalls' history. Their fighting techniques. The reasons why the Buhatt must be overcome.

Having travelled incredible distance in their craft I am now crammed into this pod with hundreds of other transformed, one of thousands of pods suspended beneath the immense fleet of orbiting battlecraft. Here we await our time of fulfilment. The time we may serve our saviours.

The pod drops. Shudders, vibrates. Rushing air noise. The wall becomes hot as the atmosphere thickens. Some of the weaker ones scream with pain and yell to gods in whom they never believed and mothers who cannot hear them.

The pod explodes just above the planet's surface. We are thrown through the air.

Bright green sky. White sun. Heat.

I land in the midst of battle. My legs flex and absorb the impact and I roll and run towards the enemy positions firing my weapons as all around me machines chug and clatter and spout ink-black plumes and spit arcs of flame.

Airborne machines engage each other. Fireballs blossom and fade. The air is burned.

The dead litter the ground, charred and broken.

Beyond the trees the gigantic emerald pyramids glint – our target.

The observer inside me indicates five hundred steps to the trees but I estimate four hundred. I glance back. Transports rise away from the clearing, their hardware loads deployed. But the machines they have bought to help us wallow and strain in the boggy ground.

Gunfire to my left. An explosion. Slashes of coloured light.

Weapons' fire. Engine roar. Screams. Billowing folds of smoke and flame taint the sky.

Two hundred steps.

Two figures emerge from the small building ahead. I fire a burst of basic projectile ordnance that kills one instantly. The other has a problem with his weapon. I open his neck with my blade arm without stopping.

His blood fills the runnel, slides off the shining edge.

An explosion in the air to my right. A machine drops fast then the ground shudders and the aircraft flattens and a gout of stained fire rises into the sky. The parched grass ignites.

One hundred steps.

Figures moving. I fire my most powerful weapons, huge bolts of energy leaping from where once flesh and bone were crude and weak.

More figures in the trees ahead. Too many, claims the observer.

I ignore it. It knows nothing.

Then I see the flash of their weapons' discharge.

Flashing lights in my eyes. Heat in my head.

The embryos they implanted are already crawling from my dying body, seeking refuge, a place to grow.

As the light fades I see so many things.

So many things. So far away.

Then a brilliant flash. Devils' breath scours the land.

And beneath a boiling cloud the emerald pyramids shatter, their shards falling like blossom petals.

My head spins.

I hear birdsong.

But there are no birds.

Not here.

About the Authors

Neal Asher lives sometimes in England, sometimes in Crete and mostly at a keyboard. Having over eighteen books published he has been accused of overproduction (despite spending far too much time ranting on his blog, cycling off fat, and drinking too much wine) but doesn't intend to slow down just yet.
http://theskinner.blogspot.com/
http://freespace.virgin.net/n.asher/

Chris Beckett lives in Cambridge with his wife and youngest daughter. He has published more than thirty short stories, mainly in *Interzone* and *Asimov's SF* magazine, and his short story collection *The Turing Test* (published by Elastic Press) was the surprise winner of the Edge Hill Short Fiction Award in 2009, beating a Booker Prize winner, Anne Enright, into second place. His novels *Marcher* and *The Holy Machine* are currently available from Cosmos Books, with a new British edition of *The Holy Machine* due to be published by Corvus in 2010.

Keith Brooke's first novel, *Keepers of the Peace*, appeared in 1990, since when he has published five more adult novels, two collections, and over 60 short stories. For ten years (from 1997) he ran the web-based SF, fantasy and horror showcase *infinity plus*, featuring the work of some 100 authors including many of the genre's biggest names. Writing as Nick Gifford, his teen fiction is published by Puffin. Keith writes reviews for The Guardian, teaches creative writing at the University of Essex, and lives with his partner Debbie in Wivenhoe, Essex.

Eric Brown has won the British Science Fiction Award twice for his short stories and has published over thirty-five books. His latest include the novel *Cosmopath* and the children's book *A Dinosaur Ate My Socks*. He writes a monthly science fiction review column for the Guardian. His website can be found at: www.ericbrown.co.uk

David L Clements is a lecturer in astrophysics at Imperial College London working on extragalactic infrared astronomy using, among other things, the recently launched Herschel and Planck satellites. As well as rather too many scientific papers he has had short stories published in the Footprints anthology (Hadley Rille Press) and Analog magazine, and has others forthcoming in other anthologies. He is also working on a novel with the working title of 'The Bourbaki Conjecture'. Needless to say, his writing is influenced by his research.

Michael Cobley was born in Leicester, 1959, went to school in Clydebank, then attended the University of Strathclyde, to study engineering. He began to write with a serious intention in 1986 and is thus far the author of three novels, the Shadowkings Trilogy, and one short story collection, *Iron Mosaic*. His new space opera sequence, *Humanity's Fire*, began with *Seeds Of Earth*, soon to be followed by book 2, *The Orphaned Worlds*, in April 2010, published by Orbit. In addition to a controlled videogame addiction, he is also an unreconstructed heavy metal fan, and finds inspiration in both.

Una McCormack is the author of three Star Trek: Deep Space

Nine novels, published by Simon and Schuster: *Cardassia: The Lotus Flower* (2004), *Hollow Men* (2005), and *The Never-Ending Sacrifice* (2009). Her short fiction has appeared in various publications including *Glorifying Terrorism* (ed. Farah Mendlesohn), *Subterfuge* (ed. Ian Whates), *The Year's Best Science Fiction Vol. 25* (ed. Gardner Dozois), and Doctor Who Magazine. A Doctor Who novel, *The King's Dragon*, featuring the Eleventh Doctor, will be published by BBC Books in 2010.

Martin McGrath is originally from Northern Ireland but has spent the last 20 years in and around London as an itinerant journalist and PR person – a life his daughter has characterised as telling fibs for anyone with money. "Proper Little Soldier" makes an even dozen published stories, with others forthcoming in *Albedo One* and *Outshine*. Like everybody else, he's working on a novel.

Jim Mortimore is an author, composer, scriptwriter, and award-winning graphic designer. He has written some fifteen spin-off novels for popular television series, principally Doctor Who but also Babylon 5, Farscape, and Cracker. His books have been published worldwide and in a variety of languages, including French, German, Japanese, and Finnish. His short fiction has appeared in various places, most recently in *Future Bristol* (2009).

Gareth L Powell is a regular contributor to *Interzone*. His stories have appeared all over the world and been translated into seven languages. His first collection, *The Last Reef*, was published by Elastic Press in 2008 and Pendragon Press published his first novel, *Silversands*, in 2010. He lives in the West Country with his wife and daughters and can be found online at:
www.garethlpowell.com

Rosanne Rabinowitz has contributed fiction to *Black Static*, *Postscripts*, *Midnight Street* and the award-winning anthology

Extended Play: the Elastic Book of Music. She lives in South London, belongs to T Party Writers and recently completed a novel, *Noise Leads Me.*

Andy Remic is the author of eight Fantasy and SF novels, currently – *Spiral, Quake, Warhead, War Machine, Biohell, Hardcore, Kell's Legend, Soul Stealers.* He's a hard-talking, hard-fighting fluffy bunny rabbit of a man, who enjoys mountain biking, film making, mountain climbing, kick boxing and red hot chilli peppers! He has an unhealthy love of chainsaws, and has sometimes been accused of literature. For more info, check out: www.andyremic.com.

Martin Sketchley is a British author based in Birmingham. Having worked in retail then catalogue publishing, he is now a writer and editor for an international publisher of global business analysis. In what little spare time he can find, Martin plays guitar in an indie-pop band and dreams of being an airline pilot.